She felt a wave of sickness coming over her,
and fought it down, not daring to give way
because they might be watching, and they
would know that she was nervous, that her
callous attitude with Ivliev was just an act.
They mustn't see any sign of weakness, or
they would know she was an enemy and not
an ally, like her uncle . . . He didn't matter;
already what he had done and what he was
were unimportant beside her overwhelming
terror for Arundsen.

Arundsen, who was being manoeuved into
following her, eased into a trap from which
he would never escape . . .

THE LEGEND

A deadly web of espionage and treason

Also in Arrow by Evelyn Anthony

THE LEGEND

Evelyn Anthony

ARROW BOOKS

Arrow Books Ltd
17–21 Conway Street, London W1P 6JD

An imprint of the Hutchinson Publishing Group

London Melbourne Sydney Auckland
Johannesburg and agencies throughout
the world

First published by Hutchinson 1969
First published in paperback by Sphere 1976
Arrow edition 1983

Made and printed in Great Britain
by Anchor Brendon Ltd,
Tiptree, Essex

ISBN 0 09 932380 X

To Anthony and Mary with love

CHAPTER ONE

Peter Arundsen had a hangover. He had spent his forty-second
birthday at one of the best restaurants in London, dressed
up in a dinner jacket, dancing to a smooth twenty-five-piece
orchestra with his wife, and on the following afternoon he still
had a hangover. It was four-thirty, and he'd left the office
early because they were going away for the weekend. He stopped outside the front door and very slowly put the key in the
lock and turned it. He was slow because he was reluctant. He
didn't really want to go in and face his wife, any more than
he wanted to get on the train at Victoria and arrive at Buntingford House. His head ached because champagne disagreed
with him; but it was his birthday and so he had to have it,
whether he wanted to or not. It had been a jolly party, just six
of them, and his wife had enjoyed every moment of it. He tried
to say, Bless her Heart, and couldn't. It wasn't his kind of
evening, that expensive, conventional evening out, but it was
very typical of the life he'd been leading for the past eight
years. Ever since he had left the Firm.

He closed the door carefully after him, so that it made a
click, instead of the usual slam. But it wasn't any use; his
wife heard him and called out. 'Pete? Is that you?'

'Yes,' he called back.

'I'm in the bedroom. Trying to shut your suitcase.'

'I'm coming.' He threw the rolled-up copy of the *Evening
Standard* on the hall chair. The big black headlines were
hidden, covered by the sports page and details of some soccer
star who'd been suspended. For kicking or gouging of some
unsportsman-like behaviour. English sport was like English
politics as far as Arundsen was concerned. Scraping rock
bottom. He had rolled up the paper instead of throwing it
away, because his wife probably knew anyway; she often
listened to the lunchtime news on the radio, and, of course,
the radio was full of it, like the newspapers. 'Dunne in Moscow', 'Trade Expert Defects to Russia'. And there was a large
blurred photograph of James Dunne, taken before the war.
Even Arundsen, who was his best friend, wouldn't have
recognised him. He went on up the narrow passage and into
their bedroom. It was quite a big room, for a London flat,

and his wife Joan had enjoyed herself making it as feminine as possible. It was all pink and white, with frilly lampshades like someone's old knickers, and two neat twin beds, properly spaced apart by a combination bedside cupboard and book-shelf in white wood with gilt metal fittings.

Three years after their marriage, when they moved into the flat after his promotion, Joan had got rid of their double bed, and Arundsen had been too disinterested to care. She was bending over his suitcase as he came in, and for a moment he had an impulse to slap her bottom; it was a neat little bottom and one of the things he had fallen for when they first met. But she wouldn't think it was funny, or sexy, if he did; the last time she had been very irritated, so he changed his mind, and said, 'Hello, darling,' instead.

'I can't get this damned thing shut,' she said. 'Honestly, why do you have to take so much with you? It's only two nights!'

'I used to travel with a paper bag till you married me,' he said. 'It's your fault.'

'There's a difference between going round the works with a toothbrush and one clean shirt, and taking three pairs of shoes and half the laundry basket for a weekend. Here, you sit on it. How's your head, darling? Had a busy day?'

He got down on his knees and began leaning his weight on the suitcase. His head pounded with the effort. She hadn't mentioned Jimmy Dunne. That was worse because he'd have to explain it all to her; he had hoped that she'd found out the details for herself. Then there were only the condem-nations and 'I told you he wasn't any good' to wait for; he was prepared for these.

'I heard about Jimmy on the news,' his wife said. 'I nearly rang you, but then I thought you'd hear anyway. I was sure there was something wrong when he disappeared on holiday like that. It's just what those other two did, don't you remem-ber?'

'Yes,' he said. 'But Jimmy's no Burgess or MacLean.'

'Then what's he doing in Moscow?'

He closed the case and snapped down the locks. 'I don't know, darling. We'd better get a move on or we'll miss the train.'

'There's plenty of time, it doesn't take more than ten minutes from here.'

When his salary went up to five thousand they had taken

6

the flat in a modern block on the Embankment; it was so central, just as Joan said, so near the theatres and everything. In fact they went to the theatre about twice a year. The cottage in Herts had been sold, and now he spent the weekends in London, reading the Sunday papers or going round to have supper with some of the new friends Joan had made. The distinction was deliberate; they weren't people with whom he had anything in common. They were all respectable, middle class, and the men were as boring as the women. He often wondered what the hell his wife did all day, now that their small son David had gone away to private school.

'Have we got any more Alka Seltzer?'

'I bought some this morning; you finished the lot. I thought you might need some to take away. Is your head very bad, darling?'

She came and put an arm round him, and kissed him on the cheek. She was affectionate and thoughtful, and a pretty woman. It wasn't her fault that he was bored with his whole life and with her. He gave her a squeeze round the waist.

'You're a good girl, Joan. I'll go and take a couple. I'm not looking forward to the weekend, I must admit.'

'Then why don't we just cancel?' She said it very eagerly. He knew how much she hated these trips down to Buntingford and the reunions with Thomson and the others. She had always been uncomfortable and ill-at-ease; the mention of the Firm and its activities embarrassed her. She was always worried that their friends would find out what he had done after the war.

'We can't,' he said. 'The Chief's expecting us.'

'You all talk about that man as if he was God,' his wife said. 'You don't work for him any more; he's not in the beastly business himself now. Why do you keep up with him at all?'

Arundsen shrugged. 'Why do people go back to their old school? Happiest days of your life, and all that sort of tripe.'

She stood back from him and her mouth turned down. It made her look hard and much older suddenly.

'You're not comparing murder and all those awful things with being at a public school! You know what I think of the whole thing.'

'I should do, you've told me often enough,' he said. 'And it wasn't murder — don't be so damned silly.'

7

'Oh no? What about that Scot, MacCreadie – you told me he was an *assassin*, during the war.'

'I was exaggerating,' Arundsen said irritably. 'I was probably drunk. We did a job, darling, and whether you like it or not, it had to be done. It still has to be done. I gave it up because you wanted me to, but I'm not going to be bloody well ashamed of it. I know you don't like the Chief, but it's only three or four times a year at the most, and I like to go there. He was one of the best men in the whole outfit.'

'He's horrible,' Joan said. 'Such a condescending snob, having us all down to that house. I hate going there. It's the same every time; you all get together and swop stories about what you did or so-and-so did, and wasn't it bloody marvellous, while I sit there, bored stiff! And you've got a wonderful audience in his niece. She just laps it all up. I suppose she'll be there this weekend again?'

Arundsen felt himself stiffen.

'I don't know,' he said. 'I expect so. For God's sake, darling, what's wrong with *her*?'

'I'll tell you what's wrong with her,' Joan said. She stood in the middle of the room, her face flushed and her mouth opening and shutting, spitting out the words. He thought how unattractive she was when she was angry.

'She's divorced her own husband and she has the nerve to make a pass at mine, right in front of me. That's what I don't like about her!'

'You're talking about three months ago,' he said. 'You must be crazy, going on like this. We've only seen the woman twice. Look here, Joan, for God's sake stop having a row with me. I'm going to wash or we'll miss the train.'

'I'm not going,' his wife said. 'I've just had enough of it. You can go on your own.'

Arundsen went to the bathroom without looking at her.

'All right; if that's how you want it.'

He shut the door and locked it. The Alka Seltzer were on the shelf; he dropped three into a glass and filled it with water. He watched the tablets leap and fizz, spending themselves in millions of bubbles until they floated on the top, fluffy and shapeless. He drank the water down, grimacing, and wiped his mouth on a towel. He had met Joan when he was still with the Firm, after Jimmy Dunne's recommendation had got him promoted and posted back to England. He had taken her out a few times and then slept with her. She had felt very worried about the whole thing, and in the end he married her. And that was when the pressure began. She wanted a child, a settled home. People in the Civil Service were always travelling; why, he'd been three years in Hong Kong and a year in Yugoslavia before that. He didn't even know how long his London posting was supposed to last. And then he'd told her what he really did, and what friends like Bill Thomson, who'd been his best man, and George Geeson really were. She had been horrified.

The Secret Intelligence Service. Arundsen was in a weak position because he hadn't told her first, and she had played on this, putting him at a disadvantage. And when she was pregnant he resigned. What she didn't know was that he had been on a two-week assignment which took him into East Berlin and brought him out across the Wall with a Pole called Rodzinski whom British Intelligence wanted to question very badly. He had cut it very close indeed on that trip; the sight of Joan with her knitting bag of baby clothes made him feel like a criminal. He had left the Firm, and the Chief had been very understanding about it. He owed it to him to go down to Buntingford when they were asked. He was a great man in his own way, and if Joan was too small-minded to see it and accept him that was just too bad. She wasn't coming. He came out after washing his hands and the bedroom was empty. His case stood in the middle of the floor, waiting for him. He picked it up and thought he had better put out a peace feeler, at the same time hoping that she wouldn't respond by changing her mind and coming after all.

'Come on, Joan. Get your things and come down. Don't let's fight.'

She was sitting in the lounge, as she called their drawing-room, reading the evening paper he had left in the hall. Her face was hostile, but there was no sign of tears. If she'd been crying he would have made a genuine effort.

'I've arranged to go over to the Nortons' for supper,' she said. 'I told you I don't want to go. You'll have a nice time holding Mrs. Wetherby's hand and telling her what a hero you were.'

He went out of the flat without answering, and stopped himself slamming the front door because of what it would do to his headache. Twenty minutes later he was in the train on his way to Sussex.

'I love coming down here,' Bill Thomson said. 'I've been all over the world and there's nothing anywhere to beat a house like this.' He half turned to speak to the woman on the terrace beside him. The sun was slowly setting, spreading wide streaks of colour across the sky; reds and pinks and oranges ran into each other, outlined by the purpling edges of clouds that were creeping up from the horizon. The terrace was a long one, built of grey stone. It ran the length of the west side of the house, and it had been added to the original Tudor structure in the late eighteenth century. It gave a splendid view over the landscaped garden on the west side of the central court. A mile-long drive led up to Bunting-ford itself, and an unbroken view of green fields and woods surrounded the beautiful red brick building, rising in its traditional E-shaped symmetry, its copper-domed tower shining like a green jewel in the light of the setting sun. It was a famous example of early sixteenth-century architecture, built by the treasurer to Henry VIII on lands sequestered from the monastery of Bunting. The great Elizabeth had spent part of her girlhood there, and the rooms she used were still preserved with some of the original furniture and tapestries.

It was a house whose beauty always took Bill Thomson's breath away; simple, stately, rich in colour; surpassing the most glittering of palaces abroad. Mary Wetherby leaned forward, her elbows grated by the grey stone balustrade. The sun was on her too, turning her dark brown hair a red colour, like old copper. She wore it long and straight; her face was beautiful with a pale skin and hazel eyes that changed to blue or green in different lights. She was thirty and divorced four years. 'Phillip loves this house,' she said. 'He'd do anything to keep it going.'

'Must take a lot of money, by his standards,' Thomas said. 'Still, I suppose the great unwashed help with their half-crowns. I'd like to come down sometimes and do a bit of guiding. I'll ask him if he'd like that.'

'I've helped him several times,' she said. 'One woman thought I was his daughter.' She smiled. 'He was absolutely furious. He hates opening the house to the public, you know; he really resents people walking through the place. But as you say, it brings in the money.'

'It's glorious,' Bill Thomson said. 'I was brought up in the country; Peggy and I had this little place near Dorset after the war. We got the garden really going; people used to stop their cars to look at it. Then she died and there didn't seem much point.'

'You live in London permanently now, don't you?'

Mary had spent a year in Washington where her husband was Naval Attaché and two years roaming America after she left him. She had never met Peggy Thomson.

'Yes, I've got a little place in Swiss Cottage. I do a bit of work at the office and it's near enough without being in the centre of Town. I don't do too badly really, but I just don't like city life.'

'It's my haven, this house.' Mary Wetherby didn't look at him as she spoke; her face was turned towards the setting sun, descending bloodily behind the skyline. 'I've no family of my own – my mother married again and she lives in South Africa – I haven't seen her for years. Phillip has been kinder to me than anyone. When I come down here I feel completely different. Safe, as if nothing could ever come through from the outside world.'

'Surely it's not that bad a place,' Bill Thomson said. He was tall and thin, nearing sixty; most of his life had been spent abroad, the latter part of it since leaving Portugal where his father worked as a wine-shipper had been spent in the Firm. They all called it the Firm. Only outsiders talked about MI6. Or gave it its initials, S.I.S. The Secret Intelligence Service. The people on the inside talked about the Firm or the Office. His wife had been in the cypher department of the newly created S.O.E. branch of Military Intelligence when he met her; they had married during the war and they had been very close. There were no children; by accident, not design. And they hadn't needed any, because they were enough for each other. Now he too had retired, like all Phillip Wetherby's weekend guests. He ran a small export business and lived in Swiss Cottage, as he said. He spoke fluent Portuguese, Spanish and French, and during the war he had joined MI9 and run an escape route across the Pyrenees for refugees, escaped Allied servicemen and agents. He had lived what he described as an interesting life, and he was conditioned to accepting circumstances as they came along without any special resentment if they were unpleasant. His wife had understood his work and waited patiently, supporting him when he needed it, never complaining. She had faced her own death from cancer with the same stoic calm. He looked down at the woman beside him, and wondered what the hell she found so difficult about life at her age that she wanted to hide from it at Buntingford.

'It can't be too bad,' he repeated. He softened it with a laugh as if they were both joking. Her shoulders moved in a little shrug.

'Bad enough as far as I'm concerned. I'd like to stay on here and never go back to London.'

'Why don't you?' Thomson asked. 'If you really want to opt out at your age.'

'Because Phillip wouldn't like it,' she answered. 'He likes to live alone, I know that. Look, there's the car coming now.'

Thomson looked at his watch. 'So it is. The Chief suggested I went down and met the Arundsens; this business with Jimmy Dunne will have shaken the hell out of him. They were very close friends.'

'I'm sorry, I didn't know that,' she said. 'Bill, can I come with you?'

'Of course.'

The car was a grey Bentley Continental, driven by a young man in chauffeur's uniform. The car and the chauffeur were one of Phillip Wetherby's conceits. He had never driven himself since the end of the war, and he insisted on what he described as a decent car. Thomson and Mary Wetherby got in; as if by consent he sat in the front and she behind. The conversation had left a strain between them. He had never liked her, without knowing why, and he had let her see it. He was sorry and annoyed with himself. Then he began to think about Arundsen and Jimmy Dunne, and he forgot about the woman in the back.

He had known Arundsen for years. Thomson was twenty years older and much more experienced; he had the war and a lot of nasty episodes behind him when Peter Arundsen joined his department in '47. And the regulars were not very welcoming to young men from University who thought they knew it all, especially since they were coming in after the show was over. That was the general attitude and Thomson shared it. He showed Arundsen the ropes and waited for him to fall on his face, which he did within three months of joining. But he knew it and he was big enough to ask for help. Thomson liked him after that; he asked him out once or twice to the pub opposite the Whitehall Theatre and liked him even more. He was not superstitious but he believed in luck. Arundsen was lucky; he felt this very strongly. He was also extraordinarily inventive. You could give him a really awkward problem, like a complete breakdown of communications with a network inside Rumania, for instance, and no means of knowing whether their agents had been blown or were keeping low, and some bastard in the Foreign Office sending memos saying they must have an answer. Arundsen would think of some crazy means of getting it; often involving his own entry into the danger zone and out again. He had luck and courage and ingenuity, which was another way of seeing the simplest solution first. When he was promoted over Bill Thomson the older man stood him a dinner. He admired him and he liked him. He liked his little wife too. She was a good sort, and she loved him. She was right to persuade him to get out, though she would never know how right. Getting Rodzinski out of Berlin was almost his last job. They'd missed him by a hair.

The station at Buntingford was full of cars, waiting in orderly rows for the commuters to come pouring out of the train. Thomson wasn't a man who had a chauffeur but he had authority with people. 'Pull in here. I'll get out and meet them.'

The chauffeur pulled the Bentley into the kerbside.

'You wait here, Mary. We'll be back in a second.'

He saw her open her bag and take out a mirror to look at herself, and this irritated him all over again. There was something about her he didn't like, and for once he couldn't put a finger on it. Men in general liked her; the last time Arundsen had been falling over himself every time they were near each other. Perhaps that was why he didn't like her. Nice, average Joan Arundsen wouldn't have a chance against a woman like that.

'Where's Joan?' He came up to Arundsen on the platform.

'In London. She couldn't come down. How are you, Bill – didn't expect to see you here; I thought you always came down early.'

'I do,' Thomson said. 'The Chief sent the car for you, so I took a ride down to meet you. Nothing wrong with Joan, is there?'

'No,' Arundsen said. 'We just had a bloody row at the last minute. She said she wasn't coming, so I said okay. Who's that in the car?'

'Mary. She took a ride to meet you too.'

Arundsen gave his case to the chauffeur who was standing

by, looking sulky. He wondered for a moment why so many professional chauffeurs under forty were queers, and then why Phillip Wetherby employed him. He had a horror of homosexuals. He opened the back door and got inside.

The first thing he noticed was her scent. With his eyes closed he'd have known she was near him because of the scent she wore. It was strong and elusive; he had never known anyone else who wore it. He looked into her face and his heart gave an irregular jump. She smiled at him and held out her hand. He could feel the blood coming up round his neck, under his collar.

'Hello, Peter. How are you?'

'I'm fine, thanks. Nice to see you, Mary.'

She moved a little, making room for him. He supposed it was the hangover, but he seemed abnormally aware of her. His head had begun to ache again with the dull pain which only a drink would settle.

'How's the Chief?' he asked Thomson.

'In good form, I think. Pretty fed up over Dunne; I'd better warn you, Peter, he won't hear any excuses.'

Arundsen looked out of the car window. 'There just aren't any. The bastard's gone bad, and that's all there is to it.'

'Is it very serious – did he know a lot of things?'

He turned back to Mary Wetherby. He liked the way her eyes changed colour according to the clothes she wore.

'He's probably the greatest living authority on China in the world, politically speaking. He spent most of his life there; his father had the Slatefield agency, and Jimmy took on the job after he left University. He got a first in Oriental languages, and God knows what he could have been if he'd stayed in England. He had a terrific brain. Instead, he went out to Hankow and joined his old man's firm.'

'We'd recruited him while he was still at Cambridge in '35,' Bill Thomson said. 'We picked up a lot of people at about that time. Being a Western commercial representative is about the best cover for work in the Far East you can get. They're welcomed everywhere. Jimmy was a natural for the job.'

'He had a complete affinity with the Chinese,' Arundsen said. 'I went out to Hong Kong in '56, beginning of '57 – anyhow, I was told off to work with Jimmy. That's how I got to know him. He was wonderful to work for; he knew exactly what the score was, and he went straight to the source. And he could; he knew them all and they all accepted him. Mao, Chou en-Lai, they were all friends of his. He had thrown in his lot with the Reds early on; he said Chiang Kai-Shek was a gangster and he wouldn't win; and he was right, of course. He went on the Long March with Mao after the Nationalist victory. There's nothing he doesn't know about the present political set-up out there.'

'No wonder Moscow's delighted to get him,' Bill said. 'He's just what they need at the moment.'

'But why does this matter to us?' Mary asked. She was looking at Arundsen as she spoke; the movement of the car as it cornered the narrow lanes had brought them close. His knee was pressed against hers and he hadn't moved away; instead he slid his arm across the back of the seat so that she was leaning against it. He looked at her mouth and wondered what it would feel like to kiss her.

'Why are the papers making such a fuss?' she said.

'Because about ten years ago he gave up his association with Slatefields – they're an American firm and they won't trade directly with Red China now, and he joined our trade section in Hong Kong. So he's an official on the staff; that makes a stink to start with! And look at the question of security! This is the third English defector within the last eighteen months, and a couple of Admiralty clerks get hauled up for selling secrets on the new sub: the Americans must be doing their nuts over it. I mean, who the hell *can* be trusted? Why did he do it – who got at him? The ramifications go all over the place. Do you want a cigarette?'

'Yes please.'

She bent forward over his lighter flame, and the scent was in her hair. It haunted him; one day he must find out what it was called. It lingered wherever she had been; he remembered noticing it in the library at Buntingford when he and Joan had last come down, and knowing that Mary had been in the room. 'We're here,' she said. The car rounded a wide sweep in the long drive and the house came into view, its copper-domed tower silhouetted against the sky. The sun was down and it would soon be dark. There was a gleaming black Austin Princess drawn up at the entrance, and Bill Thomson laughed.

'The Geesons have come, I see. Good old George; he likes

15

the soft life. You know he's done so damned well in that company that you can't pick up the *Financial Times* without seeing something about him in it.'

'I know,' Arundsen said. He liked George and his wife, but he envied him a little. He had adjusted to the peace-time scene so brilliantly. He was rich and successful, and when Joan wanted to be bitchy she liked to mention the Geesons and point this out.

'He'll be chairman of that group, you'll see,' Bill Thomson said. The car stopped, and before the chauffeur could get round to them Arundsen had opened the door and jumped out. He was not a man who pawed people; normally he disliked the habit of kissing and embracing comparative strangers which was the accepted convention. But he wanted an excuse to touch Mary Wetherby, and he held out his hand to help her get out of the car. It *must* be the hangover; he blamed his raw awareness on his aching head and complaining liver. Whatever the reason, she was causing a major reaction just by being near him. For a moment their fingers locked. He knew that she held on a little too tightly and a little too long, and Bill Thomson was looking at them. The clock in the Tudor tower above struck seven and a flight of white pigeons burst out from the roof-tops, streaking in panic across the sky. They walked across the courtyard in silence, with Bill Thomson between them, and went into the house.

It was understood that guests at Buntingford dressed for dinner. George and Françoise Geeson were already in the library when Arundsen came down. There was no sign of their host. He never appeared before a quarter to eight. The Geesons were a middle-aged couple; he had worked with S.O.E. during the war and left it with a D.S.O. for work in France. He was a slightly built man with greying hair and alert brown eyes who had made a great success in industry, applying the techniques of dash and imaginativeness which had distinguished him in the field of operations. His wife was French, and they had met during one of his tours in the South, when she had acted as his courier. They had four children, they were happy and they suited each other as well in peace as they had in the hectic years when both lived one step ahead of the Gestapo. He was successful and rich, and occasionally did what he described as an odd job here and there for the Firm when he was travelling.

16

At a quarter to eight Phillip Wetherby came into the library and everyone stood up. He looked round the room and smiled at them all; he was a tall thin man, his hair completely white, a pair of thick-rimmed spectacles on the bridge of his over-bred nose.

'Hallo there, how nice to see you all. Arundsen – my dear chap, so sorry Joan isn't well – George and Françoise.' He spoke a few words to her in exquisite French, and she laughed, pleased at the gesture. He was a man who knew the value of small touches in relation to people, he remembered details and made use of them at the right moment. It gave the impression that whoever he spoke to was special to him, a little more favoured than the rest. Mary Wetherby came in a moment later, wearing a long green dress of a material that clung over her beautifully proportioned body, her dark brown hair caught up in coils on top of her head. Arundsen felt her looking at him; he made an effort and didn't move or meet her eyes. He saw her go up to Françoise Geeson and say a few words; she had the same knack of putting people at their ease as Phillip Wetherby. It was something they shared through the same background and traditions. You only had to look at her to see the refined breeding in her face and the slim bones of her body. He hated the word 'lady' with its vulgar connotations of pre-war snobbery, but there wasn't another that fitted her. Everything about her was soft and feminine, and yet elusive. He studied the two inches of whisky in his glass, while Bill Thomson went on talking to him, and wondered whether he would have let his imagination rove over the woman in the way it was doing if his wife had been in the room.

'Well, Arundsen?' Phillip Wetherby was beside him. 'How are you?'

'Fine, thanks. You're looking very fit.'

'I am. Retirement suits me; I spend a lot of time gardening and, of course, there's the odd game of golf. Bad news about Dunne.'

'Yes,' Arundsen said. 'Bloody bad business.'

'I'd like to talk to you after dinner,' Wetherby said. 'You knew him so well, you might be able to help give a line on what happened.'

Arundsen looked at him and gave a thin smile.

'I thought you said you'd retired.'

'So I have. But I get the odd call now and again. The

17

Major-General's a very good man and we're old friends. We'll talk after dinner.'

He turned away from Arundsen then, and said, 'Anybody know what's happened to the Countess? We'll have to sit down without her soon.'

'No, no idea,' Thomson answered, and Arundsen said nothing. He had stopped seeing the Countess when he got married; she had only been at Buntingford twice since then and he was surprised that the Chief invited her at all. He disliked homosexuals and equally he despised whores. And whatever she had been in the war the Countess Katharina Graetzen was now a whore and a drunk.

'She's coming,' Françoise Geeson said. 'I spoke to her yesterday and she said she'd come down tonight. I'm sure she'll manage it, Mr. Wetherby.'

'Let's hope so,' Phillip said. 'But it's eight-fifteen and I think we should start our dinner. It's rather good tonight and we mustn't let it spoil. Mary, my dear, will you lead the way?'

CHAPTER TWO

The Countess had caught the six-forty from Victoria with so little time to spare that she ran on to the platform without a ticket. It was a full train; she had been lucky to get a seat. The last time she had stood for most of the journey. It was a year since she had been asked down to Buntingford, and when Phillip Wetherby's letter came, she went out and spent her last ten pounds on a second-hand evening dress. And she promised herself not to get drunk, or to annoy him like last time; then he might ask her at regular intervals. She was late because the man she had arranged to meet had kept her waiting, and she was so short of money that she didn't dare break the appointment. She leant back in the carriage and sighed. She felt tired and depressed, as if the episode had soiled her. For a long time she had been drifting into the casual commercial encounters like the one which had made her miss the train, and they meant nothing to her. She was broke in spite of everything and there wasn't any other way to live. She had tried taking jobs, but they didn't last. Life was like one of those children's puzzles, full of little balls of steel. As soon as you juggled one ball into its socket all the others tumbled out and the whole thing had to begin again. Her age was a secret; no one had ever known it for sure, not even the people in S.O.E. for whom she had worked before joining Wetherby. She was born in Silesia, and her title was quite genuine. Her hair was light brown, the front streaked with blonde where it had begun to turn grey, and in the high cheek-bones and fine jaw-line there was the ruins of a beauty which had made her famous in European society after the war. But the face was sallow, the skin stretched and drawn with tiredness and vicious alcoholic bouts. When she lit a cigarette her hands shook. One by one the little balls had dropped out of their sockets and now they swirled and skittered across the puzzle's surface in a hopeless confusion. Her life was a shambles for the simple reason that it had gone on too long. Youth and excitement were the Countess's true milieu. When one began to fade the other deserted with it; the twenty-six-year-old girl who parachuted into German-occupied Poland in 1944 and took part in the Ghetto rising came into the peacetime world with decorations and a dazzling reputation. Wetherby employed her, and as Foreign Office interpreter she travelled through Europe, collecting lovers and information, living on the crest of the Cold War wave. And then things slackened. She was forty, and she had slipped into the habit of getting a little drunk at parties, of sleeping with men when it wasn't necessary to the job because they told her she was beautiful. Her old employers were kind and tactful but they dropped her. She was no longer reliable. That, in her own opinion, was when she should have died. She was out of a job, and the travel agencies, interpreter stints and dress shops followed one another in quick succession. She didn't last in them because she couldn't adjust to the life. There was a sense of waste and failure which drove her to the bottle in a suicidal rush, but even this didn't succeed. She went on living and slipping lower and lower down the scale until only a very few of her old friends kept in touch, and they were not the smart ones, but the wartime or postwar comrades from the Firm. Men like Arundsen whom she had known once a little better than she should have, and the Chief himself, because he never quite forgot his people, no matter how low they sank.

She sighed again and opened her eyes, staring out of the train window at the darkening countryside as it flashed by, seeing none of it. She should have died, before it came to the gentleman who'd come to her bed-sitting-room in Bayswater that afternoon. He was about sixty, and there was dirt under his fingernails and his breath smelt of stale beer. She had picked him up at Lyons over a cup of coffee, and at the end he had grumbled and sworn at her because she asked three pounds.

He paid, but she knew she wouldn't see him again. As a mistress she had been superb; glamorous, exciting, sensual. Now she made love with sad disinterest, and only when there was no other means of meeting her expenses. She lived in a miserable bed-sitting-room and escaped from it all by getting drunk as often as she could afford. Death would have been so welcome; a different type of woman would have taken the obvious escape route via the gas fire or the aspirin bottle, but Katharina was incapable of the ultimate act of cowardice. Courage was an integral part of her nature; she had been born brave, with a love of hazard for its own sake and a contempt for physical risk. She would never kill herself.

She wondered who would be at Buntingford, and automatically she thought of Arundsen. There had been a brief interlude between them ten years ago, a meeting and a parting in which there had been comradeship and a great deal of passion. It passed by mutual consent into a relationship of affection and respect. Sentimental without possessiveness, the Countess liked to keep in touch with her friends. Unfortunately their wives resented her and squeezed her out by means of the usual feminine dirty tricks. The dreary woman Arundsen had married was no exception. She had conveyed her opinion of the Countess without saying anything obviously rude or disapproving, and Arundsen dropped out of her narrowing circle.

It wasn't his fault. The Countess didn't blame him. It was a long time since they had met; her infrequent visits to Buntingford hadn't coincided with his. He must have changed; he was a good-looking man with the fair hair and blue eyes of his Norse ancestors. A strong man, capable of passion and daring. Now he was caged, of course, like so many of his kind, tamed and disciplined to a steady job and a respectable life.

Perhaps he was happy – the Countess hoped so. She liked others to be successful, to find themselves in the alien peacetime world where she herself was lost.

'Buntingford! Buntingford!'

She opened her eyes quickly as the train drew into the station and pulled her shabby overnight case off the rack. Her second-hand dress was in it, a wild, stupid extravagance for just this one weekend, and a bottle of brandy, buried under the clothes at the bottom, just to help her get through the two days.

In the library after dinner Phillip Wetherby offered Arundsen a cigar. He had sent the others into the drawing-room with instructions to amuse themselves, and settled down with a brandy to the talk he had mentioned before dinner.

'You know, this whole business of Dunne defecting has shaken the departments very badly,' he said. 'He was always looked on as a hundred per cent reliable. He'd been in the most confidential posts in the Far East and then in London here. There's never been a whisper about him, except the "queer" allegation, but that was investigated and there was absolutely nothing in it.'

'Well, it came after Burgess and MacLean, everybody was seeing buggers under the bed at that time,' Arundsen said. 'I don't know, I just don't understand what could have happened. I knew Jimmy like I know myself. We'd no secrets from each other. I said today, I'd have staked my life on him being straight.'

'However,' Wetherby said, 'the fact remains that he's gone over to the opposition. I heard yesterday that he went through Germany; that Austrian holiday was just a blind. He took off after a week and vanished. Next we heard a rumour that he'd been seen the other side of the Wall and now Moscow's crowing from the roof-tops.'

He took a sip of his brandy; it was an old fine champagne cognac and he savoured it carefully; he was a man who did everything in moderation and disliked excess in others.

'I needn't tell you there's an awful flap on in Washington. How much did he know? why did we send him with our trade delegation when he wasn't reliable? – on and on and on.'

'I can imagine,' Arundsen said. 'But why? What got him?'

'That's what we'd like to know. That's why I wanted to talk to you, Arundsen. You were his best friend. Probably the only friend he had in the Firm – I mean someone who was near to him, not just a drinking companion.'

'There were plenty of those,' Arundsen said.

'Of course, no man who drinks like that is really stable,' Wetherby said. 'I always disapproved of that aspect of him, but then what's the good of hindsight. Enough people will be saying "I told you so" as it is. How long is it since you left us, Arundsen?'

The question came without warning; there was no change of tone. It was quite casual.

'I resigned in '60,' Arundsen answered. 'Why?'

'Quite a lot of us resigned,' Wetherby went on. 'But if there's a job to be done now and again – we help out.'

'Like yourself?'

'Yes, and Geeson, and one or two others. Would you do a job for us, Arundsen? Just one job, wouldn't take you long.'

'What sort of job?'

'Go to Germany and see if you can pick up anything about Dunne. See who he met out there – find out who picked him up over the other side.'

'I should say our old friend Ivliev picked him up in East

B. That is if he's still in charge of their set-up.' Arundsen lit a cigarette. His hands were quite steady and his mind was calm. He had already thought out what was coming next and he had his answers ready.

'Oh, he's still there; very efficient man.'

'Long memory, too. He bloody nearly got me the last time I went over there.'

'That doesn't worry you, surely?' There was a little surprise in the voice, a slight lift to the eyebrows conveying to Arundsen that he was talking in a rather distasteful way.

Arundsen smiled. 'As a matter of fact, it does. I'm married, I've a wife and a boy to consider. I wouldn't go back over that Wall for all the tea in China; or all the experts on it, either. I resigned, Chief, because I'd had it, and only a bloody fool goes on. And I resigned for good. I'm not prepared to start again.'

'You could be a great help,' Wetherby said. 'This is something you could do better than anyone we've got.'

'Look, Chief . . .' Arundsen got up. He was growing angry, and he didn't want to let it show. But he wasn't going to be made to feel a coward.

'You're talking as if Jimmy Dunne were my responsibility. He's not. He's the responsibility of the people who employed him. They're the ones to sort this out. If they haven't got a man clued up enough to go to Austria and Berlin and make a few enquiries, then they're as bloody inefficient as I thought they were. I'm not going back there. I'm not working for the Firm again, and that's absolutely final. I'm out, and from the way they run the Eastern Section since you left I'm bloody glad of it.'

'Very well.' Wetherby got up too; Arundsen had tensed in spite of himself. The older man was relaxed, almost indifferent.

'You're quite entitled to refuse. I shall probably go myself.'

'Good luck then,' Arundsen said. 'No hard feelings, I hope?'

'Of course not.' Wetherby moved away from him, opening the door. 'You were always pig-headed, my dear fellow. But one of my very best operators, all the same. Let's join the others. Mary won't be pleased if I keep you shut up too long. You're rather a favourite of hers.'

Sunday began with clouds; they lowered over the splendid trees with a full-bellied threat of rain, and then before lunch they started moving, driven like ships across the sky by a hostile wind. The sun came out, dappling the gardens with warmth, striking a green glow off the copper tower, and by midday the weather-vane was almost motionless. The wind had dropped and it was going to be a perfect English June day.

The night before had not been a success for Arundsen. The Countess had come up to him when he went into the drawing-room after his talk with Phillip Wetherby, and for a moment he had thought times were better because she had a dark red dress on, and in the shaded lights she looked quite young and beautiful.

But the illusion didn't last. He had bent and kissed her on the cheek, privately thanking God Joan wasn't there, or she'd have given him hell about it afterwards, and at once he got the brandy smell.

Her voice was rather deep, with the Polish accent clinging to certain vowel sounds; it seemed incredible that they had once been lovers. Incredible and unimportant. She was an old friend in need, and her greatest need was self-respect. He lit her cigarettes and told her lies about how little she had changed, and the sad eyes thanked him. After an hour the Geesons had rescued him; he needed rescuing because the Countess had accepted two brandies and soda from Wetherby, and she was getting to a slightly maudlin stage, clinging on to his arm and going back over old times. He had slipped away, his place taken by George Geeson. Geeson had a reputation as a ruthless industrial operator, but where his wartime comrades were concerned he had a sentimental streak a yard wide. He settled down to spend the rest of the evening with the Countess because she was tipsy and miserable and needed support. Arundsen hadn't meant to do it but he found himself next to Mary Wetherby. He was irritable and depressed; Wetherby had put him in the wrong. He had been right to refuse to go back, but his reasons were based on self-protection and this made him ashamed. A couple of years ago he might have gone. Had Wetherby been in charge of the section he would have gone without question. But not now. The Berlin/Eastern Europe section was run by a retired naval commander whom Arundsen had always disliked when they were both working there together, and the top man of all was what he described as stupid shit soldier. He was not sticking his neck out for any of them. But he wished it wasn't Wetherby who'd asked him.

He was depressed by the Countess; she looked haggard and broke, in spite of the long dress which was three years out of date. She was dying visibly and with great pain; he couldn't accept it without resentment against Fate, and a little against the peacetime world which had no place for people like her. They'd all been bloody glad of the Katharina Graetzens in the war. Now there just wasn't a niche she could be fitted into; no room at the bloody Do Drop Inn. He had turned to Mary with a kind of defiance, letting himself look at the shape of her breasts under the green dress, and making love to her mentally while they talked. It was a way of defying his wife, who had accused him of it anyway, and of ignoring Wetherby's gentle acceptance that he was a coward who wouldn't go back. Well, he wouldn't go back, and being married didn't stop a man from wanting another woman. It was partly her fault anyway; why did she wear a dress that clung at every vital point if she didn't want to be undressed – she had looked at him with an odd expression, as if he were being rude to her, and he had broken off suddenly and realised that in a way he had been. They were talking about the Countess, and Mary had said how sorry she was for her. 'You don't have to be sorry,' Arundsen had said. 'She'll make out.' It was rude and immediately he felt ashamed, because he had taken his bad temper out on her. She coloured and got up.

'I'm sorry,' she said. 'I didn't mean it like that.' Then she went away and he was furious with himself and with her, because the rest of the evening was ruined.

He had slept badly and woken bad-tempered and tired. She wasn't at breakfast, and he was so irritated he escaped into the garden. Also he didn't want to read the newspapers because they were full of Jimmy Dunne.

There were half a dozen different types of garden at Buntingford; a water garden, where rare lilies and irises bloomed, and a huge weeping willow trailed its branches in the pool, two acres of formal lawns and bed, with sudden unexpected vistas come upon through avenues of trees, with a fountain or a group of figures at the end. There was a lake behind the house, and a pavilion, built at a much later date by the same Wetherby ancestor, who had fallen in love with the classical lines of Greece and the romantic splendour of Renaissance Italy. The pavilion gleamed white through the thick dark trees, reflected in the shimmer of the lake, and swans sailed past it. But it was never used.

Phillip Wetherby's mother used to have picnic parties there, but after her death it was closed up. Arundsen was walking towards the lake when he saw Mary Wetherby pass at the end of a pergola covered in roses. She was walking slowly in the direction of the lake when he caught up with her.

'Hello,' he said. She stopped and turned; even in the open air the scent was still a part of her.

'Hello, Peter. It's such a lovely morning – I thought I'd go for a walk.'

'Good idea. Can I come with you?'

'Of course.' He thought she had the most beautiful smile he had ever seen.

He wasn't just attracted to her; that was common enough when a woman looked like she did. She disturbed him. He slid his hand into the crook of her arm. He was a man who did everything physical with firmness. She couldn't have freed herself.

'I was rude to you last night,' he said suddenly. He had always disliked apologising; he was surprised by the way the words came spilling out. 'I'm sorry, Mary. I was just feeling bloody-minded. I shouldn't have taken it out on you.'

'You didn't,' she said quickly. 'I made a very stupid remark. Who am I to be sorry for somebody like the Countess? You were quite right.'

'I'm a bit touchy about her, I suppose,' he said. 'She's come down to the bottom. I used to know her as she was. In fact,' he made the confession he had never dared to make to Joan, 'in fact we used to know each other rather well, at one stage. Not that there's anything left of it now.'

'Were you in love with her?' They had come to the edge of the lake, walking very slowly. She felt the pressure of his arm against her side. It was the first real contact they had made, and it seemed as if they had often walked together, their arms linked, their bodies lightly touching. She turned a little away from him and told herself not to be a fool.

'No, I wouldn't say I was in love with her. She wasn't the kind of woman you could fall in love with; she was bloody attractive, and she had the glamour, the lot. Everyone was after her, but there wasn't any love apart from going to bed. I suppose I never felt superior with Katharina, even when we were lovers, and a man doesn't like that.' Arund-

26

sen smiled. 'It doesn't help to know the woman is braver and cleverer than you are and probably a damn sight better able to look after herself in a bad spot. And it was all true. The Countess was as tough as they come.'

'She can't have been,' Mary Wetherby said, 'or she wouldn't have let herself go to pieces. The really tough ones survive. They don't kill themselves by inches like her.'

'No, I suppose not. But I wish there was something I could do for her. I wish Joan would even let me ask her round to dinner sometimes, just to keep in touch, but she won't.'

'It's not surprising, if she knows you had an affair,' she said.

'She's no idea,' Arundsen said. 'Joan knows practically nothing about what I used to do, and she doesn't want to know. She's always resented the Firm, and the Chief, and everything connected with it.'.

'Perhaps because you were in danger,' Mary said. They had stopped and were facing the lake; he hadn't let her go, his grip on her seemed to be tightening.

'Maybe,' she felt him shrug. 'I always felt it was some kind of resentment, like jealousy. It made life impossible when we were first married. I couldn't travel anywhere without a scene, I felt like a bloody criminal if I went on a job, and, believe me, those aren't the sort of conditions to work under. I packed it in, and settled down after David was born. but she still resents it. She hates coming down here, for instance, and it's only a few times a year.'

'Is that why she didn't come with you?'

'Yes. We had a row, and I walked out and left her in London.' There didn't seem any point in lying about it. If his wife had come with him it wouldn't have been happening. Even so, he shouldn't let it happen. 'I'm a bit of a bastard, I suppose,' he said. 'I shouldn't be telling you this.'

She half turned to face him, the long dark hair falling back from her face as her head lifted. 'I don't think you're a bastard, Peter. And I know all about bastards. I was married to one for two years.'

It was not premeditated. His mind had been dwelling on her since the previous evening, now his body moved towards her automatically, his hands closed on her shoulders and began pulling her near; he bent to kiss her mouth.

'No,' she said. 'No, please don't.'

He stepped back immediately. 'Sorry,' he said. 'Let's walk on. We can get back to the house if we go round here.' He felt rebuffed and angry with himself. He was behaving like a fool; being disloyal to his wife and unfair to the girl. They were too old to play kissing games. Love was strictly for adults and it was played to the conclusion. He had just got there way ahead of her, that was the trouble.

'Are you very angry with me?' She had stopped and put her hand on his arm.

He turned round to face her and saw that there were tears in her eyes. He smiled, and all his anger went away. This just wasn't the kind of woman you grabbed hold of in a wood. It was his mistake, not her fault. 'So long as you're not angry with me,' he said. 'Give me your arm, Mary. I'll promise to behave myself.'

She put her hand in his; he glanced down at their fingers intertwined. The feeling was going right through him again; it was like picking up a live wire.

'What sort of a bastard was your husband?'

He had heard Wetherby mention him. He existed, but there was no shape, not even a rumour to give him substance. He wanted to know about the husband very badly.

'He was charming,' she said quietly. 'Good-looking, amusing, five years older than me. Everyone said I was lucky. I thought I was very lucky too. My family were delighted. He's Phillip's heir, you know, he'll inherit the house. People said we made a perfect couple. You know, I really was in love with him.'

They had stopped again by the edge of the lake. A single swan slid past them, ruffling the water, its head held arrogantly on the arch of its beautiful serpentine neck.

'What happened?' Arundsen prompted.

She wouldn't look at him; she turned a little, watching the majestic white bird glide across the lake.

'Do you believe the story that they sing before they die?' she said. 'It's rather a beautiful idea.'

'It's a legend,' Arundsen said. 'You can believe it or not. That's the nice thing about legends. Now tell me about your husband. Why did you break up?'

'It isn't very pretty,' she said. 'You really want to know?'

'If you want to tell me.'

'He was a pervert.' In the woods to the left there was a sudden crack; someone was shooting pigeon and a great flock of them rose whirring and clattering from the trees and broke out into the sky. 'He wasn't a pansy,' Mary said. 'Not that kind of pervert. He was sadistic.'

It was so unexpected that Arundsen didn't know what to say.

'Nobody knows except Phillip,' she said. 'I got a Mexican divorce, it isn't even valid here. I didn't care, I just wanted to make some kind of gesture, to be free of him. I said mental cruelty, and got the decree. He got a ship and he was in Malta by then. You knew he was in the Navy, didn't you?'

'No,' Arundsen answered. 'Why didn't you leave him before?'

'I did, twice. But he promised he'd change and I went back. But it wasn't any good. He couldn't come near me without wanting to hurt me in some way. I don't think he could help it.'

She looked up into his face and slowly she shook her head. 'You don't want to kiss me now, do you?'

'If you cry,' Arundsen said, 'I will. And it's not quite the moment for it. Look, there's your friend's mate coming round. They are beautiful birds.'

He put his arm round her, drawing her against him, and let her compose herself, watching the two white swans sail down the bend of the lake out of sight.

'Perhaps the legend's true,' she said. 'Perhaps they do sing. I'll ask Phillip; there have always been swans at Buntingford.'

'When do you go back to London?'

Arundsen slipped his hand through her arm, and down till he was holding her wrist.

'On Tuesday. I hate going back.'

'Will you have lunch with me on Thursday, Mary?'

'I don't want you to feel sorry for me,' she said. 'I don't want you to ask me because you feel sorry for me.'

'I'm asking you because I want to, and we're not going to play games about it. Will you meet me on Thursday?'

'Yes,' she said. She smiled at him, the green lake water changing the colour of her eyes. 'Of course I'll come.'

'I'll ring you on Wednesday and fix the place,' Arundsen said, 'Come on, we'd better go back or we'll be late for lunch.' He leant down suddenly and kissed her on the cheek. 'Forget it,' he said gently. 'It's all over now.'

They began to walk upwards to the house, and as they

turned through the covered rose walk they separated. From a window in the Long Gallery the Countess watched them move through the herb garden, and saw them pause for a moment and briefly touch each other's hand. She screwed up her eyes against the smoke from a cigarette which burned away between her fingers; she smoked continuously, and her hands were stained with nicotine. She had settled into the window embrasure with a newspaper and tried to read in spite of her headache. The headache would remain until the drinks were passed at lunchtime, or she could summon the energy to go up to her room and have a drink in secret. There wasn't much brandy in the bottle and she wanted to conserve a little for when she got home. The Countess had learnt how to take as much of other people's liquors as she could get, thereby saving money and supplies for the dreary days alone. She sponged with cunning and without scruple, but only for drinks. She smoked her own brand of cigarette, the cheapest on the market, and went without a day's meals to tip the butler and housemaid at Buntingford. But the brandies and soda were like life-blood to her; she had no principles and no pride left when it came to the bottle. She stayed quite still in the window, looking down at the sunny garden where Arundsen and Mrs. Richard Wetherby had stood for a moment, making their secret communication without knowing they were being watched. The Countess had watched a lot of people and her instincts were acute. The tone of a voice, the flicker of an eye could betray a relationship, a guilt which nobody suspected. In the few seconds spent under the window the two people had betrayed themselves.

Poor Peter. He was settled and respectable, living a neat little life secured by insurance policies like the television advert. He had never said so, but she knew how he must hunger for the excitements of the past. When a man was dissatisfied and bored he soon got into mischief. And Mrs. Richard Wetherby was mischief.

'Bill?' She called over her shoulder, and Thomson pulled himself up from an armchair where he had been quietly dozing.

'Bill, come and sit here.'

'Pleasure, my dear. Have a cigarette? come on, put away those filthy weeds and have one of mine. Lovely view from this window, isn't it. Sun's really pouring down.'

'I've just seen Arundsen and Mary come in together,' the Countess said. 'What's going on there?'

'Nothing, I hope.' He looked at her and his eyes grew narrow as he frowned. 'What did you see?'

'Nothing,' she echoed him with a slight, mocking shrug. 'Nothing and something. Is he all right with Joan? Why isn't she here? He said she was ill but I didn't believe him.'

'They had a row,' Thomson said. 'He shouldn't have come down without her; she's a good girl and she's done her best for him.'

'She's a middle-class bore,' the Countess said. 'She's put Arundsen in a cage, and you know it. If she lets him out to wander round by himself then she's a fool as well.'

'Just because she's not your sort,' Thomson said, 'that's nothing to hold against her, my dear. You're not exactly the wifely type, so you shouldn't criticise. I like Joan, and in a way I understand the way she feels about all this. You talk about a cage because that's how you see ordinary life. Peter was finished. He'd had it, and he knew it himself. Best thing he ever did was to get out and get married. I hope he's not going to make a bloody fool of himself and get mixed up with someone like that.'

'You don't like her, do you?' the Countess said.

'Do you?'

'Yes; she's very nice to me. Most women are bitches, she is not. But you haven't answered my question, Bill. Why don't you like her?'

Thomson hesitated. 'Countess, I don't know. She's very nice to me too. She's nice to everyone. Damned good-looking woman, charming manner, sense of humour – you name it, she's got it. But I don't like her, and I'm damned if I can tell you why.'

'She'll bring Arundsen a lot of trouble,' the Countess said. 'I know the type and I know him. I'd like to see him spread his wings a little, but with someone different.'

'I'd like to see him get to hell back to Joan,' Thomson said crossly. 'And I shall tell him so.'

The Countess smiled, and slipped off the seat.

'And you know what he'll tell you to do with that advice? There's the gong – let's go down, perhaps we'll have a little something before lunch. Come, my dear Mr. Thomson – you may escort me.'

It was Monday morning and the weekend guests had gone. Phillip Wetherby sat in the library in his favourite chair, which was so enormous that he seemed lost in it, and so shabby that the leather was worn in two bare patches on the arms, and read the morning papers, slowly and thoroughly. James Dunne was still the big news item.

After the rumours of his disappearance the next phase had opened with his discovery in Moscow, and now personal views of him by former friends and people claiming to be colleagues, filled the centre pages of the Press with articles explaining him and trying to account for what he had done. Most of what he read was rubbish; most inaccurate of all was the inevitable inside story by the political correspondents. One story, making the cliché comparison between Dunne and Burgess and MacLean, mentioned his habit of taking massive doses of Vitamin B12 after a night spent getting hysterically drunk. This was the first authentic thing Wetherby had read. He looked at the author's name again and grimaced with disgust. A retired Foreign Office official of a minor capacity, since become a self-styled pundit on the Far East. Wetherby remembered him, not because the man was important or because they had met often, but because he had the kind of memory which stored everything and everybody in connection with his work. He had run into the writer of the article once or twice, filed him away as stupid and third rate, and only remembered him as a man Dunne used to meet in Hong Kong. He had written about Dunne's depravity and alcoholism at great lengths, and the result was to further discredit British Security for retaining such a man in a responsible position. It was grossly exaggerated, but there was still an element of fact. Dunne had been going bad for the past two years. His drinking had got visibly out of control and his stability was cracking; he had begun suspecting people he worked with of plotting to get rid of him, or sending reports behind his back. He was rude to several senior members of the Firm while he was in London, and ruder still about them when he went back to Hong Kong. These were only little signs, but if Wetherby noticed them, then it was incredible that others in authority had not. It only confirmed Wetherby's view that his old organisation had gone to hell in the last few years. Arundsen had said as much when he refused to go back to Berlin. Bloody inefficient, he'd called them, and Wetherby couldn't disagree. As a result they had lost a lot of very able operators through administrative bungling and sheer callous indifference to the risk imposed upon them. Resignations were high, especially among the older, experienced men, of whom Peter Arundsen was an excellent example. The whole system of the Secret Intelligence Service had changed into an impersonal bureaucracy, its individualists hampered by petty jealousies and departmental bickerings, its agents' confidence undermined by a feeling of inefficiency at the top and indifference to their personal safety. In the old days, when he was chief, a man like Dunne would have been withdrawn eighteen months ago. He got up and put the newspapers tidily on the table beside his chair. The door opened and his nephew's wife came into the room.

All his life Phillip had been brought up with beautiful things. The picture gallery at Buntingford was a connoisseur's dream; the Wetherby ancestor had furnished his house with some of the finest Italian primitives in England, and the prize of the whole collection was a magnificent centre panel from a Fra Filippo Lippi triptych. Phillip had a natural sense of style and grace, highly developed by the early association with beauty in all its artistic forms. He watched his nephew's wife cross the room towards him, and he appreciated her as he did the magnificent pictures in his gallery. He had liked her the first time they met because she pleased his eye. She had reminded him then of a figure in the Fra Filippo Lippi picture; not the pale, northern Italian Virgin with her corn hair and round blue eyes, but a dark, haunting face among the massed company of the saints around the celestial throne. In spite of what his nephew had done to her, she still had the same look of gentle innocence. More than her colouring or features, that expression was the secret of her beauty.

'Good morning, my dear,' he said. 'All is peace and quiet. The Geesons left after breakfast, taking the Countess with them. Everybody else caught the early train.'

'It was a very nice weekend,' she said. 'I think they all enjoyed it. Especially the Countess. She's so pathetic, Phillip. She makes such an effort to pull herself together, just to please you.'

'Unfortunately it doesn't last,' he said. 'She'll end in the gutter somewhere. Such a pity; she had a lot of good qualities. Anyway, I'm glad you enjoyed yourself. You seemed to be getting on very well with Arundsen.' He said it with a smile to encourage her. She came round and sat near him, and he noticed that she was twisting her wedding ring round and round as if she were nervous.

'Yes, I was. In fact he asked me to have lunch with him. I said I would. Is it all right if I go?'

'I don't see why not,' Wetherby said. 'I told you to be careful, but that doesn't mean you can't have any private life. Go out to lunch by all means; but don't get too involved. He's not a fool, you know.'

'I know,' she said. 'He wouldn't find any excuses for me, either. No one would, except you.' She got up and lit a cigarette; the lighter flame trembled.

'You mustn't be so morbid about it,' Phillip said. 'It's all over, my dear, and you did what you thought best at the time. *I* would have done the same.'

'Richard didn't give in to them,' she said. 'He told them to go to hell. I weakened, Phillip. I was too ashamed to face exposure. I'll never be able to forgive myself.'

Wetherby didn't answer immediately. He sat and watched her smoking, drawing nervously on the cigarette and puffing the smoke out. She had weakened. His nephew, the degenerate, had been strong. It was an odd quirk, that sudden show of courage on the part of Richard Wetherby. It showed that there was something of value in him, but unfortunately not enough. Phillip had been delighted with the marriage, believing that they would have children and Buntingford would continue on in the family as it had for so many centuries. When Mary came back from the States and told him the truth he had changed his will, cutting his nephew out completely, and left the house to the National Trust.

'You were very good to me, Phillip,' she said. There were tears in her eyes. It was nearly four years and she still became emotional when it was mentioned. 'I don't know what I would have done without you!'

'Nonsense,' he said. 'You exaggerate the whole affair. I was the only person you should have come to – after all, it was my nephew who was responsible and it was my family name at stake. You shouldn't go on thinking about it. Just because Arundsen asks you out to lunch! Tell me, are you attracted to him?'

'Yes,' she nodded. 'Very much. I wish he wasn't married!'

'Oh, I shouldn't worry about that,' Phillip said. 'Go and enjoy yourself, Mary. But if you have an affair with him don't get too confidential. Keep him at a distance, or one

34

day you might be tempted to confess all – dreadful mistakes are made that way. You know the old saying? *Post coitum omne animal triste* – well, I think it should be *indiscretio*. Be careful, that's all.'

'I will,' she said. 'I won't think of it again.'

'Don't,' Wetherby said. 'The negatives have been destroyed. It's all over. By the way, I'm going on a trip at the end of the week; do come down while I'm away if you get tired of London.'

'Thank you,' she smiled at him. 'I'll wait till you get back. Where are you going? Or mustn't I ask ... ?

'Berlin,' he said. 'I still have my uses now and again. Now there's some work to be done in the rose garden while the sun shines. Amuse yourself. I'll see you at lunch.'

She stood by the tall chimney-piece after he had left, finishing her cigarette. The sun was shining through the long windows, cut up into bizarre patterns by the mullioned window glass. The long cool room was very still; it smelt of wood smoke and the curious damp smell of age, as if Time had stopped and the room itself was a vacuum. It was all so old, so remote that it gave a sense of peace. 'If you want to opt out at your age.' That was what Bill Thomson had said, and she knew he despised her. But she had wanted nothing else when she came back from New York after the divorce.

She had been resting that afternoon in their Washington apartment when the telephone rang; stretched out on the bed with sleep pads over her eyes. They had been to a party at the Belgian Embassy the night before, and when they came home her husband had tried to make her go to bed with him. There had been a violent row, and she had locked herself in the spare bedroom and cried until the early morning. Nothing about him would have suggested what his habits were. He was young, good-looking, a typical naval officer with a fine career in front of him. He had charm and brains; the Embassy said he was the best Naval Attaché they'd had in Washington since the war. And she was beautiful and popular; everyone supposed they were an ideal couple.

They rode high on the capital's social circuit. That evening there was a smart dinner party in Georgetown, followed by an official reception for the Foreign Minister from Thailand. And another party tomorrow and the day after; the

35

sleep pads and the wretched afternoon spent dozing on her bed might take the ache behind her eyes away. When the phone rang she hesitated, but it went on ringing, as if the caller knew she were lying there listening.

At last she picked it up. A man's voice at the other end said a dozen words, then the line clicked. She had opened the door within twenty minutes as instructed and the man who had called her came into the apartment and sat down. She had never seen him before. He was a middle-aged American, unremarkable-looking, with the persuasive manners of a travelling salesman. He had smiled at her, asked her permission to smoke, and then handed her the first photograph. The woman on the bed was a well-known Washington call-girl who specialised in the kind of performance being enacted in the picture. He sympathised, he said, at her horror and disgust. It wasn't very pretty, especially since the man involved was so clearly Commander Wetherby. There was a better likeness of him in the next batch of photographs. There were six in all, and they had been taken on different occasions, always with the same woman. From the angle they were obtained by a camera in the ceiling, probably concealed in the bed hangings. After Mary had looked at them she shut herself in the bathroom and tried to be sick. But the man knocked on the door and told her to come out.

He was very sorry for her; he made that clear. Obviously she didn't share her husband's sexual tastes. She had heard him go on talking, her head hidden in her hands, sick and confused beyond understanding most of it. Only when he put his hands on her shoulder did she come to life and shrink away from him. The photographs would be sent to the British Embassy and copies to the State Department. Unless she did a small service in return for their suppression.

She remembered saying she would tell Richard, and the man smiling. Richard already knew about them, he said, shaking his head. He had been approached first and didn't seem at all ashamed of being shown up. But as his wife her position must be different. People would never believe that she too hadn't let him do that kind of thing . . .

And in the end she had asked what they wanted her to do, and this was the first stage in capitulation.

It was very undramatic; it seemed such a trifling thing

that she didn't believe him at first. He was patient, and he repeated what was wanted. At the reception for the Thailand delegation there would be a well-known Pentagon general, renowned for his hawklike attitude to the Eastern bloc. Mary knew him; they had met socially several times. In that case, the man explained, it would be only too easy for her to invite him to dinner. That was all they wanted; just a dinner party for the General. It wasn't such a terrible price to pay for that one print alone. He had put his finger on one of the photographs, and she had looked away, shuddering.

A dinner party. She had imagined all kinds of impossible situations, papers she would have to steal, information she'd be asked to glean through the British Embassy – all the fictional propositions of the blackmailer-spy. The idea of asking General Hughie Stuart to dinner was such an anticlimax that she didn't even argue.

The man got up, putting the obscene prints away in his brief-case, and thanked her for being so sensible. He would be in touch, he said. Then he had gone, and the worst thing she had to face was not the implication of what she had agreed to, but the need to face her husband when he came through the apartment door.

It never occurred to her to tell him. That meant explaining about the photographs; it meant admitting that she had committed herself to people whose affiliations were only too obvious, and she dared not do it. She couldn't have come close enough to him to confide. It was her secret and her guilt. And her fault too; she had stayed on with him trying to make the marriage work, hoping that some miracle would turn him back to normality. The Catholic attitude to marriage went so deep that it was part of her psychology. Effort, patience, loyalty, all these qualities and more were asked of a husband and a wife, even if only one side were prepared to give them. Divorce did not exist.

She had tried and she had failed. Nothing would alter Richard. In his way she supposed he must be mad, but this was little comfort. All she had left was the public image; he had only six months more in Washington. When that post finished she would leave him.

The dinner party was given for the General; her husband compiled a list of guests with British Embassy guidance, and she could remember for weeks afterwards looking

37

round the table, wondering who was working for them among the guests, while the General expounded his views of Presidential policy. There had been no clue then or later. And no word from the other side until a month afterwards when the telephone rang, and this time it was a woman. They wanted her to find out the views of a certain Senator's wife on the chances of a trade agreement with Yugoslavia.

She had said yes, and been too frightened and too ignorant to tell them lies. She repeated the Senator's wife word for word, and realised that what she was telling them came from the Senator himself. It was all done on the telephone; she never saw the man again. And so it went on; the requests varied from pieces of gossip to social gatherings where a name here or there was suggested for inclusion. On one occasion Mary was sure that she had been instrumental in introducing a senior British Treasury official to a woman who afterwards involved him in a divorce scandal that wrecked his career.

It was easy and insidious; she never knew when they would want something, and often weeks passed without a word. Once she had asked when they meant to stop, and the reply was to ring off. From the time it began she moved into the spare bedroom, and she gathered enough courage to tell her husband that after his Washington job ended she would get a quiet American divorce. That decision ended her public association with the Catholic Church. She believed in nothing but the necessity for keeping the disgrace and horror of her private life from public exposure. And now there was a second skeleton to join the original one in the cupboard of guilt. She had committed treason. Never in her life had Mary Wetherby appreciated the refinements of loneliness and isolation as she did in those months in Washington. She had become a pariah, married to another pariah, without even the comfort of being in league together. The trap was sprung and she was in it. When Richard Wetherby's new posting came through it was an appointment to a ship in the Mediterranean. They gave a farewell party in Washington, and set out together for New York. In New York they separated; Mary rented an apartment on the East Side, and he flew back to England. A week later she received the prints by Red Band messenger. She was off the hook.

She went to Mexico for the divorce; it was done very

quietly, and the question of legality didn't bother her. Technically she was rid of him, and this was what she wanted. In retrospect it was a foolish thing to have done, because the whole degrading process would have to be gone through in England if she ever wanted to marry again.

When she left Mexico City she felt a little cleaner, but not much. At twenty-seven she had nothing to look back on without misery and disgust and little to look forward to; she stayed in Mexico for two months, travelling alone from the beautiful sprawling capital to Guadalajara and on to Monterrey.

She avoided the ghastly tourist traps with their false gaiety and phoney Mexicana; from Monterrey she flew back to the States and settled in New York. She made many friends, and got a job with the U.N. as an interpreter. Thanks to a finishing school in Florence, her Italian was exceptional. The work was interesting and it kept her occupied. The next two years passed very quickly; her circle of friends widened. There were weekends in Vermont, trips to Palm Beach, and a continuing social round which had the same anaesthetic effect as getting drunk. She had no time to think, and only once the temptation to unburden drove her to St. Patrick's Cathedral and the confessional which she had renounced. Inside was peace of mind, anonymity and even forgiveness. There was a queue of people waiting, and after a monemt she had turned and walked away. Her faith was gone, but she had too much respect for what it had once represented to debase the ancient Sacrament of Penance to the level of the analyst's couch.

For some time she had been morbidly afraid to go home to England, imagining that she would be arrested when she stepped off the plane; it was this fear which prevented her from destroying the photographs. They were the only proof that pressure had been put upon her. But as soon as Mary was in England the sense of guilt overwhelmed her, as if there had been no interlude since Washington. There was only one person to whom she might go and who might understand. Phillip Wetherby had been very kind to her; he had told her before she married Richard that the house he loved would belong to their children. He had given her his mother's splendid jewellery as a wedding present and made over money to his nephew. She owed Phillip an explanation for the failure of the marriage.

She wrote and asked if she might come down to Bunting-ford and see him. That interview took place in the long library; it was teatime and already dark. A log fire burned in the Tudor grate. Phillip refused to have central heating in the main rooms because it ruined the panelling. She could look back on herself that February afternoon, wait-ing for Phillip to come in, the photographs in an envelope on the table by her bag. Up till the last moment when he came through the door she had no idea how she was going to begin. He had made it surprisingly easy.

He made her sit down, and gave her a drink, and started by saying how disappointed he was that things had turned out badly between her and Richard. Richard had not com-municated with him, except to write from Malta saying they were separated. He appreciated her thoughtfulness in coming personally to see him. And then, because she had never stopped glancing towards it, he had picked up the envelope with the photographs and asked what was inside it.

'The reason why I left him,' Mary had said. 'Please don't look at what's in it yet. Let me try and tell you first.'

Phillip had never been demonstrative; he was always remote, even cold, in his attitude to people, irrespective of how much he liked them. When she began to cry he didn't come near her. He waited patiently till she felt able to con-tinue with the story. He interrupted once or twice in the beginning.

'You had no idea he was like this before your marriage?'

'None – he was always sweet and affectionate – I almost died on that honeymoon.'

When she came to the telephone call in Washington she saw a very slight change in his expression, but it was gone in a second, and it was his only visible reaction until he looked at the first photograph. Then he turned away and she heard him clear his throat and swallow hard, as if some-thing were choking him. He turned and threw the package straight on the fire.

'I did what they told me,' she had said. 'I know what you must think of me, Phillip, you of all people, but I couldn't face people knowing.'

'Thank God,' Phillip had said, 'you didn't try. You were quite right. You're not to blame yourself.'

At the end he had told her that, of course they had the

negatives. Returning the prints was a gesture to make her feel safe. In fact they had a hold on her which they could use at any time. Once they got their hooks into people they never let them go. It was extremely lucky that she had told him. He was in a unique position to help her, it might be possible to get the negatives and any evidence they had of her working for them returned through British Intelligence channels. It might involve a bargain, but such things were common practice. She wasn't important, they'd exchange their hold on her for some equivalent advantage.

No, no, he had assured her, he would arrange something without disclosing who she was.

That night the warm, serene old house was like a womb; it enclosed and sheltered her, driving the nightmare of the immediate past and present far beyond its boundaries. She felt safe and protected, and it wasn't a feeling she could remember since she became a Wetherby. Phillip was very kind. He remarked the next morning that she looked pale and strained. He felt she should stay with him for a few weeks and relax. And he never mentioned Richard or the photographs again, except one morning six months later, when she was leaving for London after spending the week-end with him.

'By the way,' he had said, 'I got everything back from our friends. The negatives have been destroyed, so you needn't ever think of it again.'

If he had been a warmer person, Mary would have loved him as if he were the father she had lost while still a child. As it was, her sense of gratitude and dependence on him was as deep as if she were indeed his daughter. He had warned her once or twice that she must never tell a living human being what had happened. If she married again, and he hoped she had forgotten all that Catholic nonsense about divorce, she must do so knowing that she must keep this secret from her husband.

He had covered her completely, as far as he could tell but there was always a risk that something might come out if anyone enquired. The Americans were hysterical where espionage was suspected among their allies. She needn't think of it, but she must choose her closer friends with care. Especially men.

The warning hadn't been necessary until she met Arundsen. She led a pleasant social life in London, picking up with her old friends, and there were half a dozen men who regularly took her out, and tried to have affairs with her. But she was in no danger of involvement with any of them until Arundsen came into her life. She had believed herself in love with Richard Wetherby; she didn't put much trust in that particular emotion. What she felt for Arundsen was a confusion of several feelings at the same time. She was so quickly attracted to him that it astonished her; she had looked on that side of her life as finished. And she was drawn to him by the very qualities her other men friends lacked. He wasn't very smart, but he was strong, and she felt this strength. He was shy in an odd way, and he didn't seem to fit in any category. He wasn't a very good-looking or sophisticated man; he wasn't smooth, or a gentleman like Phillip; Richard Wetherby would have called him a bit of a roughneck with the patronising assurance of his own élite background. Most of all she felt the power of a personality who had made decisions and taken risks. He wasn't the kind of man to be cheated by a woman; he wouldn't take it well and the woman wouldn't get away with it. She was a fool to have anything to do with him. But she had known that from the beginning; it was too late to pretend to herself now. Phillip had said it was all right. She could see him in London, so long as she was careful. For the first time since she returned from America she was anxious to leave Buntingford.

'I don't believe she wasn't down there,' Joan Arundsen said. She had been crying, and her face was pink, the cheeks and eyelids puffy. He had come in on Monday evening, without telephoning from his office to make up the quarrel, and he had hardly said a word during dinner. He looked tired and completely disinterested in whether she was angry or not. And so the row began and she cried halfway through it, which infuriated him instead of making him feel sorry for her. And the real resentment soon flared up with her repeated question on a rising note of hysterical emotion – was Mary Wetherby in the party? Arundsen had lied because it was the easiest thing to do. He hoped to cut the scene short and eventually reach some sort of compromise which would allow him to go to bed without Joan lying beside him in the other bed, nagging and crying till the small hours.

42

'I've told you,' he said wearily. 'No, she wasn't. Isn't that enough?'

'I don't believe you,' his wife said. 'You go away for the weekend, leaving me here alone . . .'

'You wouldn't come,' he interrupted.

'Leaving me here from Friday to Monday, never a phone call to see if I'm all right, nothing. I know that bloody woman was down there, making up to you, and that's why you didn't even give me a thought.'

Arundsen leaned back and shut his eyes, letting the words flow over him, letting her cry and accuse, because she was right in every detail. He hadn't thought of her except once, and that was when he told Mary Wetherby that they had quarrelled.

The past was out. He was bored with his job, fed up with his marriage and very much alone. But when he thought of Mary Wetherby, even with his wife's voice shrilling over him, he felt as if the years were dropping away from him. He felt desire and he felt excitement, because the chance of that kind of woman came once or twice in a whole lifetime. She made him feel the man he used to be. A man with something in him, not a glorified nine to fiver in a bowler hat, reading *The Times* on the Tube and learning about world affairs from Newsweek. He could still feel his old self, just by planning to take her out to lunch.

CHAPTER THREE

Colonel Nickolas Ivliev leaned forward and tapped on his driver's shoulder. 'Move forward and draw in on the right.' The Zim car was not very big, nor painted the sinister black associated with the Russian Security patrols. It was a modest-looking model, sprayed a discreet shade of dark grey. The engine was a supercharged six-cylinder type capable of bringing the Zim up to a hundred and twenty miles an hour in just over a minute; there was a radio telephone link with the K.G.B. Headquarters at the Karlshorst, and a concealed tape recorder in the central arm-rest at the back.

The car slid forward, following a man walking on the right, and as it drew level with him it stopped. The Colonel opened the rear door and the man got in and sat beside him.

'Good of you to come, Mr. Wetherby. I hope you weren't waiting long?'

'Not at all. I enjoyed the short walk. Where are we going this time?'

'Just for a drive.' He smiled at Phillip Wetherby, showing a line of gold teeth in his upper jaw. He took his army cap off and rubbed his cropped head; he made a movement to lower the arm rest between them when Wetherby said, 'Please, Colonel. That arm rest is an old trick. I'm not an amateur, and I object to having my conversations with you taped.'

'I thought it would be more comfortable, but if you prefer not . . .'

There was a second recorder which operated in the ashtray in the side door where Wetherby was sitting, and this had been switched on since he entered the car.

'A cigarette.'

Wetherby shook his head. 'I prefer my own; they're less strong. What news of Dunne? Any improvement?'

'I'm afraid not. He's adamant that he won't co-operate with us. We've moved him from Moscow to Kalitz. What about Arundsen?'

'No luck at all,' Wetherby said. 'I asked him to come

back. I said we needed to check on Dunne's movements and contacts in East Berlin, and he refused to touch it.'

'That's very unfortunate,' Ivliev said. 'He's absolutely vital.'

Wetherby looked out of the window for a moment; the car was proceeding along the Karl Marx Allee through the centre of the city. Modern buildings rose up like cliffs on either side of the wide highway. This section of East Berlin was prosperous and modern. There was a hideous hotel, concrete and steel office blocks and multiple State-owned stores. It was a long way from the opulent elegance of the pre-war Unter den Linden, but it was an effective façade behind which the East German Government concealed the drabness and shortage which characterised their half of the great German capital city.

'I got the message about Arundsen,' Wetherby said, 'but it wasn't very clear. It didn't explain *why* you want him so badly, or how he connects up with Dunne. I'd like to hear everything in full detail. Getting Dunne to defect to you was one of my better contributions. I'm damned if I want it to go sour now.'

'It was a brilliant coup,' the Russian said. 'Made by a master, Mr. Wetherby. There was no reason to suppose that Dunne would regret his action and refuse to co-operate with us. But this has happened. For the first few days it was all right. We gave him everything he wanted, every comfort. Plenty of drink, any women he liked; he was fêted in Moscow. He seemed to thrive on it. There was every hope that he would get down to it with our interrogators and give us what we wanted. But immediately after the first session he turned hostile. He demanded to go home. We let him get extremely drunk and that pacified him. But the next day his attitude was the same. He became violent and had to be restrained. That's when we moved him to Kalitz.'

'I've heard of Kalitz,' Phillip Wetherby said. 'How very unpleasant for him. But I still don't see where Arundsen comes into this.'

'Forgive me,' Ivliev said, 'but I must take it step by step, to put you, as you say, in the picture. You needn't worry about Dunne, nobody's going to hurt him at Kalitz. He's been given a little sedation and asked a few questions, but nothing drastic will be done. It's not an ordinary case of

45

extracting information, Mr. Wetherby. What Dunne can give us is far more valuable. He's the greatest living expert on China, and the only man outside Peking who knows the inner mind of Mao Tse-tung. And of most of the other top Maoists. We don't want facts from Dunne; we can get those ourselves from our own agents. We want his knowledge of the situation, his advice. And we want it given freely. Otherwise it won't be accurate. The Soviet Union is dealing with a very dangerous enemy; more dangerous than any of your Western nations, including the United States. Dunne knows the mind of that enemy. And he is loyal to what he knows. He said very plainly, and obscenely – that he preferred the Chinese to us.'

'Surely,' Wetherby showed a little of his growing irritation, 'surely you can apply your usual methods and g$_{et}$ him to co-operate!'

'We can,' the Russian agreed. 'But Dunne is a paranoiac as well as an alcoholic. These people are difficult to handle; too much interference and their mental processes break down completely. We can condition a man to anything, but this takes time, and time is what we haven't got. It could be a year before Dunne was properly re-educated. If we get our hands on Arundsen it'll be over in a few weeks.'

'But why? Why Arundsen?'

'All things have a point of leverage. Find that point and you can literally move a mountain. Arundsen is Dunne's point of leverage. Can you accept that?'

'Not without further explanation, no,' Wetherby said 'I gave you one man, and I knew why you wanted him. Now you want another man, and I'm afraid I don't work in the dark. I see no real connection between them.'

'They were close friends,' Ivliev said. He hadn't wanted to go into details, but he knew Phillip Wetherby wouldn't co-operate without them. He never bluffed when he said no. 'We got the first clue to Dunne's tendencies when he didn't use the girls we sent him. Under sedation and questioning he's betrayed a homosexual aspect more and more. At the moment he's resisting it; Arundsen was his best friend, his drinking companion, colleague, call it what you like, as long as he doesn't have to see it as it really is. He is in love with Arundsen, although he doesn't know it. He's been repressing this for years and now that it's beginning to come out, he finds it very painful. His doctor advises

46

that he must be made to acknowledge it, and the best means of doing that is to confront him with the man himself. Then he will break down; we are assured of that. The re-educative process will be quick and easy because he will have Arundsen to depend on. When he has left Kalitz he won't feel any guilt for being what he is; he will be free of inhibition and shame, and very conscious that the Soviet Union has accepted him as his own society never did. He will be eager to work for us. I hope this makes sense to you Mr. Wetherby. Arundsen is so important that without him the whole affair will be a waste of time.'

Phillip had been looking out of the car window while he listened. He turned to the Russian and shook his head. 'Personally I don't believe in any of this psychological nonsense,' he said. 'Drugs and scientific measures I can accept, but the whole concept of the human psyche seems complete rubbish to me. However, I will take your word for it.'

'Can you get Arundsen to come here? He's got to come of his own free will; we can't kidnap him in Britain, our relations with your Government are going smoothly and they mustn't be upset. We can't take him on his own ground or anywhere in neutral Europe.'

'Why are you so set on East Berlin?' Wetherby said.

'I almost caught him once, with the Rodzinski abduction,' Ivliev answered. 'I regard him as my responsibility because of that. And I received Dunne too. This is my operation, Mr. Wetherby, and I'd like to finish it. It's your operation, also, and unless you can complete it by giving me Arundsen it will have failed.'

'I've never failed,' Wetherby said coldly. 'I'll get Arundsen for you. I can't see how at the moment but there must be a way.'

'We have every confidence in you,' the Colonel said. He reached down to the floor by his feet and produced a small pig-skin case which might have been made for binoculars. There was a flask and two small silver cups fitted inside it.

'I have some Scotch whisky here,' the Colonel said. 'I hope you'll join me.'

'Thank you,' Wetherby said. 'Just a little.'

Ivliev watched the Englishman take the silver cup and sip from it. He had been an Intelligence officer since leaving Leningrad University, and in all his forty-eight years of life, twenty-eight of them devoted to the scientific study

47

of human beings in relation to espionage he had never met anyone like Phillip Wetherby. The man was such an enigma that he fascinated the Russian. He didn't fit into any category, and being a Ukrainian and of a tidy disposition, Ivliev liked to label people. There was no explanation he could find for the fact that Wetherby, for many years the principal adversary of the Soviet Intelligence in the East, should suddenly decide to betray his own country and work for the enemy. For the first two years he had been deeply suspected; every move was watched and every action checked. But no fault could be found. He gave them information which was immensely valuable; he delivered British and American agents into their hands without a scruple. But Ivliev couldn't understand why he did it. He himself was a simple character; his own motives were clear. He did not belong to the type of Russian Intelligence officers who exist only in the minds of Western thriller writers. He was not a member of the original Bolshevik Revolution who had risen from the ranks or the lower decks and was now old enough to be disillusioned with his political creed and tempted by the fleshpots of the West. Ivliev was a man of sincere ideas and dedicated patriotism, a Russian first and a Soviet Russian second. He had fought in the final stages of the war, and marched with the occupying troops into Berlin, until he took a special course at Leningrad and transferred to the Intelligence at the end of it. He was brilliant at his job, and there was nothing he could imagine more satisfying than being a Russian in the last half of the twentieth century. He was not a cruel man, or a sentimentalist. He liked to describe himself as a policeman. He finished his whisky in one swallow, offered the flask to Wetherby, who shook his head. He was a polite man, but suddenly curiosity overcame him.

'Mr. Wetherby, there's something I would like to ask you. It's a very personal question. Would you mind?'

'Not in the least. Ask, by all means.'

'Why did you decide to work for us?'

The Englishman turned his head slightly and smiled. 'Why do you suppose, Colonel? You must have given it a lot of thought, what conclusion did you come to?'

'Nothing that made sense,' Ivliev answered. 'You are not a convert to Communism, you don't accept payment. Possibly you feel a sense of grievance against your country?'

Wetherby shook his head, and the supercilious smile became an equally contemptuous laugh. The logic itself amused him. All the temptations were there but the real one. A political ideology which he found repugnant, the unlikely bribe of money to a man already very rich, and finally the unpaid grudge.

'I'm afraid you're a long way from the truth, my dear Colonel,' he said. 'I'm not motivated by spite against anything or anyone. As a matter of fact my country has rewarded me very well for my services. It's something much simpler than anything you've suggested. The reason I came over to you was because I was bored.'

Ivliev didn't answer because he didn't believe him. The car gathered speed as it drove round the outskirts of the city, and then turned back, cruising down the Unter den Linden. 'I'll leave you in the car park at the cinema over there. A taxi is waiting for you. He'll take you back into the West.'

'Thank you, Colonel. I'll make contact in London and let you know my progress with Arundsen. And don't worry. You shall have him.'

The rear door opened, and closed. In the gloom of the car park Wetherby disappeared from Ivliev's view. The Zim did a U-turn and drove out into the street; at Ivliev's instructions it pulled into the kerb. A moment later he saw the taxi leave the cinema car park and head south down the avenue. Wetherby was checked every step and he never made a suspect move. The most famous wartime Intelligence Chief in the European theatre had been a double agent for the Soviet for nearly five years. And he explained his treason by saying he was bored. The Colonel was angry with himself for being fool enough to ask, and being made to feel a fool by getting such an answer. Bored. It was not just incredible, it was an insult. He leaned forward and snapped at the driver to take him back to Headquarters.

'You've got a very nice flat,' Arundsen said.

'I'm glad you like it. Sit down and I'll get some tea. Or would you rather have a drink?'

She had thrown her bag and gloves on a chair in the small, elegant hall, and she turned to him at the entrance to the drawing-room, a bright multicoloured silk scarf in one hand, brushing her long hair back with the other. She looked like the glossy photographs of models caught in an improbable pose; slim, burnished, unattainable. Arundsen dropped into an armchair and looked up at her. They had had a good lunch and rather too much wine. He smiled at her and held out his hand.

'I'd like a drink. In a minute.'

'All right.' She didn't come towards him, but the warm smile lit her face and gave him hope. 'I'll go and get some ice. I won't be a minute. The cigarettes are in that box there – beside you.'

He looked round the room appreciating what he saw. It was like Mary. Cool and expensive, with flashes of brilliant colour. There were a lot of flowers, cleverly arranged so that they blended into the room. He remembered suddenly that Joan never bought flowers unless people were coming to dinner. There was a fine landscape over the mantelpiece and a curious modern abstract on a long wall. He disliked the abstract because he couldn't see anything in that form of art, but just the same it blended. After they left the restaurant there was a moment of hiatus, when neither spoke or seemed to know what to do next. It was so close to becoming an anticlimax that Arundsen nearly panicked and suggested a cinema. They had stood on the pavement, hesitating, and suddenly he had hailed a cab. He gave Mary's address, and just walked into the flat with her. He wanted to make love to her very badly. All through the lunch, sitting in the touching intimacy of a small table, he had been so aware of her that he didn't want to eat. Everything about her which attracted him seemed more exaggerated; her eyes were bigger, and dark blue, like her dress, her skin paler, smoother, and the damned scent came at him whenever she moved. When she turned and smiled at him it tied a knot in his inside. It wasn't just desire; Arundsen had wanted a lot of women over the years, but he realised that what he felt for Mary Wetherby was much more complicated than a simple urge to sleep with a beautiful woman. It was too complicated to make sense and he didn't want to try. He wanted her to come back into the room before it got so bad he had to go out to the kitchen and find her.

'Sorry I was so long,' she said. 'I couldn't get the ice out.' She was carrying a tray with a bottle of whisky, a syphon and two glasses. He got up and took it from her.

'To hell with the ice,' he said. 'Come and sit down.'

There was a large modern sofa, the only big item in the

room, and he held her by the arm, guiding her to it. She let him put her in one corner of it, and she watched him pour two whiskies.

'I don't want one,' she said. Arundsen came back and held the glass out to her. 'Yes you do,' he said. 'I don't like drinking alone. And stop looking so frightened.' He reached over and took her hand, the left one with the wedding ring she still wore.

'Why don't you take that off?' he said suddenly.

'I don't know,' she said. 'It was a superstition I once had, if you took your ring off the marriage broke up. And marriage was for ever, as far as I was concerned.'

'You're not a Catholic, are you?' Arundsen asked.

'I was,' Mary answered. 'I don't practise any more.'

'Then you shouldn't stick to a superstition. Take the bloody thing off and throw it away.' He began to turn the ring round on her finger, sliding it down over her knuckle. She had beautiful hands, unmarred by the long painted nails that he disliked. The ring came off suddenly, and at the same moment he tossed it to the other side of the room. 'That's what that's worth,' Arundsen said. 'Now come here.'

It was dark when she woke, and he was still asleep, one heavy arm lying across her. She didn't move; she lay beside him watching the lights flickering through the bedroom window from the traffic passing underneath. Never in her life had she woken in this way.

The peace of exhaustion filled her mind, and a sense of deep, increasing tenderness for the man beside her. A stranger. A stranger who had taken her out to lunch and then persuaded her to go to bed with him. It sounded so sordid, the kind of cheap situation which normally disgusted her; but the reality was not like that at all. What Arundsen had made her feel was impossible to describe. The word beautiful fitted it, and so did all the other superlatives, so debased by trivial use that they were only clichés. She had been afraid and reluctant, resisting the temptation to do something she had despised in other women, and he had overcome her with gentleness. Insistent but always gentle, until she had come willingly to meet every demand he made upon her. She would never think of making love except as he had shown how it should be done. She moved at last, bending over him and kissed him. He woke immediately, and after a second's pause, he smiled at her.

51

'Anyone ever tell you you were marvellous?' he said.

'No.' The soft hair brushed his face as she shook her head; he reached up and pulled her down to him, running his fingers over her face, prising her lips apart with the tips of them. He had been very careful with her; he had never allowed his impulses to slip from control. He wasn't just satisfied and sentimental; even the rising provocation in holding her body close and kissing her couldn't disguise the fact that his emotions were in full play. He made a wry joke to hide them.

'It wasn't too bad, after all, was it?'

'It was marvellous,' she whispered. 'Thank you.'

'Don't thank me, darling,' he said. 'Just let me do it again, and don't be nervous this time.'

'I won't be nervous,' she answered. She slipped her arms up round his neck and kissed him. Her cheeks were wet where she had cried, as some women do when they are overcome by happiness. 'I'll never be nervous with you, Peter. Never with you.'

'It's nearly seven,' Arundsen said. 'I'll have to go soon.'

'I know.' She came over to him and sat on the arm of the chair. The drawing-room looked the same; the door to her bedroom was closed, hiding the evidence of the unmade bed. Everything looked the same as it had when they came in after lunch, and yet everything was different. 'Have a drink before you go.'

He reached up and squeezed her hand. 'I will, if you will.' She gave him a glass of whisky and sat beside him again, one arm round his shoulder, balanced on the chair arm.

'Do you feel guilty, Peter? About Joan?'

'No,' Arundsen said. 'I'm afraid I don't. She's not very keen on this sort of thing anyway. And it's not the old "my wife doesn't understand me" routine. It's the truth. She doesn't know and it won't make any difference except that I'll say I was working late or met a friend or something. I feel much more guilty about you.'

'Why me?' she whispered, bending down and pressing her face against him. 'You shouldn't feel guilty about me. I'm very happy.'

'Yes,' Arundsen said. 'I know you are. But it's not much fun making love and everything going well, and then the bastard goes home to his wife and leaves you sitting here. That's the part I don't like – leaving you alone.'

'You're not to call yourself a bastard,' she said. 'I told you that before. Down at Buntingford, when you nearly kissed me.'

'And you backed off,' he reminded her. 'I remember very well. You're not in a position to back off now. Bend down.'

Her body was very soft; she slid down on to his knees and he plunged into a long kiss, his hands moving over her. There was nothing artificial about her, nothing that promised on the outside and turned out to be a fake. She was supple and feminine and within seconds he was ready to take her back into the bedroom and make love to her more powerfully than before.

'You must stop,' she said. 'Please, Peter, stop now. You've got to go home.'

He swore, but she insisted and he let her go.

'Don't be angry,' she said suddenly. 'You know I'd like you to stay all night. But I don't want to make trouble for you. You ought to go home.'

'All right. But I don't want to. When am I going to see you again?'

'I don't know.' She turned away from him. Don't get involved, Phillip had said. Have an affair, but don't get emotional about it. But she was already so emotional that there were tears in her eyes because he was leaving.

'What do you mean, you don't know?' Arundsen demanded. 'You're not suggesting we stop seeing each other, by any chance?'

'We'd be better not to,' she said. 'I know we're making a mistake – anyway, I'm making one. Listen to me, Peter. I know I asked you back here – I know I went to bed with you, just like that. But I'm not a tramp. It doesn't sound very convincing after the way I've behaved, but I don't go round sleeping with men. I don't expect this to mean anything to you, but I know it'll mean something to me. And I can't afford it.'

He came up to her and held her still, both hands on her shoulders.

'I want you to understand something, Mary. Neither of us can afford to get involved, but the fact is, we are. We began it, and we're going on with it. Don't think this is any casual lay as far as I'm concerned. Anyway, you know it's not.'

He kissed her, just missing her mouth.

53

'I'll come at five tomorrow. You'll be here, won't you?'
'Yes,' she said. 'Of course I will.'

The grey Bentley eased forward and drew up at the steps of the Regulars' Club in Pall Mall. Wetherby's chauffeur got out and opened the rear door; Wetherby climbed inside it, closed the door and a moment later the car moved away from the pavement, gliding from second through to top without a perceptible difference in the movement.

'We'll go straight home,' Phillip said, and the man nodded. He enjoyed living in the country; Buntingford was exactly the kind of setting he felt appropriate to his job; he had a very comfortable flatlet with everything he needed, and the kind of employer who should own a Bentley. He couldn't have borne to work for some jumped-up company director with a vulgar house in Hampstead.

'Pleasant lunch, sir?'

'Moderate. The food's good, but the service is frightful. It's a rather second-rate club.'

It had been what Wetherby termed a business lunch, at the invitation of the head of the Firm, a retired major-general whom he didn't like. It was the sort of club frequented by admirals and senior army officers; its interior was drab, the decorations varying between the hideous apple green beloved by the military and the café au lait which was supposed not to show the dirt. Wetherby loathed going there, but he had been asked to report on his trip to Berlin.

And he had confessed to failure. The Major-General was a tight-lipped, autocratic type, his ruthless zeal and total inhumanity in personal relationships untainted by any imaginative quality. In Wetherby's opinion he was the worst possible kind of man for the job. He was unpopular with his staff, and his casualty rate was so high among agents that a lot of good men, of whom Arundsen was typical, refused to work for him. He didn't like Wetherby, but he made use of him, because he was widely experienced, with the entrée to many places where the Major-General's men couldn't otherwise penetrate and he gave his considerable services free. In return he was kept informed of most of the highly secret work which was in hand.

It amused Phillip to sit over lunch and shake his head, admitting that Dunne had slipped through from his Austrian holiday without leaving any trace. Then mischief had prompted him, as it sometimes did, to lay a clue in front of the fool sitting opposite him, and watch the fun. In the car, inching through the traffic up the Mall, he wondered whether that impulse had been over-rash.

And then he smiled to himself. Of course it was rash, but how dull life would be if there were no risks, no vulgar gestures under an unsuspecting nose. He had told the Major-General, very seriously, that he had picked up one lead while in West Berlin. Dunne had stayed at the Berghoffer for two nights; this was a small low-grade pension-cum-boarding house near the industrial section of the city, and Dunne had indeed stayed there, under Soviet supervision. But Wetherby made his gesture by saying that a mysterious man had been seen with him, and then given a fairly good description of himself. It was the sort of supercilious joke which gave his unique position such a spice. It explained how true his remark to Colonel Ivliev had been, in a way that the Russian would never have understood.

He had been bored by working for his own side, and then frustrated as the quality of the work in the East European Section deteriorated in spite of him, and then finally rejuvenated by his decision to turn double. Ivliev was a superb professional, but he hadn't yet reached the point known only to the masters of the espionage trade, where the work becomes an end in itself, and patriotism or ideologies become irrelevant. Phillip couldn't have lived without his work, and the work itself was not up to his standard. He had come to the end, and he was due to retire. Only the supreme challenge of treason was left to him, and he took it because it demanded the ultimate in professional expertise.

He thought of the Major-General, seizing on the mysterious companion who had been with Dunne. No such meeting between them had taken place; he had left Dunne in the Tyrol. The progress through to Berlin and the East had been organised by Ivliev's people. But the soldier went on harping on the man's appearance and nationality. Wetherby had even suggested that the man could be an Englishman. He was well-bred-looking – he saw the Major-General wince because he was extremely conscious of his own middle-class origins and an unfortunate public school now vanished without trace – he had grey hair and he wore glasses. 'In that case,' the Major-General said, 'we'll put a really good man into Berlin to follow it up.'

He had told Wetherby the name and details of the agent.

Hugo Riezner, a young Anglo-German, completely new to the Berlin section. And then the joke had got a little out of hand.

Phillip lit a cigar and pressed the electric button operating his offside window. It rolled down six inches. The Major-General had said in view of this information he would intensify investigations into Dunne's activities in England, especially within the three months of his last leave. If this man was an Englishman they ought to follow Wetherby's lead with scrupulous care from the home end as well as the German side of it. Very useful work, very promising, the soldier had said, and ordered them both a double brandy. Normally he was a mean host. He drank whiskies in a series of quick doubles in the bar, and outraged Wetherby's sensibilities by ordering a half-bottle of indifferent claret with the meal, and nothing with the coffee.

Over the brandy, Phillip had worked a way through this development; it had looked rather nasty for a moment. He had spent a lot of time with Jimmy Dunne; however careful they had been, it was still possible that someone, somewhere, might remember something. He was regretting his little joke at the Major-General's expense when he suddenly thought of the Countess. It was so clever that he became quite animated in proposing it.

'Just the person you need to nose out everything Dunne did, my dear fellow,' he said. 'A woman is sometimes much better than a man at this kind of thing, and Katharina is one of the most experienced people I know. Let me give it to her to do.'

The Major-General had hesitated, repeating the name.

'Don't I know about her,' he said. 'Didn't she collect some gong or something during the war?'

Wetherby had been unable to resist saying it. 'Yes, indeed. The George Cross, among a few others. She wouldn't want much money. Things aren't too good for her at the moment. I'd take it as a personal favour if you'd put this in her way. I'll talk to her about it.'

And so it was arranged. The Countess would investigate the mystery man; Wetherby couldn't imagine anything more complacent than the idea of a broken-down drunk on a trail which he could obliterate at every juncture if she showed any sign of finding anything. Not that she would. She was finished.

It was all going in the most satisfactory direction. Getting James Dunne to defect had been a fascinating, though repulsive process. He had often felt during the months when he cultivated the man that vivisectionists must feel as he did. There was no sense of compassion for the object of the operation. He had spent hours going from one scruffy pub to another, listening to the outpourings of a drunk, surely the most boring occupation known to man, playing alternatively on his vanity and his increasing persecution mania.

It had been done with such subtlety that Dunne ended, in that crucial few days in the Tyrol, by weeping like a child at the lack of appreciation for his services and the ingratitude of all concerned to Wetherby and himself.

'Bugger them all,' he had shouted suddenly, springing up and squaring up to no one in particular. 'I'll bloody well show them how important I am! I'll teach them to write me off! I'll go over to the other side! They want me, don't they? – they think I'm a bloody good operator . . .'

And so Phillip had slipped away, and Ivliev's men had come to take Dunne through the net. He was maudlin and drunk most of the time. It was the most gruelling few days Phillip could remember, because he had found Dunne so personally repulsive. But by God what an achievement! Getting Arundsen out of his safe little niche would be child's play compared to manoeuvring that gorilla.

It would be nice to do the Countess a good turn and put a little money in her way. And he had the name of the new man going to Berlin. Reizner. If he was as good as the Major-General thought, then Ivliev had better have him murdered.

When Arundsen came out of the lift she was waiting by the flat door. They met four times a week, sometimes they lunched together, always in out of the way places where they weren't likely to be seen, and then they went back to her flat for a hurried interlude alone; if Arundsen was too busy to get away he came round after his office closed. They had been meeting for nearly a month. He pushed the front door shut behind them and began to kiss her.

'I've missed you,' she said. 'Oh, Peter, I thought it would never get to five o'clock.'

'I missed you too,' Arundsen said; he was busy with her mouth, stifling the words with kisses. Instead of getting better, slowing down, it got worse. He wanted her more every time they were together. The scent and feel and thought of her obsessed him.

'I'm crazy about you,' he said. 'Absolutely crazy about you. I've been thinking of this all day.'

'So have I.' She slipped away from him, flushed and out of breath. 'Don't you even want a drink first?'

'No,' Arundsen said. 'I just want you.'

Later he bent over her and kissed her gently on the lips. 'You've changed a lot,' he said. 'You keep coming out of your shell all the time. Better and better; more and more beautiful.'

She looked up at him and smiled. Her hand reached up and stroked his cheek. 'You're a wonderful teacher. And a very powerful lover. You must have made love to hordes of women.'

'Not hordes,' he laughed. 'One or two, here and there. But none like you. No one has ever been like you. You're like a drug; the more I get the more I want.' He put his arms round her and she entwined with him, clinging close to his body. It gave her a feeling of safety as if his physical strength could insulate her from the world.

'Do you know what I'd like to do?' he asked her.

'Tell me.'

'I'd like to go away somewhere with you. I'd like to spend a whole weekend alone with you. Probably keep you in bed from Friday to Monday!'

'Don't you like me otherwise?' She asked the question smiling.

'No,' Arundsen laughed at her. 'It's just sex with me, that's all.' Women always played this game, but it was the first time it hadn't jarred on him. She wanted to be reassured; he liked to tease her before saying what she knew already.

'You know, I couldn't bear it, if that's all it were,' she said suddenly. 'Would you be very angry if I said I loved you, Peter?'

'No,' Arundsen held her closer to him. 'No, but I'd be surprised. There's not much to love about me.'

'You don't realise,' she said. 'You don't see yourself as you are.'

'Oh yes I do,' he said. 'That's just the trouble. The hell of it is one day you'll see it too, and then you won't want me any more. I'm middle-aged, I've got a dull job, I don't love my wife and the only thing I care about is you. Haven't I told you I'm in love with you?'

'In a lot of ways,' Mary said gently. 'But not in words.'

'Well, I'm telling you now,' he said. 'I'm in love with you and I love you; I've never said that to any woman in my life before. But I don't know what the hell to do about it.'

'Thank you, darling. Thank you for saying it to me.' She turned and kissed his shoulder.

'It still doesn't answer the question,' he said. 'What's going to be the end of it? You say you love me – I think you must be crazy, but I believe you – so what do we do?'

'Why think about the end?' she said quickly. 'Why can't we just be happy now?'

'I've got a tidy mind.' He stroked her hair as he talked. 'When I find something I really want I like to keep it. I want to keep you, Mary. One day you'll get fed up or meet someone else and then *Kaput*! You'll be gone.'

She sat upright and looked at him steadily.

'I'll never be gone from you,' she said. 'You're the only man I've ever loved in my life. You needn't be afraid of losing me. I'm the one who's afraid of that happening. You're everything I've ever looked for, Peter. You're strong and you're gentle and you make me feel so loved – and so safe. But we can't change the situation. You're married, you've got responsibilities, a child – you can't walk out on them!'

'I know I can't,' Arundsen said. 'The hell of it is I don't think I'd be missed if I did go. Joan and I haven't got anything left. David's all right, he's at school anyway.' He got up, moving across the room, collecting his clothes. She lay back, watching him dress, her arms linked above her head.

'Why couldn't I have married you in the first place?' she said suddenly. 'Why did I have to marry Richard Wetherby and you marry Joan? We could be so happy together. Just lying here, I can imagine how I'd feel, being your wife.'

He came and sat on the edge of the bed. He bent his head down and kissed the soft place between her breasts.

'You look sad, darling. I'm going to take you out to dinner tonight,' he said. 'I'm not going home and leaving you here alone. I'm going to ring up Joan and say I won't be back till late.' He went out of the bedroom, and she heard the telephone jingle as he picked it up and began to dial. She dressed, trying not to listen to the lies he was telling. She took a black silk dress out of the cupboard, and made up her face. He liked her hair hanging loose and long, and she sprayed her arms and neck with scent.

She had always been fastidious; good grooming and elegant

clothes were part of her natural background. Now she did everything with his approval in mind. She used little lipstick, because when he kissed her it was messy, and he was always kissing her when they were alone. He made love to her in little ways, they were always in contact, holding hands, linking arms, sitting close together. And yet he used her very carefully, as if she were intrinsically precious to him. This was one of the reasons why she loved him, and she knew it. All she had experienced inside her marriage was inseparable from being hurt, mentally and physically. With Arundsen she knew the deepest submission and the sublimest satisfaction from it. Firm and yet gentle. A strong man who knew what he wanted and what she wanted too. It was the answer to what she had been searching for all her life, and the antidote to the years of married hell.

He had never asked for details about her life with Richard Wetherby. He had left it to her to tell him if she wanted to; he was there and ready to listen when the moment came, but because of Washington it never could come. He wasn't a man who would forgive treason. If he ever knew it, it would be the end. She went into the drawing-room to find him.

'I fixed it,' he said. 'I said I'd met a chap from the old office, and he'd asked me to have dinner with him. It's all right, you needn't look like that. She believed me. She's quite happy.'

'I wouldn't be,' she said. She came and put her arms round his waist. 'I'd know you were lying and I'd be miserable. I do hope she isn't, Peter. I had that sort of thing done to me, too.'

'What didn't he do, while he was at it?' Arundsen felt himself growing angry. 'Never mind that. We're going to go out somewhere nice; out of London. I know a very pretty place near Reading. Would you like that?'

'I'd love it,' she said. 'I'll get my coat.'

They had a corner table, near the inevitable inglenook fireplace which was filled with flowers in a big brass bowl. There were fresh flowers on the table, and candles. It was warm and intimate, and they held hands under the table while they chose from the menu. Arundsen hadn't felt like this for so many years that he seemed to be in his first youth. Just being seen with her was an excitement. Everybody looked at her; he liked the feeling of ownership. Most of all he liked the way they could relax together, and how the talk flowed between them without any effort. It was natural, like the silence.

He had spent a long day at his office, and the boredom of what he was doing made it seem interminable. Nothing mattered but the woman beside him. He had never thought of leaving Joan before. Now he thought of it constantly. His mind had begun to play with ideas, selecting and rejecting one scheme after another which might show him a way out. It would be difficult and even messy. Expensive too. But it could be done.

'Are you enjoying it?' he asked her.

'Yes. Every moment. I'm very happy, Peter. It's such a funny feeling. I'm not used to it.'

'I'm going to make you used to it,' he said. 'Pour out the coffee, I've had an idea. Why don't we really go away somewhere for a few days?'

She took two cigarettes out of her case, and lit them both, handing one to him. 'Darling, how can we? How can you get away?'

'Business,' Arundsen said. 'I've been told for years how important it was to get on, be enthusiastic and all that sort of jazz. I'm going away on business for a weekend. Men only. How about Paris? Do you like Paris?'

'I went there with Phillip a year ago,' she said. 'It was rather lonely. He went off seeing people most of the time. I spent a fortune shopping, I remember that.'

'Well, you won't be allowed to do that if you come with me,' he said. 'When I'm not making love to you, which will be most of the time, we'll do a proper rubber-necking tour! I know dozens of nice places to go. I'll take you to Malmaison and show you the rose gardens.'

'What about Versailles?' she asked him. Their hands clasped on the table top, and they both laughed.

'Versailles too. Anything you like. Shall we do it?'

'Yes,' she said softly. 'Yes, darling, I'd love to go with you.'

'Paris is a bit trite,' he said after a moment. 'We could go to Stockholm or Copenhagen – they're beautiful cities. We don't have to go to Paris if you'd rather see somewhere else.'

She looked at him and smiled. It made him feel as if someone had punched him hard over the heart when she looked at him like that.

'You're very silly, for such a clever man,' she said. 'Don't you know I'd go to Bournemouth, and enjoy it, just to be with you? It's not the place I care about.'

'I love you.' He said it quietly, not looking at her. 'And I'm going to make you happy. Paris will be just the beginning for us. Come on, my darling, let's get the bill.'

It was nearly ten years since the Countess had been inside the Ritz bar; after Wetherby's telephone call she had leant against the shabby papered wall in the entrance hall of the lodging house and given way to panic. She couldn't meet him there. She had no proper clothes, her hair wasn't done; she had a miserable hangover and an empty stomach. The Ritz bar had nothing to do with her life any more. The communal phone in the dirty little hallway, the depressing bed-sitting-room three floors up – this was what she had grown used to, and where she felt at home.

'You finished with the phone, dear?' It was one of three girls who shared the two double rooms on the ground floor.

'Oh, yes. Here.' The Countess pulled herself together and went back upstairs.

She was afraid. Buntingford was one thing, but meeting the Chief in one of her old haunts was quite another matter. She went to the mirror on the chest of drawers and looked at herself. She spoke in Polish, and the reflection glared back at her.

'You're a coward. A drunkard and a slut and now a coward. Go and make yourself respectable, or you'll be late. Damn you.'

She left the Bayswater house half an hour after the phone call. She wore a plain dark coat, which had taken some time to brush, and a red hat shaped like a turban, which hid her hair. She had put on her last pair of perfect stockings and high-heeled black satin shoes, which she had hardly worn. It didn't really matter so long as she didn't disgrace him. Nobody would ever recognise her, even if some of the old smart faces were still there. She took the Tube, gritting her teeth against the noise which rattled through her head, and the jerking movement of the train which teased her uneasy stomach. She had always hated Tubes; it was a curious legacy from the war, that the enclosed little carriages snaking at speed underground gave her a feeling of claustrophobia. She and two members of the Polish Resistance had once spent four days hiding in a disused sewage tunnel, and she had never liked being below gound level since. It was the rush hour and the Tubes were crammed with struggling crowds. The traffic above would be crawling, especially since it had begun to rain. She almost ran up the stairs of the Tube station at Green Park, and then paused for a moment on the pavement, letting the people pour out from behind her.

She crossed over from one side of Piccadilly to the other, and glanced at herself in the mirrored back wall of a display window outside the great hotel. She had often stayed there, frequently dined there in the splendid restaurant or the grill.

It was good of Phillip to ask her to meet him in such a place; a different kind of man would have suggested somewhere cheap, appropriate to her changed status in the world. She straightened herself, and walked through the swing doors; turning right, she began walking down the steps into the bar. A waiter came up to her.

'Madame?'

'I'm meeting Mr. Wetherby. Is he here?'

'Yes, madame. In the corner over there. Come this way, please.'

He got up and came to meet her; when she held out her hand he kissed it. 'My dear Countess,' he said. 'How nice to see you. Come and sit down.'

'You know, it's nice to see this place again,' she said. She had drunk one brandy sour, and was being deliberately slow with a second. But her head had cleared and she was relaxed, nostalgic. The pink lights were kind to her; she looked much younger and the jagged lines of strain and alcohol were smoothed away in the soft glow.

'It brings back so many memories. I don't see a single face I know.' She smiled at him. 'Just as well, they wouldn't recognise me after all these years. You said you wanted to talk to me about something important? Will you tell me what it is?'

'It's only an idea,' Phillip Wetherby said. 'It may not appeal to you at all. You have your life, you probably won't want to go back over old ground.'

'My life.' The Countess leaned towards him. 'You know what my life is. Don't let's talk about that. What do you mean, go over old ground?'

'Come back to work for me.' He stubbed out his cigarette in the metal ashtray, pressing out the last little spark in the blackened stub. 'It's quite an important job, really, and we need someone like you. Someone with experience.'

'You mean you're asking me to do a job for you – like the old days?' She stared at him, and suddenly the illusion vanished. She looked old and anxious, with the wretched eagerness of the unemployed.

'Yes,' Phillip said. 'That's what I do mean. We need someone to investigate the three months James Dunne spent on leave here in England. We want to find out if he had any friends or contacts, and who they were. It'll be quite a long job, I think. The regulars have already done some of the preliminaries, but they didn't get very far. I'll have to fix up about the salary, that's if you decide to do it, of course. But it won't be too much of an insult. I'll see to that.'

The Countess put one hand up to shield her face. Her eyes had filled with tears and they were overflowing. She searched her bag and brought out a paper handkerchief.

'Forgive me,' she said, and wiped her eyes. 'You don't know what this means to me. I'll be all right.' She turned her face to him and smiled. The edges of her lids were red and her mouth quivered.

'Would you take it on?'

'Yes,' she said. 'Oh yes, I would. And don't worry about the salary, don't ask them for too much or anything like that. I'd do it for nothing!'

'Never do anything for nothing in this world, Countess,' he said gently. 'It's a bad principle. I didn't realise you felt so keen on getting back into the business. I'd have put something in your way before.'

'I feel as if I were drowning and you'd pulled me into the last boat,' she said. 'I let you all down before, I won't do it again, I promise you. I won't touch a drink!'

'You shouldn't worry about that,' Phillip Wetherby said. 'You'll have to meet people, make contacts. Don't make an issue of the odd brandy. You'll do splendidly. And once you're working for us there'll be other jobs after this one.'

'I am so grateful to you,' she said simply. 'Forgive me for getting emotional. It was just a shock for a moment. I lived for my work; it really was the breath of life to me. I never thought I'd get a second chance. I'll do it, and I'll find out everything you want. Can you give me a few details?'

'I thought we might go into the grill and have some dinner; I can talk to you about business then, I've got a list of dresses you might start with – and some money, in advance. Can you dine with me?'

'Yes,' she nodded, holding herself tightly in control. 'Yes, I'd be delighted. I've no engagements for this evening.'

'Good.' He smiled at her, and offered a cigarette. His gold lighter clicked and the little flame flared.

'There's no hurry, it's only seven-thirty. We must have another drink.'

CHAPTER FOUR

The Countess paid off the taxi at the end of the road. She had few enough personal belongings and they all fitted into one rubbed old suitcase with the faint outline of her initials on the lid. The leather was good and it would never wear out. In the old days she bought the best: clothes, shoes, luggage, scent. She was well paid and her expenses were extravagant. There had been a general feeling in the department that she deserved the good things of life because of what she had done and was even then doing. It seemed so unreal that when she thought about it, it was as if everything in the past had happened to someone else.

She began walking down the street to the corner; the name of the district suited it. World's End. It was the shabby declension of Chelsea; the houses were shabbier, the shops more mundane and the inhabitants moved rather than swung through their days. Dunne had spent his last leave in the area. She had passed the house where he had a room and stopped at the house two doors down. There was a card in the ground-floor window. 'Bed & Breakfast.' The notice was printed in bold black type. Underneath it was a sentence written in ink. 'No coloureds'. The Countess walked up to the front door and rang the bell.

There was a bed-sitting-room on the first floor overlooking the street. The landlady was a harassed woman in her fifties, clean and hard-working, and not, as she explained to the Countess, prepared to take just anyone.

The Countess understood her; she had been mistaken for a prostitute before. She wasn't offended; she was even a little amused. There wouldn't be any more desperate pick-ups and the stealthy progress upstairs with them, hoping no one would come out of their rooms at the wrong moment.

She had a job, and a post-office savings account which Wetherby had opened for her with an initial payment of five hundred pounds. The bed-sitting-room was clean, with a single divan covered in dark flowered cretonne, an uncomfortable-looking armchair in the same material, a Victorian mahogany table of squat ugliness, a ceiling and a bedside light; one modern standard chair which looked pale and incongruous

66

in a corner, and a print of Lady Hamilton as a Bacchante over the mantelpiece.

There was a gas fire, and a gas ring. The landlady's name was Mrs. Johns, and the rent, she said, was seven guineas a week, breakfast included.

The Countess turned and smiled at her. 'It's very nice. I'll take it. I would like to pay two weeks in advance – is that agreeable to you?'

Mrs. Johns said yes, thank you very much, it was. She always asked for a week's rent anyway, but if the lady liked to pay for two – well, that suited her. The Countess gave her the money, smiled at her again, and Mrs. Johns, deciding that she was certainly a lady, in spite of being foreign and rather come down in the world, relented enough to smile back.

'Are you very full?'

'I've only this room and a back lower ground vacant at the moment,' Mrs. Johns said. 'I didn't think you'd want to see that. It's a bit dark, you know. Cheap, of course.'

'No, this is just what I wanted. I expect people come and go though fairly often. Do you have students here?'

'Now and then, but I like regulars. As I said, I like to know what I'm getting. Some of these young ones are really dreadful. I've two gentlemen who've been here for eighteen months, and the lady above since last Christmas time.'

'How nice,' the Countess said. 'I'm sure I shall be one of your regulars too, Mrs. Johns. Thank you so much.'

It was ten days since she had accepted the job from Wetherby. A man from the Major-General's office had called to see her three days later, and given her the description of the man she had to find out about. When she told Wetherby he seemed irritated; she understood how he resented a piece of unnecessary interference, like that visit; she was working for and reporting to Wetherby directly. After their dinner at the Ritz she had begun to limit her drinks. It had been an exhausting effort of will to cut out the first two fingers in the early morning. By lunchtime she was shaking and sick with the need for it. But the effort encouraged her to make others.

She bought half-bottles, and made them last two days. There was a flask in her handbag, and it was full. Its capacity was just over a half, and she had set herself strict limits as to how much she nipped from it a day. And there was no bottle hidden in the bedroom to top up the flask. That in itself curbed her because she was inhibited by the need to go out and buy more, rather than unlock the wardrobe or search under the mattress. She owed Phillip Wetherby too much to let him down. Her own promise haunted her, made in the half-forgotten environs of the Ritz bar, her resolution buttressed by two champagne cocktails.

'I won't let you down this time. I promise, I won't touch a drink.' That was a boast, and she knew it. A promise which was impossible to keep. But to cut down was something she hadn't been able to do for years.

Phillip had given her hope when she had lost both it and self-respect. She had something to do which was important, and this time she was going to do it, out of gratitude to him. She unpacked her clothes and put them away; there was a new cloth coat which she hung up in the cupboard and a new coat and skirt. She had bought carefully, refusing to be extravagant because Phillip had been generous. There was one hanger with the cleaner's name stamped on it, and two hooks in the wardrobe wall. A piece of frayed American cloth covered the shelf at the top. Everything was put away within ten minutes except a cardboard box on her bed. There were three small flat leather cases in it, and it was a long time since she had felt able to open them and look at what was inside. She took the English one out, held it for a moment and then snapped it open. The bronze Maltese cross dangled from its blue ribbon. The George Cross had been awarded her in 1945; her name was on the back of it. The other two medals were the Croix de Guerre and the Legion d'Honneur.

She had made a parachute drop into Poland with two other agents, both men, in the spring of '44. The object was to organise Polish Intelligence and relay information back about the casualties and supply losses of the German armies on the Eastern Front. The retreat was in its final stages; the three agents had contacted Polish Resistance and formed a group which liased with London. They had also established relations with the advancing Russians. Katharina had been a witness of that last-minute uprising in Warsaw; she had lived through it and fought through it, while the Soviet armies waited on the other side of the Vistula until Polish patriotism was extinguished in blood and the city itself was destroyed.

The Russians had promised to advance and help the Resistance. Instead they delayed deliberately, allowing the

German forces time to annihilate all opposition, and then taken up the battle when it was too late for Warsaw.

Katharina had brought one of the two men back out of the burning shattered city; he was wounded and his companion had been killed in the first forty-eight hours. On two occasions she fought off German patrols with grenades and Sten-gun fire. In a deserted field twelve miles from the city outskirts she had hidden in a ditch, nursing the agent, who died in the pick-up plane on their way back to England. That was what she won the George for; the other decorations came for later work in Paris and in Normandy.

Two men had been in that house eighteen months. They would have been there when Dunne was living two doors down. She would start with them in a casual way. There was a small restaurant at the end of the street, and two pubs within three minutes' walk. Dunne was known to have used all three. The department's investigators had talked to everyone in the neighbourhood in the first few days after his defection, but people were wary of questions. They either invented something in order to draw attention to themselves or omitted things because they didn't think they were important.

She had a better chance of drawing information out of anyone who knew him than any of the Special Branch or the Firm's touts, because she knew what she was looking for. A special friend, a close companion.

Anyone who fitted the description of the Englishman seen with Dunne in his last hours in West Berlin.

Arundsen had booked rooms for himself and Mary at the Carlton Hotel; he remembered it from several visits in the late fifties, before he got married. It was a luxurious and cosmopolitan place, patronised more by the French than by foreigners. Its position on the left bank was not central enough for the rich tourists, but its chef was famous. He met Mary at London Airport on Friday afternoon, and held her hand through the short flight to Orly. They didn't talk very much; she looked at him and smiled, and the old feeling of a body blow to the heart made him grip her hand harder, without saying anything.

'I hope to God the weather's good. It should be perfect so long as it's not too hot.'

'Stop worrying,' she said. 'I don't care if it's snowing.

We've got three whole days together, darling, that's all that matters.'

In the hotel they registered under separate names, and went into their rooms which were on the same corridor. Five minutes afterwards he knocked on her door.

'Darling,' Mary said, 'why didn't you book a double room for us?'

'Because if I'm getting a divorce you're not going to be cited. Come and kiss me.'

'I love you,' she said. 'I want you to know that.'

He held her very tightly in his arms and kissed her with increasing urgency. Then he pushed her a little back from him, and brought both hands round to cover her breasts. 'I believe you do love me,' he said. 'Now I want to show you how much I love you.'

She woke first, as she always did, and lay beside him, drifting on a slow tide of remembered pleasure, discovering how it felt to love him as well as be in love with him. He had a strong body, and she was aware of how carefully he controlled its strength so that she was never hurt. He was not a man who talked very much when he made love; and she found herself responding to him with a stream of words, both passionate and tender. Every time they were together the relationship developed further. Nothing was stale or a disappointment because it was never quite the same. And this was love, Mary thought, one arm across his chest, her head resting on his shoulder. This was what she had never known and had ceased to believe could exist. This excised the guilt and the anxiety of his being married, because she was so happy that she felt completely selfish in these moments. And he was happy too, because she made him so. This mattered to her very much, her ability to please him, to give back something of what he had given her. At times like these she could forget her marriage; she could almost pretend that Richard Wetherby had never existed. She had told Arundsen little by little the miserable details of those two years. His acceptance made her love him even more, because she was so grateful for the understanding. He let her unburden herself, as if he could take some of the pain and regret upon himself, and she had found a single, terrifying impulse growing stronger the more they were together. She wanted to tell him about Washington. She wanted to turn to him one day, on an occasion like the present one, and tell him that she was a coward and a traitor, but would he please, please try to understand that too, and go on loving her. . . .

'Hello, darling,' he said.

She lifted her head and kissed him. 'Hello.'

'Do you want some dinner? Poor sweetheart, you must be starving.'

'You always feel hungry, don't you?' She laughed at him and stroked his hair. 'Your hair sticks up like a little boy's and you wake up thinking about food!'

'If you don't get up,' Arundsen said, 'I'll start thinking about something else.'

'All right.' She bent over and kissed him, then threw back the bedclothes. He watched her moving through the room; she was slim and graceful, profoundly erotic in the casual search for her clothes.

'I've changed my mind,' he said. 'I don't think I want dinner after all.'

'Oh yes you do,' Mary said firmly. 'You're taking me to dinner and to the Folies Bergère. You promised!'

'Taking coals to Newcastle, that's what it is. All right – I promised. But do me a favour, darling. Put some clothes on!'

They had dinner in a small restaurant called La Bonne Auberge, and it was so good that the time passed and they didn't use the tickets for the Folies after all. It was a warm and brilliant Saturday in July, and he had hired a self-drive car to take them down to Malmaison, where the roses would be coming into their full glory of first bloom. On the way down Mary turned to him and said suddenly: 'I've never been so happy in my life.'

'I haven't either,' Arundsen said. He overtook a fast little Peugeot with speed and skill and brought the car back into the straight. 'I've never known anything like this. And I'm not going to let it go. You'll just have to marry me. My mind's made up.'

'You said we wouldn't talk about that this weekend,' she said. 'Please, Peter darling, you know it's impossible.'

'Nothing's impossible if you want it badly enough. And I want you; for ever and ever amen. We won't talk about it now, sweet, because Malmaison is just a hundred yards off this road. I'm going to take you through the rose garden where Napoleon made love to Josephine, and propose to you and you're going to say yes, and shut up arguing.'

71

The Empress Josephine's favourite retreat was more like a large country house than a palace. The rooms were on a small scale, and Mary and Arundsen walked through them with a group of tourists, and a guide. The decorations were surprisingly fresh; the red and gold bedroom with its superb Empire bed and hangings looked as if it was still occupied.

'She must have been tiny,' Mary whispered. 'The bed's so small.'

'As a matter of fact she was average height,' Arundsen answered. 'Napoleon was the short arse – sorry, darling – five foot nothing in his socks. They slept sitting up, that's why all the beds are short by our standards. Bloody uncomfortable by the look of it.'

'You know a lot of things, don't you?' she said. 'You've done so much, been to so many places and you know why Josephine slept in a small bed. You're a very remarkable man!'

'I'm a dreary executive in a city firm, and I've no money. Don't get carried away by the cowboy bit after the war. I wasn't anything special. Come on, let's leave this lot and go into the gardens. They're really beautiful.'

They walked through the formal beds and banks of roses; the air was so full of their scents that it was almost too sweet.

'Look,' Mary said. They had stopped by a long low bed of magnificent floribunda. 'Orangeade. Phillip adores them; he told me he was going to take out three beds at Buntingford and put these in instead.'

'Seems such a long way away, doesn't it?' Arundsen said suddenly. 'You know, if I hadn't had a row with Joan that Friday afternoon we wouldn't be here now? Funny, isn't it.'

'Not very,' she said. 'I don't like to think about her. I feel so guilty. Don't start talking about divorcing her, please darling. It'll spoil this perfect day we're having.'

'All right, I won't,' he said. 'But it's got to be faced sometime. You can't run away for ever.'

'I can,' she said gently. 'I'm not very good at facing up to things. You'll find that out one day. Look, there's a fountain. Let's go down there and sit down. I'm dying for a cigarette.'

'Me too,' he said. 'And don't look sad. You won't have to run away from anything, or face anything. I'll do it for you.'

Kalitz was a small village about five hundred versts south

72

of Moscow. It had once been part of the half a million acres owned by a Muscovite prince before the Great War, and in the first decade of the twentieth century he had built himself a spring hunting lodge outside the village. The Prince had died just before the Revolution, and his widow and children disappeared with the advent of the Soviets. Since Stalin's death the old sprawling stone building had been repaired and altered to fit the special requirements of the K.G.B. It was a place where only special prisoners were detained, and it was staffed by the military and by a team of doctors. An electrified fence twelve feet high surrounded it, and all approaches were barred to the general public for a radius of a hundred and fifty versts. The village itself had been depopulated and closed down; the inhabitants were resettled a week's journey distant from the area. If the exterior of Kalitz was forbidding, the inside was a deceptive contrast. The rooms were pleasantly furnished; there was every comfort for the K.G.B. officials and some of the prisoners' quarters were comparable to a good middle-class European hotel. Only the outside locks on every door and the bars, albeit wrought iron, outside the windows, spoilt the illusion that this was not a prison more dreaded than the Lubyanka. On the top floor the house had been converted into a series of small cells, with a central medical ward. These rooms were bare, padded and soundproofed. They remained occupied for intervals by everyone who was brought to Kalitz and refused to co-operate immediately.

The more drastic medical treatments, including intense courses of E.C.T. which impaired the memory and prepared the victim for accepting alien ideas, often produced reactions of violence or euphoric conditions where the person had to be restrained for his own safety.

Many, under prolonged interrogation and drugs, tried to commit suicide. All, with one or two exceptions, left Kalitz either mentally impaired or carefully indoctrinated. Those who succumbed completely to the methods and became impossible to take out of the little cells were lethally injected and their bodies incinerated in a separate building built within the grounds.

James Dunne had been at Kalitz for nearly three months; he had not been taken to the ultimate treatment section at the top of the house, he was still confined to his pleasant first-floor bedroom, and it was in this room that Colonel Nickolas Ivliev came to see him.

Dunne was sitting in an armchair when the Colonel came in. He didn't look up or pretend that he was aware anyone was with him. Ivliev, who was very experienced in the effect Kalitz had on different people, assessed his attitude as being bloody-minded, but essentially dejected. He was a big man, who had lost weight since coming to Russia. He had refused to shave or wash in the beginning, but this period of protest had been succeeded by another; he wouldn't eat. The principal medical officer had removed all alcohol for thirty-six hours, and only restored it when Dunne gave in and promised not to go on hunger strike. Nobody had been harsh with him, or threatened him with anything. He had been kept steadily sedated and gradually weaned from a bottle of whisky a day to measured doses during the daylight hours which his male nurse brought him in a medicine glass. He was allowed to smoke and read selected classics and there was an unlimited supply of paper and pencils. He had a personal interrogator who spent two hours with him every morning, afternoon and evening. The talks, question, refusal, counter-question, abuse, patient explanation went on till they became something which Dunne looked forward to; at that point they stopped without explanation and he saw nobody who would talk to him for a fortnight. The nurse brought his food and drink; his room was cleaned out, and no one said a word. He had been quite glad when his interrogator opened the door one morning and the old routine of human contact was resumed.

Ivliev pulled up a chair and sat down, facing Dunne.

'You're looking well, Mr. Dunne,' he said.

Dunne raised his head and glared at him. He had seen Ivliev several times since his reception in East Berlin, but his visits to Kalitz had coincided with regular injections of sodium pentothal, and Dunne didn't remember him.

'Who the hell are you?'

'Nickolas Ivliev. We met in East Berlin, when you came over. I travelled with you to Moscow. Don't you remember?'

'No,' Dunne said. 'I don't bloody well remember anything. You've come to wield the big stick, I suppose?' The eyes were very bloodshot and weary; he had spent a lot of time weeping the last few weeks, and the contours of his face were slack. He looked as if his features were slipping, becoming blurred, like his personality.

'No,' the Colonel said quietly. 'I haven't. We're your

friends, Mr. Dunne. We've tried to tell you that. We didn't kidnap you, you know. You came of your own free will.'

'So you tell me,' Dunne muttered. 'You people tell me a lot of things. I don't believe any of them.'

'Not even that you're a homosexual.'

He lit a cigarette and waited. Dunne was very powerful; he stood six feet three and still weighed fifteen stone. Two men were outside the door of the room, in case Ivliev needed them.

He got out of his chair and stood with both trembling hands clenched into fists, but he didn't move near the Colonel.

'You're a lair. Fuck off out of here! Go on, before I break your bloody neck!'

'Sit down, please, Mr. Dunne,' the Colonel said. There was a moment when Dunne did nothing; he went on standing, holding himself together, swallowing over and over again as if there was a large lump stuck in his breathing tract. 'Sit down,' Ivliev repeated. 'I didn't mean to offend you. I'm sorry.'

'You know what you can do,' Dunne said, but he sat down in the armchair again. Ivliev drew on his cigarette. He made a smoke ring and blew it gently across the space between them. 'You Westerners are such odd people,' he said suddenly. 'You make a sin out of something which is as old as man. You make it shameful and guilty, and hound each other without mercy. We don't think like that. To us, Mr. Dunne, a man has a right to be what he's born; a right to prefer men to women if that's what suits him. There's nothing wrong with your being homosexual, and you know you are, don't you? You've accepted that, and stopped being middle class about it?'

'I'm not a bloody queer,' Dunne said. 'You keep telling me I am, but I'm not, and if you say it again, by Christ I'll break your bloody neck. I've warned you!'

'All right, I'll put it to you differently. You've no wife and no family. You're a lonely man; you gave the best years of your life working for British Intelligence, and they didn't appreciate you. You were going to be sacked, you know that, don't you? Phillip Wetherby knew it; you were going to be thrown overboard, after all your work, because they didn't think you were any good. You were a drunk, remember. You were even investigated because they suspected you of being homosexual. These were your own people, Mr. Dunne. Not very grateful, were they?'

Dunne put his head down and covered his face with his hands. 'They were sods,' he said suddenly; when he looked up his face was red and wet with tears. 'Sods; I was the best Far Eastern man they ever bloody well had. Twenty years I worked in China, selling to the Chinese from Peking to Hangkow, and finally ending up in the Trade Department. I *ran* the operation for them!'

'I know,' Ivliev said. 'You should have got out long ago, like your friend Peter Arundsen. He sends you his best wishes, by the way.'

'What do you mean?' Dunne stared at him, his mouth falling a little open, the corners quivering. 'What message—how the hell would Peter get in touch with you?'

'How did you get in touch with us,' Ivliev countered. 'It's not difficult, if a man's discontented. You should realise that. He's not too happy at the moment. I know you were very fond of him, I expect you'll be sorry to hear his marriage is breaking up.'

Dunne's eyes had begun to blink compulsively. He reached out and stuffed a cigarette into his mouth, soaking the end with saliva; his big hand trembled as he tried to light it.

'I'm not surprised,' he said suddenly. He seemed to have forgotten that Ivliev had made him angry. Arundsen had been in his mind so much lately, and in his dreams too, in the most disturbing, terrible nightmare situations which brought him awake and yelling. He hadn't been able to fight it when his subconscious took over; he was finding it almost impossible to keep it within bounds on a normal level. He was lonely, just as that little bastard opposite had said, and he'd always been lonely. Arundsen had been his one real friend.

'I'm not surprised he's left her,' he said again. 'She was a stupid little bitch; not half good enough for him. Nag, nag, nag, that's what she used to do. Every time I went there she was on at him about something. I couldn't bloody well stand her.'

'She was probably jealous of you,' Ivliev said. 'Knowing how fond of you her husband was. Women are very petty about friendships between men. Anyway, he's left her. I understand he's been unsettled by your coming over to us.'

'He'll think I'm a . . .' Dunne said. His head lowered again. 'He doesn't understand how I felt.'

'He does,' Ivliev said. 'He's very sympathetic. That's why he sent you the message. And that's why I came, Mr. Dunne. I have some news for you. Arundsen wants to defect.'

For a moment Dunne's brain cleared; the confusion and emotional turmoil opened like a curtain, allowing his natural intelligence to come through the gap. 'That's not true,' he said. 'That's just not true, Colonel. I know Peter. He wouldn't come over to you in a thousand years. He thinks you stink!'

'And if I prove it to you,' Ivliev said gently. 'If I come here within the next few weeks and Arundsen walks through that door, will you believe me then? Will you accept his opinion that we're the people to work for, if there's any future for the world?'

'You're telling me he wants to come?' Dunne asked. The moment of clarity was passing; emotions which had been repressed his entire adult life were welling up in him like swirling pools of water, threatening to flood him completely. He felt as if he would drown in his own tears if he let go.

'He does,' Ivliev said. 'He's sick of the old life. He knows what he wants now. Your leaving did it. It takes something like that to make a man see the truth. Just as you're seeing the truth my friend. Arundsen wants to come over because the way you were treated has made him realise that he could conceivably find himself in the same situation. He'd like to come and talk to you, discuss joining us over here with someone he knows. Would you be prepared to meet Arundsen soon?'

'Yes.' The man seemed to sink into himself; his shoulders contracted and he sobbed into his hands. 'Yes, yes, I'd like to see the old sod again – talk about old times, have a few drinks . . .'

'I think you'd settle down with us very happily, if there were the two of you,' Ivliev put his cigarettes away and fastened the top clip of his high collar. 'We'd give you a flat in Moscow and a small dacha for weekends outside. He could work in our Foreign Ministry in Western affairs, while you work in the Far Eastern Section. I think you'd like that, Mr. Dunne? But I've got to be sure. We don't want you upsetting Arundsen when he comes over; he's a valuable man too. Would you like that?'

'Yes.' The word came out at last, through the rough, gutteral crying. 'Yes, by Christ I would. I'd love to see him again, the old sod. We'd have some fun, like we used to . . .'

'Then leave it to me,' the Colonel said, 'and I'll arrange it for you.' He took up his cap and went to the door; he tapped once and it was opened immediately.

A small military plane flew him to Moscow. He went direct to K.G.B. headquarters on the corner of Rysinskiev Square and made his report to the General.

Dunne was ready; the staff at Kalitz had handled him in exactly the right way. He produced the dossier with the medical evidence, transcripts of Dunne's unhappy maunderings under sedation, his conversations with the interrogator, the mundane evidence of his sexual expression in dreams. It was Arundsen all the way through. And that morning the final crust had broken. He had admitted it to himself in his tears, even though he covered it up to the Russian with his babblings of a good time and a few drinks. If Arundsen were with him he would be able to adjust. He would give them everything they wanted.

The General asked only two questions. How could Arundsen, whose record of heterosexuality was beyond question, be persuaded into a relationship with Dunne?

A shock course at Kalitz, and the senior psychologist had assured Ivliev that he would emerge conditioned to any situation they required, provided they accepted that he wouldn't be any use to them in any Intelligence capacity. The course was very strenuous. The General nodded. It wasn't very much to ask, for such a valuable return as the services of James Dunne. Drunks and wives and mistresses and useless homosexual attachments had been brought to Russia before, in order to satisfy the whims of traitors. The memory of Guy Burgess made Peter Arundsen seem a trifle to contend with. Then he asked his second question.

When would Arundsen be available? The little flat eyes bored into Ivliev like tiny laser beams.

Within the next month, if all went well, Ivliev promised.

The General didn't even blink; he suggested that this was optimistic, and Ivliev hesitated. Perhaps two months, he conceded. But no longer. It couldn't be any longer because Dunne would deteriorate under the present system if it went on too long. Years of alcoholism had affected his brain and he suffered from high blood pressure.

He was more likely to supply them with the advice and insight they wanted for a comparatively short period, a year or even six months, carried on the crest of an emotional wave of gratitude and release from a lifelong repression. But these euphoric phases didn't last. The General must bear in mind that they weren't dealing with an ideological defector; the subject was a paranoiac without any basic affinity to anything. Even with Arundsen to play with, the Colonel said coldly, he would eventually crack up after a time.

The General had always considered Ivliev one of the brightest men in the Service. He had listened to him without interrupting, while he explained Dunne with the exactitude of an insectologist describing the life-cycle of a bed bug. Very brilliant and detached. He would have to be promoted after this. Which was a pity, because the General didn't like him. There was something about his clinical inhumanity that offended the General. He preferred the pathological cruelties of Beria and Stalin. Russia understood excess; it was part of the soul in which the General didn't believe on a metaphysical level. The younger generation seemed to have been born out of test-tubes.

He asked Ivliev another, final question. They were depending upon Wetherby to deliver Arundsen. If he failed to do so, what would happen then?

The last resort, Ivliev answered. Arundsen would be kidnapped in England, provided the General agreed. He was a little surprised to see the General smile for the first time in the interview.

The General shook his heavy shaven head from side to side very slowly like a bear with an ear-ache. He did not agree. In fact he expressly forbade any such action. Ivliev had set the whole operation up with his English contact. If it failed, and Dunne couldn't be put to use, he must bear the responsibility. Arundsen must come to Berlin of his own volition. Then he dismissed the Colonel. Inhuman and rash, too. He found himself hoping that the younger man would make a mistake. Then demotion, not promotion. Perhaps even a suggestion that he had been less than diligent in the way he conducted this very important affair. The General lit a long black cigarette and let his thoughts continue on these pleasant lines.

Bill Thomson was his own boss; he exported pottery from Devonshire, which found a profitable market in America. He wasn't a rich man, but he was comfortable and able to please himself. He went abroad for holidays now simply because he was so lonely since his wife had died. He went to

Spain, which they had both loved, and to North Africa, and he spent every Christmas in Ste Paule de Vence with a French family who had helped with the escape route during the war. When Joan Arundsen telephoned him he spent some minutes chatting about trivialities, waiting for her to come to the point of her call. Her voice was thick, as if she had a cold. Thomson thought it more likely that she'd been crying.

She had broken into his conversation and asked to see him urgently. And he had invited her to lunch with him that day without asking what was wrong, because of course he knew. Arundsen was making a bloody fool of himself, and he could guess with whom. It was so obviously going to happen during that weekend at Buntingford.

Arundsen had dropped out of sight, and the tearful voice down Bill's telephone was closely connected with his sudden silence.

He took a taxi from his office to a pleasant French restaurant at the back of Covent Garden. As a conservative type of man with no pretensions towards snobbery, he insisted upon comfort as well as good food. He liked to sit in a soft-seated chair and have enough elbow room to cut his meat; he also disliked a predominantly pansy staff, and arty lighting which concealed what was on his plate. His favourite restaurant was Simpsons in the Strand, and the little restaurant hidden among the vegetable lorries and glass emporia of the fruit market was his second choice.

He was sitting at a table against the wall, sipping a glass of sherry, when Joan came through the door. She was smartly dressed and wearing a hat, which he thought suited her. He got up and gave her a kiss on the cheek. Close to, her eyes were red and the lids puffy.

'Sit down, my dear. Very nice to see you. Now, how about a drink before we eat, eh?'

She put her bag down on the floor and looked at him. 'I could do with a bottle,' she said. 'You're a darling, Bill. I'll have the same as you. Sherry, please, not too dry.'

'Now,' he said. 'We'll order first and then you start from the beginning.'

Joan didn't bother trying to choose. She looked down the menu, and chose hors-d'oeuvres and then an omelette because they were easy, and anyway she wasn't hungry. She felt both guilty and ashamed, now that she was sitting opposite Bill Thomson. He was one of Arundsen's old friends, and while she had liked him, she had never actively encouraged him because of that. She had wanted to break Arundsen away from them all. She had failed so completely that Bill Thomson was the only person she would turn to in the present circumstances, and hope that he would help her.

'Why did you want to see me, Joan?' he said. 'What's the matter?'

'I don't know how to start,' she said. Her eyes began to fill with tears, and she took a deep drink of the sherry.

'It's Peter.'

'Yes?' Thomson said. 'What's he been up to? Come on, dear, I've known you and Peter a long time. I'm very fond of you both, you know that.'

'I know you are,' she said. 'You like me too, Bill. I've always sensed that, and I like you. You're the only one I do like, out of all his old friends. That's why I've come to you. I just had to see someone about it, and I know you're fond of him . . .' She trailed off and fumbled with her handkerchief behind the shelter of her bag.

'What's wrong?' Thomson asked, although he would have put a five-pound note on the table that he knew exactly what it was.

'He's having an affair,' Joan burst out. The hors-d'oeuvres was set in front of her without her noticing. 'He's been away to Paris, told me a tissue of lies about going on a business trip, and all the time he had this woman with him.'

'How did you find out?' Bill said.

'By accident. I rang his office to find out what time his plane was landing Sunday night. We'd been quarrelling like mad for days, and I thought I'd go and meet him, just as a surprise. To make it up. His secretary didn't know a thing about it. There wasn't any business trip; the other partners weren't going anywhere. Oh, she realised there was something wrong and tried to cover up, but it was obvious.'

'What did you do?' Bill said. Business trip to Paris on a weekend. He could hardly believe that Arundsen had been so stupid.

'I had a rough idea when he was getting back, so I just went down to London Airport and hung around, watching every flight from Paris coming in. And I saw him, and this woman with him. Walking arm in arm. Do you know who it is?'

Bill Thomson shook his head.

'Mary Wetherby!'

'You're sure?' he asked her. 'You're sure they didn't just meet on the plane? It's possible, you know.'

'No, don't give me that, Bill. I'm not a complete fool. He's been working late at the office every night for weeks now. He doesn't even talk to me any more. For the last fortnight he's been sleeping in the boy's room. I tell you, he's mad about that bitch; he even talked of leaving me, and I believe he really wants to. After that Paris business I started following him in the evening when he left the office. Every time he went to the same block of flats. She's listed there, at the front door.'

'I'm very sorry.' Bill reached out and patted her hand. This made her cry properly, and he let her go on for a moment, until she pulled herself together almost angrily.

'I'm really sorry to hear this,' he said. 'I think he's not only a bastard to do it on you, Joan, but a prize fool as well.'

And this he genuinely meant. Married men had affairs, and he accepted that Arundsen had fallen for a beautiful woman, with class and sex appeal and all the rest. But it was criminal to be so clumsy about it. But perhaps it was deliberate. Perhaps he didn't care if Joan found out, if his marriage broke up. He must be really twisted up if that was true. She was a nice girl, Joan Arundsen. Not very bright, or out of the ordinary; he knew she resented Arundsen's friends and his past, and he understood why and didn't blame her. She felt unsafe so long as a connection remained. She had been jealous and afraid. All his sympathy was with Joan at that moment, and that was when he knew why he didn't like Mary Wetherby. She fitted in with Arundsen's past. And she shouldn't have done because she wasn't involved in it any more than Peter Arundsen's wife. But she fitted. As he had said to the Countess, there was something wrong about her. He felt quite cold suddenly. 'What can I do?' he asked Joan Arundsen. 'I'll do anything I can.'

'Could you talk to him?' she said. 'I can't do it, Bill. I'd only lose my head and start a row, and it'd all go to pieces. I think he'd walk out on me anyway; I think he's just waiting for the excuse.'

'You don't want a divorce? That's definite?'

'No, I don't. I want to keep things going. We've got David to think of – it'd be just terrible to break up the home.

And she's no good to him, Bill! She can't love him, it's just novelty to her! I'm not going to give him up!'

'All right, I'll talk to him,' Bill said. 'On one consideration. You don't say anything. You stop following him and pretend that you know nothing, see? Leave it to me. I'll get hold of him and talk some sense into him. He's damned lucky to have you, Joan, and it's about time he realised it.'

'Well, he doesn't,' she said bitterly. 'I've done my best to make him happy, Bill, but he isn't – he's restless and fed up, always harping on the old job and the old friends – Christ,' she burst out suddenly, 'I don't know why he ever left it if it was so marvellous! And what was marvellous about it? Just tell me, you were in the same sort of thing – what was so special about chasing round the world, being in danger, getting a rotten salary and no security? But that's what he's hankering after all the time. That's the whole trouble. He's sorry he resigned.'

Bill let her calm down before he answered. The outburst only put into words an aspect of the Arundsen's relationship which he had vaguely suspected. Arundsen was not happy out of the Service, and his wife would never be happy if he were still in it. She had no appreciation of what his work had meant to her husband, or she couldn't have talked in terms of a rotten salary and no security. She didn't understand the man in the area where understanding was essential. If she had understood or even tried to see his point of view, there wouldn't have been a Mary Wetherby. He wondered if it was worth trying to explain to her how Arundsen felt and why. She blew her nose, loudly, as women only do when they're past caring about appearances, and asked him for a cigarette. She had finished all her own just going round the flat that morning. Bill lit it for her, saw that the tip was waving like blown straw, eluding his lighter flame for several seconds. She was near to breaking down completely and he decided that this was not the time to play marriage counsellor. But one thing needed establishing. It would strengthen his arguments with Arundsen if she answered the right way.

'Do you still love him, Joan? Even after this?'

She puffed and exhaled, sniffing back tears. 'Yes, I suppose I do. I know I said about David and not breaking up the home, but apart from that, *I* don't want a divorce. Maybe I'm not up to much in some ways – I'm not very – well – over-sexed or something, but I don't want to lose him, Bill.

I suppose,' she said sadly, 'that means I certainly do love him. The bastard!'

'Right,' he smiled, and made a signal to the waiter. 'Leave it with me. Do you know what my Betty always did if we had a row?'

'No,' Joan Arundsen said. He was paying the bill as he answered her.

'She went out and bought herself a new hat. Come on, my dear. I'm going to put you in a taxi.'

'You're an angel, Bill,' she said, as the taxi drew up in front of them. 'I'm so grateful to you.'

'Nothing to it,' he said gently. 'But we'll have to have a chat about Pete, you and I. After I've seen him, anyway. Be a good girl and don't say a word.' She reached up and kissed him quickly on the cheek, and then bolted head first into the taxi, where she withdrew to cry all the way back to her flat. He started walking back along the Strand, taking his time in the bright afternoon sunshine.

Talking to Arundsen was not going to be easy, Or pleasant. Bill knew him very well, and could claim to be a close friend, but what he was going to say to Arundsen might very well put an end to all relationship between them. He was becoming more and more angry as he thought of it. He was sorry for Joan, because she was a type of woman he liked. Normal, uncomplicated, albeit possessive and a bit stupid, but genuine to the marrow. There were no secrets about her, no dark corners. But she and Arundsen had drifted, because of his job, and because she couldn't and wouldn't admit that he was entitled to miss his old life and chafe against the monotony of belonging to the bowler hat brigade. Arundsen enjoyed excitement; he liked being apart from other people, an outsider on the inside of the conventional world. He liked the sense of hunting alone and still being able to seek refuge with the pack. And that was what made Buntingford such a significant part of all their lives. It was all that remained of the pack, the exclusive society of men who worked for the Firm. Arundsen had left too early; it was still in his system like a recurring malaria. He had been forced out of it by pressures which he subconsciously resented, and the focus of that resentment was his wife, who behaved as if his former career had been burglary.

It was a pity that she lacked imagination. It wouldn't be easy to explain how Arundsen felt. It wasn't something an outsider could appreciate without a real affinity for stepping into alien shoes.

Joan Arundsen didn't have this quality. But the other woman did. That was what had attracted Arundsen initially more than her appeal or her looks. She was sympathetic to him. She could make herself a part of that life of silence, conspiracy, boredom and excitement. She fitted in; it was as if she had honorary membership. And it was not because she was Phillip Wetherby's niece by marriage. She provided what Arundsen lacked at home; an instinctive feeling for what had been the most important years of his life. The more he considered it, the more difficult he felt it would be to break up such a relationship. But he had a duty to try, and duty was something Bill Thomson never avoided. Later that afternoon he dialled the number of Arundsen's office and asked him to meet him for a drink.

'This week's a bit difficult,' Arundsen's voice sounded abrupt on the line. Thomson could imagine it would be; he was all fixed up with Mary Wetherby for every evening. He wouldn't be put off; he was going to see the stupid bastard and try to set him straight.

It was important, Bill said, and he only needed half an hour. The appointment was made, grudgingly by Arundsen, for two days later, at a pub at the top of Holborn.

'Excuse me,' the Countess said. 'I'm so sorry to trouble you, but are you the owner of this house?' The woman who had been Jimmy Dunne's last landlady opened the front door a little wider; the Countess had a compelling smile which ment that the question didn't presage a complaint.

'Yes, What can I do for you?'

'I have rooms at No. 42, and I've been expecting a very important letter today. I know it was posted and it hasn't arrived. I'm going down the street asking if it was delivered to any of the other houses – you haven't had anything addressed to a Madame de Bruin, have you?'

The Countess asked with confidence. She had written the letter, addressed it to that number herself and posted it the night before.

'Why, how funny, I did get a letter this morning,' the woman said. 'I've nobody here of that name – I was just going to put it back in the box. Are you Madame de Bruin, then?'

'Yes, I am. How very lucky for me that you kept it. It's so important to me.'

The front door had opened wide and she stepped into the narrow hallway. Her letter was on a table, apart from a small pile for the boarders and a couple of brown envelopes containing circulars or bills.

'I'm a widow,' she said. 'And this letter could mean quite a difference to me. Times aren't what they used to be,' she added.

'No, they certainly aren't,' the landlady agreed. She was a cheerful woman, nearer sixty than fifty, and she loved a gossip. As one widow to another widow with an interesting letter, she immediately invited the Countess to come in and have a cup of tea.

They sat together in the gloomy little back kitchen, and the Countess blended into the scene as naturally as she had done in embassy drawing-rooms. She had a way with people, women as much as men, when she set out to gain their confidence. She looked very handsome and engaging as she sat sipping tea across the plastic-topped table.

The landlady, whose name was Eileen Hunter, began to ask her questions and was rewarded with some fascinating information. Madame de Bruin seemed eager to talk about herself, and this was a quality Mrs. Hunter appreciated in people. Other people and their business were a source of constant interest to her. Above all, she hated the close-mouthed ones, the lodgers who kept themselves to themselves, as she described it.

It was only human to stop off and have a cup of coffee or a few minutes' chat now and then, It kept the spice in life, especially if there wasn't anyone to talk to for long hours during the day. She liked the look of the Countess; she was friendly and, as a widow, probably lonely too. 'So you're French,' she said. 'Always liked the French myself. I had a lovely French gentleman here once; he had the nicest way of talking, always called me Madame.' She giggled. 'Made me feel like a brothel-keeper, dear, to tell the truth.'

They both burst out laughing. The Countess offered her a cigarette, and asked her about herself. Mrs. Hunter blossomed. An hour passed and in that time the Countess had learnt a great deal about the late Mr. Hunter, the present complement of lodgers and the inability to get the second-floor lavatory cistern fixed. On her way out of the kitchen, the Countess paused. She had seen two empty light-ale bottles at the back of the dresser.

'I suppose you don't go to the Fox occasionally?' she said.

'Well, sometimes I do, dear. Makes a change to get out for an hour. When there's not much on the telly.'

'I go there,' the Countess said. 'Why don't you meet me there and we'll have a drink together. Helps to pass the evening. My room is rather dreary, or I'd ask you to come up there.'

'It would be,' Mrs. Hunter said. 'She hasn't an idea in her head how to run a place, that woman. Charges the earth too. That's a nice idea. We'll have a little drink and a chat at the Fox.'

'Tomorrow evening, then,' the Countess smiled. 'I'll be there about seven. And thank you for keeping my letter. We'll have a little celebration. On me.'

The first three weeks had yielded a mass of trivia about Dunne, all of which was already known, and in her first report over the telephone to Wetherby the Countess had to admit she had made no progress. She had spent her time in the three local pubs, the two restaurants, getting into talk with everyone. Everyone she met was only too willing to discuss Dunne; even the lodgers in her own boarding house whom she had asked in for coffee with her landlady one evening, had spent the best part of an hour discussing him, and then admitted that they'd only seen him twice in the street. It was slow and discouraging, but she persisted. She had had an objective, which was to penetrate the boarding house where Dunne stayed without arousing suspicion or making her interest in him appear more than curiosity. That had now been achieved.

The barman at the Fox was an old man with thin grey hair carefully combed across his balding head, and the wary eyes of a queer to whom the heterosexual world has been unkind. He served the drinks and washed the glasses, and looked at the giggling young women in their thigh-displaying skirts with sour disgust. He liked his regulars, like Mrs. Hunter, who popped in for a glass of beer and talked away to him as one old woman to another. And now there was another regular, who had been coming in twice a week for the past two months, drinking the same two drinks, a brandy followed by a long cold lager chaser, and then going out again. She was such a good-looking woman, though a bit part worn, as he said to himself, and he kept an eye on her to see if she was trying to get a pick-up. But she never looked at men or spoke to them. She just seemed lonely, and whenever he took her order she smiled very nicely and passed the time of day. He had the feeling that she didn't despise him for being different. The young ones made him feel a worm, and some of the hard-faced old cows who came in with their husbands and knocked back doubles like navvies were just as bad as the sniggering mini-skirted tarts. He was an unhappy man, and eaten by loneliness like a cankered apple. When he saw the foreign lady palling up with Mrs. Hunter he felt more friendly towards her. They began lingering at the bar, including him in their conversation. He warmed and began to hang about and join in.

And then inevitably they were talking in full flood about James Dunne. Mrs. Hunter was in her element. She described him again and again for the Countess's benefit. 'No gentleman, dear, that's for sure. He used to come in at night so drunk he woke the whole place up! Never had a word to say to anyone, spent half the day sleeping it off. I didn't turn him out because, well, I've got a bit of a kind heart, I suppose, and he never did me any harm. Always paid his rent on the dot. And it wasn't as if he was permanent.' She repeated the story of how the police came and all the questions they asked, and the mess they left his room in, everything pulled to bits, even the carpet taken up.

The Countess listened and said how fascinating. Had he any friends? Only a lonely man would drink to that extent. She looked into the mirror running at the back of the bar, and exchanged a tiny smile with her own reflection. She was over the shakes and the sickness for it now; she had enough to keep her steady but not an ounce beyond. And she wasn't lonely any longer. She was alive again, and on a job.

He hadn't *any* friends, Mrs. Hunter said. She said this very definitely, and the Countess, who was watching the barman, noticed a flicker pass across his face, almost a blink of contra-diction, which disappeared like a match flame suddenly extinguished by a breath.

He knew something which the landlady didn't know. But he wasn't going to say it. Whatever it was, he kept it back, and she knew suddenly that he would have kept it back from the official questioners too. She bought him a drink, and kept quiet while Mrs. Hunter went on telling the same stories over again. Mrs. Hunter had nothing to contribute; the

Countess felt she had exhausted her, but she was useful, because she was a link with the old homosexual behind the bar. And he knew something about Dunne. From that evening he was the one the Countess began to cultivate.

CHAPTER FIVE

Arundsen insisted on taking Mary out to dinner somewhere they could dance. In fact, he insisted, they were going to a nightclub. Mary said yes, as she did to everything he wanted. She would have made love all night, or gone out, or done whatever he suggested, simply because she was so much in love with him that his contentment was all that mattered. It was a strange feeling, this submission to the needs of another human being. It had no root in fear of losing him, or in the common female masochism of wanting to be bullied. She just loved him and liked doing what he enjoyed.

'I'll have to change, darling. I didn't think we were going out.'

'Well, we are,' Arundsen said. 'We're going out to celebrate.'

'Celebrate what?'

'Knowing each other for three months. Go on, go and get ready. I'll get myself a drink.'

Whe she was in the bedroom he played with a glass of whisky and water, turning it round and tipping it one way and another, making the ice perform acrobatics as it melted.

He had spent half an hour with Bill Thomson as arranged. There was no quarrel; Bill had been calm and even sympathetic, but Arundsen knew him well enough to recognise an act when he saw one. It spoilt the effect of what Thomson had to say. His wife was miserable and he was taking a bad risk on his marriage.

He had sat there without answering, letting Bill tell him Joan knew there was something going on between him and Mary because he'd been so clumsy about the whole business. Arundsen hadn't said anything till Bill made a remark about picking the wrong woman. He had never had an angry word with the older man in all the years they'd been associated. He kept his temper and said simply that if he criticised Mary in any way, he, Arundsen, would walk out.

'All right then,' Bill said, and he wasn't acting any more; he showed his angry partisanship for Joan Arundsen. 'All right, walk out on me. Walk out on your wife and your boy too, just because you can't stop playing James bloody Bond and come down to earth. You're in your forties – it's time you grew up! And it's not growing up to sleep around with a wrong one like Mary Wetherby!'

That was when Arundsen stood up. 'I told you, I'm going,' he said.

'You don't like the truth,' Bill Thomson got up with him. 'You're making the biggest bloody mess of everything and she *is* wrong. She's no good, Peter. Pack it in and go back to your wife while she'll still have you.'

'I'm not going to smash your face in,' Arundsen had said quietly. 'You're too old. And anyway Mary wouldn't want it. She's always said how much she liked you.'

He had pushed past Thomson and gone out, catching a taxi as it cruised slowly on towards the traffic lights at the end of the road. He gave Mary's address and banged the door shut. The driver turned round to say something, but changed his mind. The passenger was a big man, and he looked in a nasty mood. Arundsen was still angry when he let himself in and Mary came to him, slipping her arms round his neck. Angry and shaken, too, because Joan had found out. He had no right to be taken off balance because his wife knew he was having an affair. It didn't make sense to kiss Mary in the way he was doing, and feel guilty about Joan. He had wanted Joan to know. He wanted the thing to come to a head so he could be divorced.

But it was a shock, just the same. She must be very hurt. He broke away from Mary, holding her at a distance; he wasn't going to hide from it by making love to her. She wasn't an escape route from his twinge of conscience and he felt it would debase her to be used. Perhaps he had debased her already.

'Darling? What's the matter – why don't you let me kiss you?'

He put his arm round her, and rubbed his face against her hair.

'Because I'm taking you out,' he said. 'And if we go on we won't go anywhere.' So she had gone to change her dress and while he waited his mood altered. He wasn't angry with Bill any more. He meant well; even trying to blacken Mary was mistaken kindness. And if Joan knew, she knew. It had to come sometime. On an impulse he went to the bedroom door and opened it. She was dressed, examining herself in a long mirror. Arundsen thought how beautiful she was and how curiously distant. He had known greater intimacy with her than any other women; there wasn't an inch of her skin he hadn't touched or a crevice of her body which he hadn't explored at will. But still she was remote. In those few seconds he might never have known her at all. She turned and as soon as she saw him, she smiled and held out her hand. 'Do I look all right?'

'You look marvellous,' Arundsen said humbly. 'Don't I ever tell you how beautiful you are?'

'Often,' she said gently. 'Very, very often. But not when I'm dressed.'

Black suited her; the material was simple, the cut exquisite. Her neck and upper arms were bare, and the reddish brown hair was drawn back under a wide velvet band. She wore pearl ear-rings and a long single row necklace. 'Have you decided where we're going?'

'We're going', he said, 'to the Savoy Grill. I've always hated it, but not so much as I hated the restaurant. The food is magnificent, the service superb, and I've always been with my wife and her latest batch of stockbroker friends. Going with you, I know I'll appreciate it. Then we're going to a nice dark smoochy night-club, where I'm going to make a pass at you. Ready?'

'Yes, darling,' she said. She slipped her hand through his arm, and they let themselves out.

'I love the Savoy and if you choose a really dark night-club and give me champagne I may even ask you back to my flat.'

The dinner was excellent. It was as if he had never been there before. There was no Joan talking about nothing in a bright little voice, pitched a trifle too loud; no dull-faced 'friends' who had to be played up to and impressed. No business talk, which bored him to exasperation; no pontificating over the menu. He remembered his birthday party celebrated in the restaurant in that same hotel: it was like a nightmare. Sitting with Mary beside him on a comfortable banquette, eating some of the best food in London, holding her hand under the table, he was so happy that he asked her to marry him again.

'Darling,' she said, 'you're not even divorced.' She smiled and tried to make it sound like a joke.

'I'm going to be,' he said. 'I'm very sorry, darling, but

I've made a bit of a mess of things. Joan knows about you and me. I don't know what she's going to do.'

'We haven't been very discreet,' she said. 'You probably won't believe me, but I don't mind at all from my point of view. I do mind for her.'

She turned a little away from him and began searching for her cigarette case. He put out his hand and closed it almost roughly over hers, snapping the bag shut.

'You're not to mind!' he said. 'I told you, my marriage has been over for years. You didn't break it up; you haven't any reason to sit there with tears in your eyes, blaming yourself on account of Joan.'

'You would have been all right if you hadn't met me,' she said. 'It is my fault. And I feel awful.'

'Look at me,' he said. 'Come on, turn round and look at me.' She did so, slowly, and for the first and only time in their relationship he held her wrists under the shelter of the tablecloth, and hurt her.

'Stop it.' He said it very quietly. 'I love you and you love me. I'll get a divorce and we'll get married. Or we'll live together if your Catholic conscience won't stretch to the register office.'

'If I had a Catholic conscience,' she said suddenly, 'I wouldn't have done what I've done already. I only gave it up because I couldn't live up to it. And that's the first time I've ever admitted *that* to myself.'

He had let her hands go free, and she was slowly rubbing her left wrist where her watch had made a mark. Washington, she thought. How easier in retrospect to have shown some courage, the courage evinced by Richard Wetherby for all his dreadful tendencies. She could have told them to go to hell. Instead she had acted on behalf of a political system which she had hated all her life. The first treason, like the first adultery, is always the hardest. She had read that somewhere. There's a permanent soiling, like a blood-stain which never comes out afterwards.

'I didn't mean to be rough,' he mumbled it, ashamed because he had hurt her. She looked at him and shook her head.

'Poor darling. You didn't hurt me. And I wouldn't care if you did. I love you so much, and I don't want to bring you any harm. I don't want to break up your home and end up by giving you nothing in exchange.'

'You can give me everything. All you've got to do is say "yes".'

'That's really so?' The changeable blue eyes were raised to him, they were clear and deep like water. He wanted to kiss them closed.

'It is,' Arundsen said. 'At least, will you think about it – seriously? I want to know, because of fixing things up with Joan.'

'All right,' Mary said suddenly. 'All right, darling, I will. Just give me a day or so.'

The subject dropped and they relaxed again; he took her to a small night-club near Dover Street which had been famous in the last years of the war and for a decade after it. He used to go there when he was young and had some money. By that time it was less smart, and had built up a clientele of off-beat characters from the theatre and the literary world, the night owls who ate and drank and talked their way through the first hours in the twenty-four. Arundsen had liked it very much; a group of people from the Firm used to meet there with their wives or girl friends. He remembered taking the Countess there as the taxi turned in at the entrance down a cul-de-sac. He wondered how she was and reminded himself to look her up. To hell with what his wife thought; he didn't have to worry about her any more.

He hadn't been there for nearly five years, and it had changed so much he almost turned round and took Mary somewhere else. But it was too late; they were ushered in, his name looked up on a membership list which he guessed to be quite fictional, and then given a good table at the back of the room. There used to be a small sextet who alternated with a mongrel South American group. Now a discothèque, managed by a girl in a skirt that barely skimmed her crutch, blared out the latest hit records. A mass of people swayed and jerked on a tiny dance floor. The lights were pinkish, and there were waiters everywhere. He ordered champagne, sent the bottle back when it arrived because it wasn't cold enough, and asked if the old manager Louis was still there. No, he was told, Mr. Louis had left two years ago. He now had his own club with a gambling room. Louis had been a friend of the Countess, a compatriot Pole with a fine war record and an elastic sense of peacetime honesty. He was said to have run prostitutes and even drugs after the war; by the time Arundsen used to come to his club, he was respectable.

The idea of Louis in a gambling club made Arundsen feel sorry for the customers.

They sat together quietly for a time; Mary drank a little of the champagne, which was now properly chilled and sitting regally, if a little tipsily, in its shining ice bucket on the table. 'Marry me.' The words of the lyric came through the frantic drum-beats of the record that was playing. 'Marry me. Love me. Marry me.' For weeks it had been like water dripping on a stone, wearing away at her subconscious. She had put it aside without difficulty the first time he mentioned it. 'Have an affair', Phillip had said, 'by all means, have an affair so long as you don't get too involved.' He had been mistaken in giving that advice. Women always got involved if it went on for long enough. He had misjudged her feeling for Arundsen. She had probably misjudged herself. Phillip thought she needed amusement; he used the word affair in its butterfly sense, a bright, insouciant meeting of two Noël Coward creations, so brittle and transient as to be almost unsexed. What she had needed was precisely what Arundsen had given her. He had loved her and made her love him. The question of involvement no longer obtained. It was now a matter of degree. She had begun to believe him when he said his marriage was finished. It wasn't completely self-delusory, because on their first meeting – how many months ago – when Joan was with him at Buntingford, she had seen that there was no rapport between them. There were no friendly whispers, no shared looks like there were with George and Françoise Geeson; not even the solid relationship of the MacCreadies, shy and undemonstrative as they were.

There had been a vacuum with the Arundsens; all she had done was fill it. The temptation to marry him had begun to grow after their trip to Paris. Now the nightly meetings, the snatched hour or two at lunchtime, left her strung up and miserable, so that she often cried when he had gone. For three years she had lived alone; seeking spasmodic shelter with Phillip as if the great house were a womb. She had lived as much as possible without a past because there was no memory that didn't carry pain or disgust at its core. Worst of all was her disgust with herself. She had betrayed her religion because, as she admitted to Arundsen, it asked too much of her. She was too weak to accept what it had to offer in exchange for courage. She was not the stuff of martyrs. She looked at Arundsen, at the line of nose and jaw, the fair hair creeping slightly back from the forehead, and saw the strength which was enough for both of them. He was not afraid of consequences; he could face them and with him she might even learn to face them on her own account. But there was one consequence he might find very difficult. The consequence of an old act of cowardice; the fact of her despicable little treason.

He took her on to the tiny floor and they danced, held very close together. The warmth of his body lulled and stimulated her; she felt his hands pressed into her back. They were strong hands and the light hairs on the backs and down the fingers were so blond they were invisible except under a light. His mouth was pressed into her cheek in a kiss that lasted while they danced; she could feel the taut muscles as they moved together. They groped their way back to the table and he poured some champagne into her glass.

'How about going home?'

'In a minute,' Mary said. 'It's rather fun being here. I've never danced with you before. You're very good.'

'My mind wasn't on it,' he smiled, and settled back. He took her hand and kissed the back of it, grinning at her. 'I'm having a very happy evening. Darling, I hope you're happy?' They wouldn't go yet. He had recovered control of himself.

'You know I am.' She leant against him, waiting for a moment, groping for a way as they had done between the close packed tables after they left the dance floor. Phillip's cynical dictum came into her mind. *Post coitum omne animal indiscretio.* But not *post coitum.* She would never tell him after they had just made love, when he was sleepy and suggestible. It might be the only brave thing she had ever done in her life, but she was going to tell him in cold blood and face to face. And she had felt her way a little. And oh, dear God – in the stuffy smoke-hazed room, the bellowing inarticulates of the twentieth-century love cult booming and battering through the amplifiers. Mary prayed in just those words, Dear God, let him answer in the right way. Let me see that I can tell him. Because if I can't, it can never be right . . .

'I was thinking the other day,' she said, 'about you and Jimmy Dunne.'

'Oh?' he sounded surprised. 'What made you think of that?'

96

'I don't know,' Mary hesitated. 'I wondered why you liked him so much. From what Phillip said you were completely different.'

'We were,' Arundsen answered. He didn't mind talking about Jimmy Dunne to her; he didn't mind talking about anything because she seemed to understand, to be a part of it all. 'We couldn't have been more different, as a matter of fact. He was a loner and a boozer – Christ, could he sink it! – but absolutely brilliant on the job. But when I went out to Hong Kong I was pretty young and green and I suppose he enjoyed showing me the ropes. He took a lot of trouble with me, actually. And I got to like him, Mary. We used to go out together; I was chasing the girls and he was looking through the bottom of a bottle of Scotch. We had some marvellous times together. He was one of the best talkers I've ever met, when you could get him to talk. He'd had a fascinating life. It sounds a dreadful cliché, but he was a real man and a damned good friend. Joan couldn't stand him. He popped up in London once or twice after we were married and came round sloshed to the wide as usual. She couldn't cope with him at all; I suppose I can't really blame her. When he was pie-eyed he'd use the worst language you ever heard in your life. Every second word. I don't think you'd have liked him either.'

'I don't think I would. But still you did.'

'Yes, I did,' he said. 'You know a funny thing – Phillip asked me to go back to Berlin and see if I could pick up any clues – who contacted him, why he went over, that sort of thing?'

'No,' Mary said; subconsciously her hand had tightened on his. 'You didn't go, did you? You told me once you were nearly caught there.'

'So I was. Bloody nearly went into their little air-tight bag. There's a gentleman called Ivliev, head of the Berlin section of the K.G.B., who'd have a special kind of red carpet laid out for me if I ever went back there. No, darling, I'm afraid I told Phillip I was retired and that was it. He probably thought I didn't want to go on Dunne's trail, but that wasn't the reason.'

'Wasn't it?' she asked him. She put a hand up to her neck of her dress as if it were uncomfortably tight.

'No,' Arundsen said. 'Those bastards have a long memory. I did Ivliev a dirty trick when I got that Pole out; I heard afterwards he nearly went inside himself. I told you before, darling, I'm no hero, and I'm too old to play cowboys. I wouldn't cross that Wall again. Not that I'd have picked up anything. Jimmy knew how to cover up.'

'Knowing him so well,' she said slowly, 'could you ever forgive him for what he's done? Could you find any excuse for him?'

He was lighting a cigarette when she asked the last part of the question. He blew out the match and drew on the cigarette till the tip glowed red. He turned and looked at her.

'Excuse? For someone who turns traitor and works for them? Believe me, darling, he may have been my friend, but to me he's just the scum of the earth. He's gone bad, and as far as I'm concerned I'd put a bullet in him if I ever got the chance.'

She didn't answer. She finished the residue of her champagne, put her cigarette case in her bag and checked the small change for the cloakroom. She did everything slowly and casually, but she felt physically numb and sick, as if she had suddenly been told of a death. When she turned back to him she managed to smile.

'Darling,' she said, 'I'm rather tired. Could we go home now?'

It was a Sunday, and from 2.30 until six Buntingford was open to public view at half a crown per head. Three yellow and green coaches were pulled up in the paddock to the right of the main entrance drive, and half a dozen private cars. Two families were picnicking under a plane tree, in spite of the cool wind and overclouded August sky. The month was nearly over, and it had been damp with low temperatures. Excursions were doing a fine trade, and at the weekends Buntingford was thronged with visitors. There were guided tours at half-hourly intervals. Three estate office workers took turns with Phillip Wetherby in showing groups of thirty to forty people round the house, reciting the patter of the new trade, the exposure of the private and exclusive to the public curiosity. Few of the crowds who inched through the Great Hall and gaped up at the sixteenth-century oriel window were interested in the architecture; the list of dates and names connected with the house meant nothing to nine-tenths of them.

Sir John Bray built the great brick mansion in 1520; it was

his son who entertained Elizabeth I on three occasions at a cost of fifteen thousand pounds per visit and was almost ruined in consequence.

Phillip was taking the 3.30 tour and he recited the set piece in a loud monotone, pausing to point out the dais at the end of the Great Hall where the family and their royal guest had their meals, his eyes flickering over the rows of faces with cold distaste. There were half a dozen children of varying ages, and a persistently wailing toddler who drowned out whole passages of what he was saying. He cleared his throat irritably and began on a louder pitch. They moved through the Great Hall and up the fine Tudor staircase to the Long Gallery. This was a vast room, running the length of the east side of the house, its oak-panelled walls hung with portraits of some early members of the Bray family and the ancestors of Phillip Wetherby who had come into possession of Buntingford in 1689 through marriage. There was a fine suit of seventeenth-century German armour and a collection of early weapons. Phillip decided that it was a waste of time elaborating on the flint-pieces, hagbutts and cross-pieces to an audience who wouldn't know the difference between a Reigsburg halberd and a child's catapult.

'Excuse me,' a man said from the front-line group. 'What's that up there? Third from the left – it's a very early French crossbow, isn't it?'

Phillip stopped and slowly looked round. The man had moved a little forward and was craning upwards, his back arched to look at the weapon which was one of the earliest items in the whole collection.

He was a very ordinary man in an open-necked cellular shirt and creased drill trousers. He spoke with an East London twang.

'Yes,' Phillip said, 'it is. Very rare, about 1514.'

'Could have been used at the siege of Orleans,' the man said.

'Why, yes,' Phillip nodded. 'It could indeed. Ladies and gentlemen, let's move down and through to the Queen's bedroom. This way please.'

The crowd paused at the door leading to the bedroom occupied by Elizabeth Tudor; Philip stood back to let them through. The man who had asked about the crossbow was the last to pass him. He smiled.

'Very interesting, your armour. We need Arundsen by

next month. It's dead urgent.' He passed through and joined the rest of the tour.

'Life can turn out very odd,' the barman said.

'It certainly can,' the Countess raised the teapot. 'More tea, Arthur?'

He had told her his name was Arthur Bartrum, but this was after she had spent almost a month buying him drinks and talking to him in the saloon bar of the Fox. It was a considerable achievement to have won his confidence so far as to edge on to a Christian name basis. The next step had been taken a week earlier. Katharina had asked him to have tea with her, and this was the second invitation. She had let him know that Madame de Bruin was not her proper name; one evening she had shown him a photograph of a Silesian castle, which was not, as it happened, remotely connected with her family, and whispered that it was her old home in France. Her late husband had been a Count, but now that he was dead and there was no money, it seemed pointless to use the title. Alfred was not only queer, but he had the passionate desire to rise in the social scale which compensated so many men of his tendencies. He was not just a snob, he was the high priest of snobbery. His bitchiest epithet was to call someone 'common'. He had pretensions to refinement; he dressed very discreetly in the style which he believed disclosed the gentleman, regardless of his job; he spoke with the care of someone who has spent a lifetime acquiring an accent different from his own. He went to art exhibitions and cultural films, and read the 'heavy' Sunday papers. He worshipped the Royal Family and what he described as the old aristocracy, as if by sheer enthusiasm, he might qualify for honorary membership. When he discovered that the Countess was titled the last vestiges of inverted suspicion were swept away. He felt like touching her for luck; she was the first aristocrat he'd ever known, even though she wasn't English. He was flattered by her attitude of conspiracy, as if they were outsiders in a vulgar world to which neither belonged. When she invited him to her dismal bed-sitting-room, he was almost emotional. And he became confidential when they talked, because, though she was a woman, she was safe. She had no designs, she was too much of a lady to behave like the common cows he usually came into contact with, and she was so intelligent, so understanding. Mrs. Turner was a nice old thing, bit of a bore and a talker, but above all so *stupid.* He called Katherina Countess when they were alone, and as he held out his cup for more tea, he went on about the strangeness of life and quoted an example.

'As I said,' he continued, 'it's very odd. Now take me, I'm a lonely man. I remember you saying how lonely that Jimmy Dunne must have been to drink so much, and I thought at the time – what a perceptive woman!'

The Countess watched him above her teacup. She shook her head. 'I said he must be lonely,' she said. 'I know a lot about lonely people. It must be terrible to have no friends at all, like Mrs. Turner said.'

'Mrs. Turner!' Arthur sniffed. 'Mrs. Turner doesn't know what she's talking about. She goes on and on about that poor man, and I can't help feeling sorry for him in a way, and everybody listens to her and thinks she knows about him. She doesn't know half what I know.'

'You're a very sensitive person,' the Countess said gently. 'You'd notice things that someone like Mrs. Turner would never see. You tell me about Dunne. What did *you* think of him?'

He hesitated; he had never mentioned this before. The men from the Special Branch had come down like locusts, swarming all over the area asking questions, and he had told them the very minimum. The man who spoke to him was a brusque young detective sergeant, who showed that he didn't think much of people like Arthur. Arthur wouldn't have helped him if he'd been Perry Mason, and Mason was one of Arthur's favourite television characters. If he was so bloody superior, let him find out for himself.

'Well,' he said, 'you're a woman of the world, Countess, I haven't had a happy life – nor an easy one in many ways. And it takes someone like me to know another one.' He gave her a little smile, and rubbed one finger up and down his cheek. She knew what he was, and he was not ashamed of her knowing. She was sophisticated, well bred. Only the ignorant despised him, because they were crude and without sensitivity. She understood that being what he was he had suffered a great deal.

'That man was different; you know. He was coarse and he drank, and honestly, his language was enough to make you sick, but I knew what he was.' He smiled again and shook his head. 'I suppose that's why I feel sorry for him. There's a sort of fellow feeling.'

'If he was different, then,' the Countess said, 'did he have a friend. Is that what you think?'

'I don't think, my dear lady, I know,' he said. 'He had a friend, and a very special friend he was too. I only saw him twice; just twice, but it stayed in my mind – I couldn't get over it.'

'Why not,' she said. She passed him a plate with some small cakes and chocolate biscuits on it. He took a cake, and nibbled at it. He reminded her of a thin grey rat, with the half-eaten pastry in two fingers of his left hand. 'What was so special about this friend? Was it a man?'

'It was a gentleman,' Arthur said. 'And when I say gentleman that's what I mean. He came into the pub one night looking for Dunne, and Dunne made him have a drink. He didn't want to hang round the bar; I could see that, but Dunne was tight as usual, and he kept insisting. They sat at a corner table, and the gentleman bought one round of drinks. I had a good look at him, I was so fascinated. You don't see that class of person in the Fox. His clothes! My God, you should have seen the way he was dressed! Such style – I served him, two whiskies, I remember very well, and he asked for Passing Cloud cigarettes. We didn't have any, so he just paid for the drinks.'

'What did he look like?' The Countess had taken a cigarette out of her bag and she lit it. She leaned back and smoked with an expression of interest on her face. 'Was he young?'

'No. No, no, not young at all. Sixtyish I should say. Very distinguished-looking, like an ambassador. Wore glasses, which spoilt it a bit. Honestly, Countess, it should have been an eye-glass. He was that type; one of the old school. I've seen enough phoneys to pick out the real thing. What a man like that was doing with someone like Dunne I can't think.'

'Perhaps they were the same. Perhaps this gentleman was different too. Was he English?'

'My God, I should say so. We're the only country in the world that breeds them like that. I wouldn't have said he was one of us. Not by the way he spoke to me, anyway.'

'And you saw him again?' she said. 'This is quite fascinating. Do go on, Arthur, tell me everything about it.'

'He never came to the pub again,' Arthur said. 'But I saw him just once after that. I was in a bus going down to my sister-in-law's place at the Oval, and I saw him sitting in the back of a big car, a Rolls I think it was, while we were at a traffic lights. It was only a moment but I've got eyes like a hawk, I can tell you, and I knew him at once.'

'How very strange,' the Countess said. 'What could a man like that have in common with this Mr. Dunne?'

'Well, only one thing, I suppose,' Arthur said. 'Though I must say, he didn't give any message to me. That's why I didn't say anything to the police. There is a fellow feeling, you know. I didn't want to start the dogs of the law on anybody's heels. Let them do their own sniffing out. I said nothing. After all,' he shrugged, 'why should I? Why should *I* help them to pry into other people's private lives? It's not the law's business. People should be allowed to lead their own lives.'

'Of course they should,' she said. 'It wouldn't have made any difference. It might have brought trouble on this other man. He could have been married. He could have been in some official position.'

'That's what I thought,' Arthur said. He had finished the cake and he brushed the crumbs on his plate into a tiny pyramid.

'There's a lot of married men find out about themselves when it's too late. Let the police do their own snooping, that's what they're paid for.'

'Just as well you didn't mention it,' the Countess said. 'It's all over now, anyway. And you might get the police coming back and making trouble because you didn't tell them. I shan't say anything to anyone, and don't you tell anybody else.'

'I won't,' Arthur said. 'As a matter of fact, I asked Dunne about his gentleman friend, and he got very cagey. It must have been someone very important.'

'Yes,' the Countess said. 'It probably was. Did he tell you his name?'

'Oh no, very cagey, as I said. But he did say he was going to Paris for a few days. He said his friend was going to be there too. That's all he ever told me.'

'And did he go?'

'Yes,' Arthur said. 'Yes, he went. As a matter of fact, he sent me a postcard. I've still got it. Might be worth something one day with his writing on it.'

'I'd love to see it.' The Countess leant forward eagerly; she held out the packet of cigarettes, but he shook his head.

'No thanks; I must be going now. I've got the postcard at

home. I'll bring it in tomorrow and show you, It's only a Paris street; not very exciting. Will you be down for a drink tomorrow?'

'Yes, I'll come in about six-thirty.'

'Seven,' he reminded her. 'It's Sunday. Thank you for the tea. It's been a pleasure. You must come to my little place sometime and I'll ask my brother and sister-in-law. They've heard so much about you.'

'I'd be delighted.' The Countess got up and opened the door for him. She held out her hand and he shook it limply. 'It makes all the difference to meet a few nice people,' she said. 'Please invite me. And bring the postcard tomorrow. I'd be fascinated to see it. Don't forget.'

She closed the door and waited for a moment, listening to the creak of the stairs and the final click of the front door as he let himself out. Then she began putting the teacups on the tray, and emptied the dusty cakes into a cardboard box to throw away.

It was the same man as in Berlin. English, elderly, very distinguished-looking, spectacles. He had appeared just once, and Arthur had seen him, and remembered him because he was such a gentleman and Arthur was such a snob. She pushed the tray and the dirty china to one side, and lit another cigarette. The man was very rich, according to Arthur; even if he had been wrong about the clothes – and pansies were seldom mistaken about that sort of detail in another man – he had then seen him in a Rolls, going eastward towards the Oval. Sitting in the back of the car. The way Arthur had described it, he was being chauffeur-driven. That could mean an official car. It might have been an Austin Princess. The Foreign Office. The Treasury. Any one of half a dozen Ministries. The Services weren't to be overlooked either. Generals and admirals and air marshals were just as likely to succumb to blackmail or treason as civilians

She sat back and slowly finished her cigarette; she felt very calm and cold, which was the old sign like a sixth sense, that she was on to something. She opened her bag and took the flask out of it. There were three inches of brandy in the bottom, and she took a deep swallow. That was enough, and she had earned it. There was nothing to do until she saw the postcard, in case it provided a further clue. Just a Paris street, the old queer had said. Nothing exciting. But she wanted to see what was written on the back. That might give a further clue. She thought of going out and telephoning Phillip Wetherby to tell him that she had picked up a lead on the mysterious man, and it was the first lead uncovered in England. Everybody had investigated Dunne's contacts in the area without finding anything, while Arthur held his tongue and his grudge against the heterosexual world. Phillip would be pleased; the Major-General would be pleased too, but if she knew the way he ran his department he'd send his own private bloodhounds down to complicate her work and try to take the credit. She decided to say nothing. Nothing to Phillip, because she wanted to give him the dénouement in one; nothing to the department because she wanted to finish this job herself. Other jobs would depend on her success. If she found the Englishman she would be taken back into the service. She would be alive again.

She took the tray along to the bathroom and washed up the china in the hand basin with a squeeze of detergent which the landlady left on the window-sill. She dried everything and put them away in her room.

She put on some lipstick and slipped a cardigan over her shoulders. She often ate at the Indian resturant a block away, because it was a place where a woman could sit by herself without attracting attention. The Countess liked the Indians; they were polite, reserved people, and they had accepted her as a regular. She felt suddenly hungry. She didn't even think of getting herself anything more to drink.

Arundsen left his office very early. He had spent the night with Mary, as he often did now that Joan knew all about them, and all through the working day he had been thinking about what had to be done.

He was ostensibly living at home. He slept in his son's bedroom, ate the breakfast his wife put on the kitchen table, said goodbye to her, and then went to his office. The best part of every evening, and now several nights a week, he spent with Mary. It couldn't continue, and the real reason he decided to talk to his wife was because she was looking so miserable. He often said to himself that he not only didn't love her but there wasn't even liking left. This was not true and Arundsen knew it. He felt a first-class shit when he looked at Joan and he frequently called himself one. She had lost a lot of weight. She got up in the morning and he couldn't avoid seeing that she was haggard and red-eyed, as if she spent more time crying than sleeping. And she didn't say a word to him; no reproach, no quarrels, nothing. She knew and she was suffering in silence. He couldn't stand another day of it. She was out when he came in; he called her and went through the flat very quickly, opening doors. For a moment he panicked when there was no answer; women sometimes did the craziest things. But there was no huddled body in the kitchen with its head pillowed in the stove; he realised that everything was electric, anyway, and felt a fool.

Half an hour later she came into the flat; he heard the front door and a rustle of paper, as she put whatever she was carrying down on the hall chair. Joan was a very tidy woman; neat in her house and fastidious in her personal habits. She put everything away in every room, except their cramped little entrance hall. This was always piled with her coat, handbag and parcels. It had always infuriated him to come in and pick his way through the mess. When she opened the door and saw him, she jumped.

'Peter! You're very early.'

'I wanted to talk to you,' Arundsen said. 'Come and sit down.' She looked at him for a moment, and then walked to the armchair opposite and sat down, crossing one leg over the other, her hands on the arm-rests and an expression of agonised strain on her face. Even before he said anything her eyes began to fill. She knew what was coming. Bill had prepared her. He wouldn't give the woman up. If he said he was leaving she had to be calm and dignified. It was the only way, Bill Thomson had insisted. And she was going to try, at least.

'Joan,' Arundsen cleared his throat. He felt as if he were being strangled. 'Joan, we've got to have a chat about things. We can't go on as we are.' He saw her wipe her eyes and he winced. 'Come and sit here,' he said suddenly, putting a hand on the empty sofa seat beside him. 'Come on, darling, let's not hurt each other more than we have to. Come and sit with me.'

She moved awkwardly and slowly; she was within inches of him, but he didn't dare to do what he wanted, which was to put his arm round her and tell her not to cry. You can't tell a woman you're leaving her for someone else and then offer to blow her nose. If he touched her she would turn into his wife again and the whole performance would end up differently. He didn't move and neither did she.

'What do you want to say to me, Pete?' she said at last.

'I think you know,' Arundsen said.

She nodded. Be calm, Bill had said. Whatever you do, don't abuse him or Mary Wetherby. I know him, and that's the worst thing you could do. He's a bastard when he's up against the wall. Don't put him there or you'll lose him for ever. She made the effort of her life and didn't say anything.

'I've met someone else,' Arundsen said. 'I'm terribly sorry, Joan.'

'I know you have,' she said. 'I know who it is.' She turned and looked at him and the lack of reproach in her face was like a slap. 'She's very attractive. I suppose you've just got tired of me, that's the trouble. I'm not going to say anything nasty to you. We've got beyond that. I've made a mess as far as you're concerned, and nothing can alter that.'

'It's not your fault,' he said angrily. 'For Christ's sake how could it be you? It's me – I'm the one that's let you down! And I told you, I'm sorry. I'm not good enough for you anyway; I never was. You need a different kind of man – somebody settled, stable. I'm just a bloody overgrown schoolboy, still.' He put his hands up to his face for a moment; he felt sick with shame and self-disgust; at the same time he longed for her to behave as he had expected she would. To shout at him, to bring her left hand up and smack him hard across the face – she had done that several times when they quarrelled badly – he wanted her to accuse him and call Mary names, to do anything rather than put him so desperately where he belonged. In the wrong. In the shit a foot deep.

'I don't need anybody different,' she said, and she began to cry properly. 'I need you, but you don't want me any more. You want this other woman and I've got nothing to offer you. Pete. Nothing compared to her.'

'Oh for Christ's sake,' he almost shouted at her. 'Stop it! It's not that. There's nothing wrong with you – look, darling, I've made a mess of the marriage. I'm asking you to let me go. Will you let me go, Joan? I'm no good to you as I am. Get rid of me and find yourself somebody else. Please, please don't cry. Look at the way we've been living – it's been hell for you. You can have your evidence, you can have the money, anything you want. In a year's time you'll be thanking God you're out of it.'

'Are you going to marry her?' she asked it with a rising note of bitterness. 'You want a divorce so you can marry her?'

'She won't marry me,' Arundsen said suddenly.

There was a silence which Joan broke. 'Why not? Christ Almighty, Peter, what's all this about if she won't marry you!'

'She's a Catholic,' he said slowly. 'She doesn't want to break the marriage up.'

She got up from the sofa and looked down at him and shook her head. Her handkerchief was bunched into a soggy ball in her right fist. 'Now look,' she said. 'Look, don't give me that. I've taken all I can from you over this, and I've tried to be reasonable. But don't tell me she won't marry you because she's a Catholic and Catholics don't believe in divorce because I shall have hysterics. I shall have bloody screaming hysterics right now!'

'It happens to be true,' Arundsen said. 'I think she'll change her mind when the thing's done. But she's said no, and I believe she means it. I've been straight with you, Joan. I haven't lied. That's the position.'

She took a deep breath. She should have hated him; she was seeing him so clearly from her vantage point of standing upright, looking at him sitting down. She could see the hair on top of his head which wouldn't lie flat at the crown; he was rubbing his face with his hands, looking up at her, his face creased with anxiety and guilt. He was so guilty that she felt ridiculously sorry for him, as if it were her son and not her husband slumped in front of her, burdened by his own unkindness and infidelity. She had never known until that moment how much she really loved him. And for all her lack of imagination and her narrowness of outlook, she found both magnanimity and wisdom.

'If she loves you,' she said, 'she'll marry you. And that's what you want. Anyway, it's what you want at this moment. All right. You go to her. I'll start divorce proceedings, but not for three months. You'll have three months together, and you won't have to be torn between us because I'll keep right out of your life. At the end of three months you may feel differently. If you do, darling, I'll still be here. That's all I've got to hope for. I'll go down to my mother tonight while you pack up.' Then she walked into their bedroom and shut the door. Twenty minutes later she left the flat. He was in the kitchen, on his second glass of straight whisky, and he didn't know she had gone till he heard the front door bang shut.

The Fox was always crowded on a Sunday evening. The

saloon bar was thick with smoke and body heat; when the Countess came in she coughed as the atmosphere went down into her lungs. She pushed her way through the wedge of people round the bar. There were girls with hair cropped so close to their heads it reminded Katharina of the prison cut which was one means of keeping the head clean of nits, and men with ringlets tumbling over their velvet shoulders. The world, in her opinion, was undergoing some curious period of sexual gestation. Whether it produced a super specimen of Homo Sapiens or a composite monster, part hermaphrodite, part beast, was anybody's guess. Personally she didn't wish to guess or even care about the outcome. The painful need of periodic wars to spring clean the human race was more apparent every year. She reached the bar, hemmed in on both sides by bodies and waited for Arthur to see her. Arthur had been waiting eagerly; he loathed Sunday nights, because he hated crowds and rush, and the young women seemed more obnoxious than on a weekday. He was looking forward to a few words with his friend. He had the postcard in his inside jacket pocket. He had searched through his letters and one or two theatre programmes and odd Christmas cards for quite a time before he found it. But it was there, slipped in the middle of a batch of coloured postcards he had collected over the years from friends. He was very sentimental about such things. He kept his old love letters like a woman.

'What a crowd,' the Countess said. Now that the moment had come she felt quite shaky. She couldn't bear the suspense of those few minutes when she had to talk and hide her eagerness to see the postcard. More terrible still was the fear that he might have thrown it away, or decided not to bring it. Homosexuals were erratic; even the most mundane were apt to fly off at extreme emotional tangents for no visible reason. She gave in and ordered a double brandy.

'It's hell on these weekends,' Arthur said. 'Absolute hell. I don't know how much longer I can stand it.'

'You mustn't leave,' the Countess said. 'The place wouldn't be the same without you. I'd never come here if you left.'

'A lot of people say that,' Arthur mellowed. She was such a nice person, the Countess. But then there wasn't any substitute for breeding. 'I didn't forget,' he went on. 'I brought that card to show you. But there's nothing to it. Just a street and his hotel.'

It was a plain postcard, a photograph of a square in Paris

with a statue of an equestrian general in the middle of it. On the top left-hand corner there was an arrow drawn in ink, and a cross above a building. The Countess turned the card over and read what Jimmy Dunne had written. It was dated nearly eight months earlier.

This is the pub I'm staying in, and I think the old Fox is better. See you next week. J.D. The name of the square was printed at the top of the postcard in tiny letters. 'Place Malakoff.'

Dunne had stayed at the hotel in the Place Malakoff on the 18th of October the year before. And he had told Arthur that his friend was going with him. It was such a fantastic piece of luck that she found herself laughing. 'That's quite a souvenir,' she said. 'It even mentions the Fox – you must take care of that, Arthur. It could be valuable one day.' She leaned forward a little; her brandy glass was empty, and now she desperately wanted another. 'Thank you for showing it to me. You must let me buy you a drink. What will you have?'

'Oh, no,' Arthur said. 'No, why should you, I mean . . .'

'Please,' the Countess said, and she really meant it. 'Please. I insist.'

'All right then.' He looked pleased. 'I'll have a whisky.' A hand came out and touched his arm. He jerked back as if something had bitten him, and glared. 'Just a minute, sir. I'm attending to this lady. Can't do two things at once!'

He turned back to the Countess and grimaced. 'Damned cheek,' he said out loud. 'What do they think I am, an octopus? Now, dear, what about you? Another brandy? You haven't had your chaser tonight.'

'Just the chaser,' the Countess said. 'You know me, Arthur, I only have one.' She drank the glass of beer quickly, because the thirst for a brandy was scorching her mouth. She knew the time had come to get out.

It was cool and pleasant outside the pub. She began to walk back to her lodgings, taking her time. It was a chance in a million that Dunne had sent a postcard showing where he was staying. He wasn't the kind of man who'd put his address on a postcard anyway. She had expected a typical tourist view of the Invalides or the Eiffel Tower, with nothing more instructive than a postmark and perhaps some clue in the message. The date when he was there, at least. Now she had the hotel; all she had to do was go to the Place Malakoff and find it.

And begin from there. People who stayed at hotels had to

register. Dunne's name would be in the book; so would his friend's name. She stopped halfway down the road by a telephone box, and then remembered that she didn't have any change. She didn't want to phone Phillip Wetherby from the lodgings because the telephone was in the hall and the landlady could hear everything that was said. The Countess went on to the house and let herself in. She tapped at the landlady's door. 'Mrs. Johns?'

The door opened; the noise of the television blared out into the corridor. 'Yes? Oh, good evening. What can I do for you? Alan, turn that down, will you?'

'I'm going away tomorrow morning, just for a few days to see my husband's brother,' the Countess said. 'I meant to tell you yesterday, but you were out. I'll be back by the end of the week. That'll be all right, won't it?'

'Quite all right,' Mrs. Johns said. She glanced behind her into the room; she was anxious to get back to the television programme.

'I'll pay the next two weeks' rent tomorrow morning, just in case I stay a little longer,' the Countess said. 'Good night.'

The next morning she bought a small overnight case, cashed a hundred pounds, half of it which were in travellers' cheques, and took the midday flight to Paris. She had decided not to let Phillip know where she was going. It would all be part of the surprise.

Phillip dined at eight; he never entertained except at the weekend. The routine at Buntingford had been the same since before the war. He went upstairs at 6.30, bathed and changed into a smoking jacket, drank a glass of sherry in the library, and then dined alone in the panelled dining-room.

He didn't serve himself; however frugal the meal, and he was a man who ate as moderately as he drank, the butler who had been with him since 1948 served him, and then brought him coffee in the library, where he spent the rest of the evening reading or watching a portable television set before he went to bed. Phillip had been thinking during the meal; he hadn't noticed whether the omelette was a cheese or fines herbes and he left his coffee on the side table afterwards till it was cold.

They wanted Arundsen by next month. He had been taken by surprise; he had imagined there was a reasonable margin of time to arrange something and indeed he had been planning a second approach to Arundsen. Now there wasn't any time at all; if Arundsen refused again he would be alerted against any other method of decoying him out of England. Phillip had been reviewing all the obvious possibilities and rejecting them because they needed time, and this he hadn't got to spare. By next month. Something drastic would have to be done. Something would have to be engineered which would bring Arundsen running into the trap of his own free will. When the answer came it was so obvious that he was quite irritated at not having thought of it before.

Arundsen wouldn't go to Germany for him or for the Firm, but he would go for Mary Wetherby. If Mary Wetherby was in danger, Arundsen would go.

He finished his brandy and sat back. They were living together in Mary's flat. She had told him so on the telephone, and he had made it clear that he disapproved. It was getting too close, too intimate. She was in love with Arundsen; that was obvious and he didn't like it. One day she would confess to him and he knew Arundsen would get every last detail out of her, including his deal with the Russians. Mary had imagined it was done through the sub channels which were used by both sides when they wanted to communicate. In fact he had asked for the negatives direct, and they had been handed over to him in London. He had destroyed them himself. It was a million to one chance against anyone enquiring too closely into his part in it, but he had learnt that these were the odds which sometimes paid off.

The time had come to break up the affair between Mary and Arundsen anyway; the whole plan would dovetail in the tidiest way.

The problem he had to solve was how to get Mary into East Berlin, and then sit back and wait for Arundsen to follow her. When he went up to bed he had solved that problem in his mind, and the next morning he telephoned her flat when he knew Arundsen had left for his office, and asked her to come down and see him that afternoon. Something very urgent had come up and he needed her help.

He told the chauffeur to meet the 2.20 train from Victoria and then spent the rest of the morning in his rose garden.

CHAPTER SIX

'You mustn't blame yourself,' Phillip said. 'It's not your fault.'

'They couldn't blackmail you if I hadn't given them the evidence,' Mary answered. 'Of course it's my fault, Phillip. You put yourself in their hands by helping me.'

'I was a fool,' he said. 'I should have known they'd keep a couple of those negatives back. Don't look so upset, my dear. I'm only sorry I have to tell you, but the point is I need your help. I'm in serious trouble. I wish I didn't have to say that. I hate sounding melodramatic, but unless I do what they want they'll expose me for dealing with them and covering up your activities in Washington.'

'I know,' Mary said. 'Oh God, Phillip, I'll do anything for you, you know that!'

Behind her the bright September sunshine filtered through the narrow mullioned window, dappling the carpet with reflections of the stained-glass crests of Bray and Wetherby that were a famous feature of the house. They were in Phillip's study, up above the main entrance. It was a small room, irregularly shaped, the original solar room and part of the fifteenth-century building which the Tudor millionaire had incorporated into his great mansion. It commanded a magnificent view of the surrounding countryside; his desk was placed in the wide window embrasure so that he could look out over the courtyard on to the sweep of parkland, studded with huge trees

To Mary it was like a noonday nightmare. Phillip's guarded message had brought her down to Buntingford immediately, but she had imagined it concerned Richard Wetherby, or even her living with Arundsen; she had been safe for four years, or so she believed, until he told her that he was being blackmailed by the Russians. They had kept back some negatives and a tape recording of her telephone conversation in Washington which convicted her of passing information. Now they were putting pressure on Phillip because he had dealt with them on her behalf. It was all her fault, all directly the result of her cowardice. When he told her he hadn't made it a reproach, had Mary knew what his long record with the Service meant to him.

'What do you want me to do?' she asked.

Philip waited for a moment. It was going very well; she had accepted everything, simply because she was an innocent amateur. A professional would have spotted half a dozen holes in his story. Why hadn't he asked to see the negatives before he accepted their word? Tapes were flimsy evidence, unacceptable in any court because they were so easy to cut up and doctor. And surely someone as skilled as he was would have covered all traces of that deal two years ago . . . But Mary didn't see any of it.

'I want you to take something to East Berlin for me.' He said it slowly, as if it were difficult for him to ask.

'There's something they want, and I dare not go myself. I'm too well known. Our people would hear of it and get suspicious. You needn't worry,' he said, and he gave a little smile. 'The information isn't valuable, but they think it is. I wouldn't go that far, even to save myself or you. But will you take it for me?'

She got up suddenly and came towards him.

'Don't do it, Phillip. Don't give them anything! I was a coward in Washington; I didn't face up to it, and what good did it do to give in? Now you're compromised, and that *does* matter. They'll never let you go, just as they never let me go. Sometime, someday, maybe in a year or two, they'll come back at you for more. It'll never end. Look, please listen to me. Don't have anything to do with them. I'll go to the Major-General and tell him the truth! If he wants to take action against me it might be the best way out for us all.'

'Who exactly do you mean by "all"?' Phillip said. His voice was flat and cold.

'I mean you and me and Peter Arundsen,' she said desperately. 'It'll clear you; they won't be able to blackmail you when I've confessed, and Peter will go back to his wife. He won't touch me with a barge-pole when he knows. And maybe my conscience will leave me alone. Let me do it. It's the best solution all round.' She went to the window and leant against it, her eyes closed as if all the strength had gone out of her. 'Please, Phillip. Let me be brave for once.'

'I see,' he said. 'Of course what you really mean is that you're living rather squalidly with a married man, and your Catholic conscience is beginning to prick, isn't that it? You want to confess all, my dear Mary, and put an end to that situation at the same time – and you can't see how much harm you would do to others while you relieved yourself! And it would only be temporary, because these grand gestures run down very soon after they've been made. You talk about being a coward in Washington – well, I disagree. What you did was to protect our name from being dragged in the dirt by giving a few harmless parties and repeating scraps of gossip anyone could have picked up. And you were right! I would have done exactly the same thing myself. My family name and our reputation means everything to me.' He had been speaking angrily, when suddenly his tone completely changed.

'The day I have to explain those photographs to the people I worked with for thirty years I'll blow my brains out.'

She burst into tears. She knew he hated emotional scenes and despised a woman who made them, but he himself was responsible. He had always seemed so calm, so remote in his self-confidence. Now he had stripped himself; his work and his good name were all he had left at the end of his life. If they were taken from him he was just a lonely and despised old man.

'God forgive me,' Mary said. 'I wish I were dead.'

'I didn't think I'd have to beg,' he said quietly. 'You often said you'd do anything to pay me back. Now you can do something. The only favour I believe I've ever asked you.'

'I'll do it,' she said. She had stopped crying; she wiped her eyes and made an effort. He noticed that she was very white, and as she lit a cigarette her hands were trembling.

'I'll go to Berlin for you.'

He came up to her and put a hand on her shoulder. 'I knew you would,' he said. 'And I'm very grateful to you.'

'When do I go?'

'At the end of next week,' he answered. 'I'll let you know the details a little nearer the time. But you mustn't say anything to Arundsen. Not a hint that you're going away even for a day! He's still with you, isn't he?'

'Yes,' Mary said. 'He is. He wants to marry me.'

'Are you going to marry him?'

'No,' she said. 'I've made a big enough mess of my own life without ruining his as well.'

He drove down to the station with her and she saw him standing on the platform, watching as the train drew out.

He had been very convincing that this was the end of it,

this trip to Berlin. He assured her that he knew what he was doing; in America she had been a frightened amateur, easy to trick. He was in a position to buy them off for good. In fact there was a code of ethics between all Intelligence Services; the cheap spies, the expendables, these had no protection; his indifferent shrug when he mentioned them had chilled Mary. But where people like himself were concerned they dealt with their opposite numbers on the other side. They wouldn't cheat him as they had cheated her. She needn't be afraid. It would be a weekend trip to West Berlin, with a day visa to the East. Nobody would suspect her; hundreds of tourists crossed over from the West every day. When she got beyond the Wall the K.G.B. would meet her and she could deliver what they wanted. He promised to let her know more, and offered to fob off Arundsen with an excuse that she was staying for a few days. Or with a cousin who was ill. She was not to worry; Phillip had emphasised that. She wouldn't be in any danger and nobody would ever find out.

He was deeply grateful to her. For a moment he had bent forward and his face had brushed against hers. It affected her all the more because she knew what the gesture meant to him. On her wedding day he had only shaken her hand.

The train bumped on its track line back to London, the green countryside sliding past the dirty windows. Mary remembered the spotless American trains; fast, efficient, geared for the passengers' comfort. The noisy swaying little diesel chugged and rattled on its way, and her head began to ache. When she got back Arundsen would be waiting for her, and she would have to lie. It was the first lie she had ever told him. 'I had lunch with a girl friend. I went shopping. I went to an art exhibition.' Anything except the truth.

Three weeks earlier she had tried to break with him; she had friends in Italy whom she hadn't been to see since she was married. They still corresponded and she had written, asking if she could come and stay with them. She had cried while she wrote the letter, because she didn't want to go. She wanted time to pretend that the truth about her wouldn't really matter if he knew it, and so why make it such an issue – she wanted to keep him somehow because she loved him so much, and yet she knew it was impossible. Some women could live with a man and keep themselves apart for their whole lives, without feeling any burden. To Mary, the need to confide, to throw herself on his mercy, was an unbearable temptation. But if the strain was crippling, the fear of his rejection was far worse. 'I'd put a bullet in him.' That was what he felt about James Dunne, who was his friend. It wasn't hard to imagine what he'd feel about his wife.

Italy seemed the solution; she had always loved the country and felt at home among the people. She could talk to her friends; Italians adored other people's love affairs. She might even go to church again, just to see if comfort could be found. She had made the arrangements and booked a ticket direct to Genoa; her friends had a villa at Santa Màrgarita. The day before she was leaving, Arundsen had arrived at the flat with his luggage.

'You're not leaving me.'

That was all he said, and then he made love to her. In the morning he had watched her unpack her cases and send a cable to her friends, cancelling the visit. He had sensed what she was going to do, and so he had just moved into her flat and taken possession. It had been possible to pretend after that. They lived together as if the miracle had happened and they were married. No past behind them, no displaced wife and son to shadow him, no memory of Richard Wetherby to sully her. She cooked him breakfast in the morning and waited for his key in the flat door at night. Sometimes he rang her from the office and she met him for lunch at a restaurant in the city. He looked younger, more buoyant; she felt contented to be overwhelmed by him, as if his authority over the situation could stave off the future. But it was still a pretence, and she knew it. It was theft, this part of their lives, stolen from his family by a woman who could never take their place. The end had to come, and now, sitting in the train on her way back from Buntingford, Mary knew that Berlin was the end. After she had done what Phillip asked she could never see Arundsen again.

The Place Malakoff was a small rectangle cut out of the heart of a busy Paris shopping sector; there were nineteenth-century houses down three sides of it, their stucco façades crumbling slightly, and a small paved square with a statue of the French general, after whom the place was named, riding an improbably rearing horse, in the middle. There was only one hotel. The Countess stopped the taxi at the far end of the place and began to walk towards the entrance. It was not fashionable, but not cheap. Paris abounded in small hotels, slightly above pension level, where the accommodation was fifty years out of date, but the food was superb. The inside was dark and smelt stale, as if nobody ever opened a window. She went to the desk, and a man in a black coat, with a rumpled white collar and stringy black tie, came out of the little office behind the desk. The Countess had her story ready. She took a head and shoulders photograph of James Dunne out of her bag and put it on the desk. 'I am from the American magazine *Look*,' she said. 'I am doing an article on Mr. Dunne the Englishman who's gone over to the Russians.'

'Yes,' the hotel manager said. 'I read about it.'

'Would you look at the photograph,' the Countess said. 'You do recognise him, don't you?'

The man glanced down and then looked up at her; his eyes were hostile. He disliked foreigners and running a hotel meant keeping one's nose out of other people's business. If she wanted information she would have to pay for it. Americans could afford to pay.

'I don't think I do,' he said.

The Countess took the photograph back. 'That's a pity. We were told he stayed here. My magazine is paying a thousand francs an interview to people who knew him. Is there another hotel near the place?'

'No, madame.' The manager's attitude was transformed by the mention of money. 'No, this is the only one. May I see that picture again, please. Just to be sure.'

A few minutes later the Countess was sitting in his office, drinking coffee and smoking, while he talked about the three nights Dunne had spent in the hotel.

'We get a lot of single men staying here, you see,' he explained. 'Some Americans, quite a lot of English. I will not have Germans here. We're always full to them. I lose business, but it doesn't matter. I lost my son in the war. So, madame, I probably wouldn't remember much about Mr. Dunne, in spite of all the publicity, except that he was such a strange man. And so drunk. The maid would go in in the morning and he would be in bed – so drunk! And by mid-afternoon he was still there. She couldn't clean the room.'

'What did he do in the three days?'

'Slept, ate in the restaurant one evening, went out. He never spoke to anyone, that I remember. Certainly not to me.'

'Did he have any friends? Did anyone book in at the same time?'

'No.' The manager shook his head. 'He came alone. But wait a moment – the second night somebody brought him home. I remember it well because he was so drunk that I had to help get him upstairs; the other man couldn't manage him alone.'

The Countess was writing it all down in a notebook. Now she glanced up at him, her pencil writing.

'What was the man like?'

'English. Very grey hair. Very much a gentleman. I used to be at the Carlton before the war – I was learning, you know, and the English who stayed there were like this man. They thought they owned the earth. They're nothing now. Just like the Dutch!' He said it with pleasure; he had never liked the English, and he was glad to see them going down.

'Dunne didn't use his name?' She felt a sudden spasm of sickness; it was so close now, a single word away. It was the same man. The gentleman unknown.

'No,' the manager said, shaking his head. 'They were talking, at least Dunne was mumbling something. The other man said very little. My English isn't very good. I didn't hear anything like a name.'

She made a meaningless squiggle on the pad. It was too much to expect; it would have been too easy. She kept the bright, interested look on her face and asked the second leading question. It was even less likely to be answered than the first. Whoever he was, he knew his job. He hadn't stayed in Dunne's hotel; only a fool would have expected it. He had met Dunne outside, and only shown himself because Dunne was too drunk to get back on his own.

'This man could be important,' she said. 'It gives a new angle to the story – very mysterious. You wouldn't know where he was staying? Did he come by taxi? How did he leave?'

'He came in a taxi. And he left in it.' The manager paused, closing his eyes in concentration. The Countess dabbed at her damp forehead and said nothing.

'He gave the driver an address. Wait a minute – The Deux Mondes! That's it – the Hôtel Charles, Avenue de L'Opéra!'

She wrote it down, trying not to hurry. Then she opened her bag and counted out fifty pounds in N.F. notes.

'You have been very helpful,' she said. 'I will get this written out, and if I need any more I shall come back. There will be an extra fee, of course.'

She walked out into the place; the sun was shining, and two girls were sitting on the bench beneath the general's statue, eating their lunch and talking. They were young and pretty and very animated. The Countess watched them for a moment and smiled, as if the sight of them made her happy. The Charles. It was a medium-sized hotel, patronized by people who liked comfort and class without the excessive luxury of the Carlton or the Ritz. Again the unknown had behaved like an expert. He had stayed somewhere where he wouldn't stick out obtrusively because the clientele was good, and at the same time avoided the milieu of the Place de la Concorde, where he would normally gravitate. He knew what he was doing. What he hadn't allowed for was Dunne's post-card to an old queer in a Fulham Road pub. She walked back to her own pension, enjoying the hot sunshine, the noise, the dust and fumes raised by the traffic jamming every street; she enjoyed everything suddenly, as if she had been born again and were seeing the world for the first time. She lunched at a café near the pension, and drank two glasses of red wine. She hadn't touched a hard drink since leaving London. Then she went into the pension and telephoned the Sûretè. The man she asked for was a wartime associate; they had not met since the year the war ended, but he had written to her once, telling her that he was married and had joined the Sûreté. He arranged to meet her that evening.

They went into the manager's office at the Charles and sat down. The assistant manager had come in, been shown the man's Sûreté card, heard what he wanted, and gone out to find the manager. Duclos was a good policeman. He did not take bribes, and he never complained about working long hours; he was patient and meticulous, and he loved his work. He didn't look like the typical French gendarme in plain clothes; there was no Maigret or Lucas image about him, no raincoat, slouch hat or dead pipe hanging from his mouth. He dressed soberly, like a respectable businessman, and he carried a brief-case. He accepted the change in the Countess because he accepted the change in himself. She had been rather unreal because women were not normally brave and resourceful and sexually appealing except in books about the war. Or the Resistance, where so much nonsense had been set down as fact. The Countess was part of his past as a young man, fighting with the Maquis in the Normandy campaign.

Now she was old, and there was a beaten-up look in her eyes which made her very real indeed. He had changed from a Maquis hero into a middle-aged *flic* with polished shoes and a brief-case, like a commercial traveller. He was going bald, and he had a son of sixteen.

'It's very good of you to help me,' she said. 'I've got to see every name on that register.'

'Are you glad to be doing this work now?' he asked her. 'Don't you feel like retiring?'

'No. When I retire I shall die,' the Countess said. 'You haven't retired either, my friend. People like us never do.'

'There won't be any difficulty,' Duclos said. 'They will bring the register for last year. If you need any more information – a little pressure put on the man at the Hôtel Malakoff – I'll be happy to oblige you. By the way, will you come round this evening and have dinner with us? I want you to meet my wife and boy.'

'I'd be delighted,' the Countess said.

The manager brought the hotel register with him. He made it clear to the Sûreté man that his was a very respectable hotel with a high-class clientele, and that any suggestion of scandal would ruin his business. He also hinted that he had friends in the Sûreté who would not like him to be embarrassed.

Then he put the book down on the table and waited. There was a long list of names for the weekend of the 18th October the previous year. She went down them slowly, checking the addresses and nationalities. There were English and French and American names and half a dozen Germans. Apparently the management of the Charles didn't have the same policy as the little Malakoff Hotel. Duclos bent over her shoulder, running a finger down ahead of hers.

'French, French, French, Belgian – English. Wetherby. Mr. Phillip and Mrs. Richard. Hargraves, Mr. and Mrs. David. American – you're sure you don't want an American?'

The Countess had stopped reading. She raised her head and blinked at him. 'What were those names you just said?'

'Here, at the bottom of the page. Dated Saturday, the 19th. Wetherby, Hargraves, Justin – an American.'

'Show me,' the Countess said. 'Where does it say Wetherby?' She followed his finger with her own; they moved down the page and stopped opposite the entry written in Phillip's clear, bold handwriting. Phillip Wetherby, Buntingford,

Kent. British. Mrs. Richard Wetherby, 21 Avening Close, London S.W.1. British.

'Have you found something?'

She went on looking at the two names, going up and down from Phillip's to his niece, and then back to Phillip again.

'Let's go on to Monday,' she said. She cleared her throat because her voice sounded odd. Sunday was blank. There were no British subjects among the five, and only two men, both with addresses in Düsseldorf. She turned the page back and looked at Phillip Wetherby's signature.

'You have found something,' Duclos said. The Countess looked up at the manager.

'Two people called Wetherby stayed here on October 19th. Do you remember them? Are they regulars here?'

'No, madame, the name means nothing to me. We have a lot of people passing through on their way to other places. I'm afraid I don't recall them.'

'Thank you,' the Countess said. 'You've been very helpful. If you could please tell me when they checked out of the hotel?'

She had gone back to her chair; she lit a cigarette and held the flame to it with both hands. She drew a deep breath of smoke into her lungs and said to Duclos, 'I don't think I've found anything for a moment. It's just a ridiculous coincidence. Could I have a list of all the British subjects listed in that weekend? They can have one typed out in a few minutes. It'll save time. I had better check on them all.'

'Of course,' Duclos said. 'I'll tell him.'

A quarter of an hour later they were in the Avenue de L'Opéra. The Countess had a list of names in an envelope, with the date of departure typed against each. The Wetherbys had checked out on Tuesday morning. She turned to Duclos on the pavement's edge. All around them the lights were glittering and winking against the darkening sky. The cars and taxis roared down the wide street, released from the rush-hour jams between five and seven, lights blazing like predators in search of pedestrian prey. People were going out to restaurants, cinemas, pursuing the pleasures of a city which could offer pleasures in all its varieties.

'Would you mind if I didn't come home with you?' the Countess asked. 'I have a lot of work to do on this. I shouldn't waste time. Can I come tomorrow?'

'Tomorrow will be fine,' Duclos said. 'You'll like my wife. And my boy. He's in his last year at the Lycée; he's going to be a doctor. Do you want a taxi?'

'No thank you.' The Countess held out her hand, and he made her a little bow, and kissed it. 'I'll walk; it doesn't take too long from here. What's your address?' He gave it to her and she said she would be with them before eight. Then they separated, and she watched him push his way through the crowds and disappear down the Métro. She hated Tubes; it reminded her of the unpleasant little journey from Bayswater to Piccadilly the night Phillip asked her to the Ritz and gave her the job. She began to walk towards the river.

'Katharina telephoned today,' Françoise Geeson said.

'Oh yes.' Her husband looked up from his evening paper. 'Is she coming round? We haven't heard a word from her for ages – is she all right?'

'I don't know,' his wife said. 'She phoned from Paris. She sounded rather odd, not quite herself.'

'Probably *futu* as usual; what the hell was she doing in Paris? What did she say, darling?'

Françoise came over to him with a glass of sherry. They lived in an expensive neo-Georgian house in the West Kensington area. Françoise had good taste but she was careful; there was no vulgarity or waste. She liked pouring out a drink for her husband when he came home in the evenings; he was tired, and it relaxed him, like reading the newspapers. She was a considerate as well as a loving wife, and he was entirely happy with her. He took the glass and made room for her to sit beside him. 'What did she want?' he said.

'She wanted me to do her a favour,' Françoise answered. When they were alone they spoke French. 'She wouldn't explain anything and I didn't press her. She sounded very agitated, and not at all drunk. She asked me to send her a snapshot with Phillip in it.'

'What on earth for? Snapshot of Phillip? You sure she was sober?'

'Absolutely certain. She gave me a pension address, and asked me to post it express. I sent on off this afternoon. We had some taken last summer; there was quite a good one of him standing by the lake. She particularly asked for one where he was full face. Do you know anything about it, Georges?'

'I heard a rumour she was doing a part-time job for the Firm,' Geeson said. 'Something to do with Jimmy Dunne. I didn't take much notice of it; she's so unreliable, poor girl, nobody'd give her anything important to do. I expect it's just a nice way of giving her a hand-out. She's dead broke.'

'Well, that was all.' His wife gave a little shrug. After a moment she said, 'Darling, you don't think she could have got on to something do you? Why should she go to Paris – she must be working on something. Who told you she was on part time . . . ?'

'Chap in the "5" section. Apparently she'd been issued with some money, and he remembered her and made enquiries. Wasn't anything much in it. Things get exaggerated. It's just a hand-out, that's all. She deserves it, it's taken them long enough to do anything for her.'

'The General doesn't do much for his own staff, much less for someone who never worked for him. I don't think he'd let money go to Katharina if she wasn't really earning it. Probably it's Phillip helping her.'

'More likely,' Geeson said. 'She never would take a penny from me; I offered it several times. Phillip could dress it up through the Firm, find some odd job here or there for her to do. By the way, darling, did you accept for the weekend?'

'I'm sorry,' Françoise answered. 'I meant to write today. I forgot about it.'

'Don't bother, I'll ring him up,' Geeson said. 'I'll ask him about Katharina at the same time. I'm going to have another sherry.'

'I'll get it for you.'

It took the Countess three-quarters of an hour to walk from her pension to the Place Malakoff. The envelope with Phillip's photograph had arrived that morning; it was an enlargment, taken full face with the lake at Buntingford behind him. She hadn't slept the previous night; her head was throbbing with tiredness and anxiety. She hadn't wanted a drink so badly for weeks.

The Countess had tried not to believe it; all through the evening when she left Duclos she busied herself drawing up another list of English visitors to the Hôtel Charles during that October weekend, and even prepared a second one, with a few American names on it, for submission to London where they could all be checked. But she was wasting time and she knew it. Her professional instincts were too sharp for self-deception to succeed. Piece by piece the puzzle took its shape, and the final picture showed one man and only one who fitted all the circumstances. A gentleman born, such a typical Englishman of the upper class that even the manager of the Hôtel Malakoff had recognised him as easily as poor old Arthur in the scruffy saloon bar of the Fox: grey-haired, distinguished, spectacles, a chauffeur-driven car. Arthur had called the car a Rolls instead of a Bentley; even the direction it was taking was right for Buntingford.

The description fitted the man who had last been seen with Jimmy Dunne in West Berlin, and the friend who had brought him back to his hotel in Paris, the friend he had told Arthur he was going with. The friend had given the Hôtel Charles as his address. And Phillip Wetherby was staying there; his niece was unimportant, she was just brought along for cover.

It was Phillip who had been with Dunne; the Countess knew this when she asked Françoise Geeson for a photograph, but all her life she had checked and re-checked everything before she passed it on as evidence. There was always the chance that she was wrong, and she clung to that hope as if it were the last thing left to her. If Phillip was the man, and the manager of the hotel identified him, then he was the answer to the whole riddle of why Dunne defected, and who had been behind him. Dunne respected Wetherby, just as they all did. He would be flattered and then influenced. Once she accepted Phillip as the unknown man, the whole process became clear. Phillip Wetherby had gone over to the opposition.

He had suborned Dunne on behalf of the Russians, and conveyed him to the doorstep into the East. She turned out of the Boulevard Nazare into the little place and walked slowly up the three steps into the hotel. She felt weary, as if she had been physically bruised. There had been a moment during that long walk when she had almost torn the picture up and turned for home. She didn't want to find him out. He was her chief and her friend; he had been good to her. Then she understood why he had pulled her out of the gutter and given her the job. He thought she was too far gone to be a danger to him. Better a drunken wreck he could keep his eye on than a smart operator from the Major-General's team nosing around after clues. That was clever too. Very clever. His only mistake was to under-estimate the power of her gratitude. She had made one final effort to deserve his charity, and that effort had been enough to discover him. The manager came out of his office, and, recognising her, he smiled. She didn't smile back or waste time. He had been paid once and he would be paid again. She dropped the photograph of Phillip on the desk, as she had done with the picture of Dunne.

'Do you know this man?'

He didn't hesitate; he looked and straightened up immediately.

'I know him,' he said. 'It's the Englishman, the gentleman who brought M. Dunne back here that night. I told you about him.'

'You're quite sure? Look very closely. Don't say yes if there's any doubt.'

'There is no doubt,' he said. He was irritated by being questioned. 'That is the man. I'd know him anywhere. It's not an ordinary face.'

'No,' the Countess said, 'it isn't ordinary. Here are five hundred francs extra. Thank you.'

'There's nothing more you want?' He thought how deceptive first impressions were. When he saw her first he thought her good-looking, with a certain chic about her. Instead she was haggard and old, and the hands stuffing the picture back in her bag were shaking so badly she couldn't shut the clasp.

He gave a little shrug and then opened the door for her as a gesture. He didn't think she would come back again, but it was possible.

She went to the corner of the place and stopped a passing taxi.

'Take me to a bistro.'

'You have any preference?' the driver asked over his shoulder.

'No,' the Countess said. 'Anywhere will do, anywhere I can get something to drink.'

'What's the matter?' Arundsen said. 'There's something wrong with you, what is it?'

'Nothing, darling. Nothing's the matter. You shouldn't have come back today; you won't have time for lunch, or anything.'

He had telephoned her that morning, wanting her to meet

him for lunch, and she had said no, there were some things to do in the flat. It was the middle of the week following her visit to Phillip and she hadn't heard any more from him. The strain was beginning to show with her and Arundsen; when they were alone she tried to be gay, and responsive, but the effort of deceiving him kept her awake after they had made love, crying into the pillow; it was almost over, and the pain couldn't be contained. The weekend after next, Phillip had said, and that weekend was almost on her. She didn't want to go to lunch with him, and submit to the scrutiny of his anxious love. He was sensitive to her in a way he had never been with any other woman, never with Joan even at the beginning of their marriage. But he watched Mary as if he were afraid she might elude him some day; he told her once that he felt at times as if he might walk into the flat or wake up in the morning and find that she had vanished. She wouldn't agree to marry him; she wouldn't discuss his divorce from Joan, and everything pointed to impermanence between them when he wanted certainty. He made love to her now as if the force of his desire could guarantee possession of her in the future. But as they lived together, Arundsen sensed that somewhere there was a reserve which he had never broken down. Until it was breached and the last area of privacy invaded, so that nothing remained unmastered by him, he would never be sure of her. Her refusal to have lunch had worried him; he feared another plan to go away, like the attempt to go to Italy, and he had come back unexpectedly during his lunch hour.

'I'm worried about you,' he said. 'In the last week you've changed. You've drawn away from me, Mary. I know you have, I feel it. Tell me the truth – has Joan been in touch with you? Is that it?'

'No, of course it isn't,' she said. 'And I haven't changed, darling. You're just imagining it.'

'It's your bloody religion, isn't it?' he said angrily. 'That's at the back of it all. You think you're doing something awful because I'm married! Oh, I know you say you've given it up and all the rest of it, but it never lets you go. You're all brain-washed from birth!'

They were sitting together, and she moved away from him, withdrawing the hand he had been holding.

'Please, Peter, don't say things like that about my Church. I have given it up, and I told you once that the reason was probably because I wasn't up to its standards. That should be good enough for you. It didn't stop me having an affair with you. I can't give you any more proof than that.'

'It's stopping you marrying me,' he said. 'You can't deny that.' She shook her head, and the angry stiffness went out of her.

'It isn't stopping me,' she said. 'I wish you'd believe that. It's nothing to do with the Catholic Church.'

'Then what is it?'

She had often imagined what it would be like if the moment came to tell him the truth, and she had never been able to set the scene. And now it had come about quite naturally and inevitably as such moments always do. They were not in bed, their bodies warm and slack with intimacy; there was no physical contact to make it easier, no covering darkness to hide his face or hers. It was 1.30 in the afternoon in the drawing-room of her flat, and they had just been quarrelling.

'What is it?' he said again. 'What is the reason, Mary?'

She got up and took a cigarette out of the box; she wouldn't let him light it for her. It was very quiet in the room; even the traffic noises outside seemed to have stopped, as if the streets were empty.

'You talked about Dunne once, when we were in that night-club. I was asking you questions, do you remember?'

'Yes,' Arundsen said. I remember.'

'I asked you if you could find any excuse for what he'd done. And you said you'd shoot him if you got the chance. "I'd put a bullet in him." I'll never forget how you said it. That's why I couldn't ever marry you, Peter, because that's how you'll feel about me in about a minute.'

He had got up, and he was staring at her, making no move towards her. 'What the hell are you talking about? What *are* you talking about?'

'I worked for the Russians in Washington,' Mary said. She was watching him and there was no change in his face at all. Nothing moved; he might have been wearing a mask. All the noises came back into the room at once; a taxi hooted and cars accelerated down the road. On the landing the lift clanged and whined on its way down from the floor above.

'Would you say that again?' Arundsen asked her.

'You heard it the first time,' Mary said; she thought her voice was steady, almost unemotional.

'I worked for the Russians; I got them information, introduced people at parties. I was being blackmailed.'

'How long did this go on?' It was like an interrogation, but the eyes were changing at last; she saw disgust in them, and pain.

He hadn't asked her what the blackmail was; he didn't care. Already he had discounted all excuses. There had been a wretched hope, so frail that she had hardly dared admit of its existence, that he might take it differently. He might have shouted at her, hit her – she would have welcomed that – and then been prepared to listen, to try to understand. Instead he looked at her with contempt, as if a racist had suddenly found his woman had mixed blood. She found a chair quite near and she sat down on it, the cigarette hanging from her fingers, and the tears coming slowly down both cheeks, without a sound of crying. 'I did it for six months. I told you, I was being blackmailed. They had photographs of Richard . . .'

'They've had photographs of a lot of people,' Arundsen said. 'You could have gone to the Embassy. You could have got help.'

'I was ashamed,' she said. 'I tried to tell you, I tried that night when we were talking about Dunne. But I lost my nerve; I knew how you'd feel about me. I knew you'd never be able to forgive me. And I was right, wasn't I? Would you still like to marry me, Peter?'

'Have they ever contacted you again? When was the last time you heard from them?'

'When we left Washington. Richard got a posting, and I stayed on. I just got a packet with the photographs inside. That was three years ago.'

'It's too late to do anything about it then,' Arundsen said. His mind was working professionally, refusing to think on a personal level. He noticed she was crying, and he ignored it. He felt sick, as if he'd been fouled in the stomach. He couldn't see her except impersonally, because if he did he would go over and knock her off the chair, just as a start.

'It's too late for everything,' she said. 'I tried to leave you, Peter; I tried to stop you breaking up with Joan. I should have told you but I couldn't. I loved you; I knew you'd take it like this.'

'I ought to turn you in.' He said it slowly, and she saw his hands curling inwards until they were fists. 'But I won't. You've done the harm now; you're not in a position to do any more.'

129

He went into the bedroom, and she heard the drawers being opened as he sorted out his clothes. She didn't wait to see him go; she went into the kitchen and shut the door, and waited. After half an hour she came out and went to the bedroom; the door was open, and she saw that he had taken everything. The flat was empty; she hadn't even heard him go.

Phillip lunched at his club in London twice a week. He drove up from Buntingford on Tuesdays and Thursdays and spent the late morning with his stockbroker, before going on to the Garrick Club for lunch.

He had not altered his routine since George Geeson telephoned him. He had done nothing in a hurry, because that was the way to make a serious mistake. Françoise Geeson had sent the photograph the same day as the telephone call. It would reach Paris the next day, and as that day was Tuesday, it was probably safer to take action from his club line than from Buntingford on an open telephone line.

He was not accustomed to strong feelings; it made him very uncomfortable to be afraid. He was also angry with himself. He had been over-confident, and this was inexcusable. The whole unpleasant tangle was the result of his little joke at the Major-General's expense. He had begun it all by giving him a gratuitous clue from sheer mischief. The Countess had found out something which the previous investigators had missed. She had gone to Paris, where Dunne had gone a year before and he had followed, taking Mary with him as a blind. And she had asked for a photograph of him. That could only be because she had also found someone to identify him. She had connected him with Dunne, and this was the chance in a million which should never have come off. Geeson was not suspicious; luckily the Countess hadn't said anything to his wife beyond the request for his photograph. They thought she was drunk, and he laughed the whole thing off and said of course she was. He had given her a few pounds and a fictitious job to help her over some financial difficulty. He had sounded very sympathetic over the telephone and asked where she was staying. He might have to settle the bill. It was such a pity about her, but there was nothing anyone could do. Anyway, they would have a chat about it over the weekend. There was a pay telephone in the lobby of the Garrick Club; Phillip excused himself from his lunching companion, a former colonial governor with whom he had been at school, and slipped into the pay box. He dialled a London number. It buzzed half a dozen times before it was answered.

'Is that 739 8274?'

'Sorry, wrong number,' a man said on the line. 'This is 739 8374.' The identification had been established.

'Listen carefully,' Phillip said. 'Get through to Paris. This is a disposal job; extremely urgent.' He gave the Countess's name and address to which Françoise Geeson had posted his photograph.

'I repeat, it's extremely urgent.'

'Paris will deal with it,' the voice said. 'Urgent rate.'

Phillip went back to the dining-room and finished his lunch; he enjoyed the ex-governor's fund of anecdotes, even though he had heard them before. It was curious, because at school they had hated each other.

Paris had an excellent disposal unit; the city was a clearing house for all sorts of political fugitives and stateless drifters. He had stopped worrying about the Countess after the telephone call.

The time had come when Mary found it was impossible to cry, and that was the worst thing about being in the flat. She had gone to bed at last, exhausted. The room was dark and quiet, and she fell asleep immediately. Arundsen had gone. The hours had passed as she moved round the flat, aimless, and weeping, but the telephone didn't ring, and it grew dark without his key turning again in the front door lock. It was a silly thing to hope for, because he had left the key on her dressing table. It was ridiculous to imagine that he would relent, ring up – make any effort towards her even to say goodbye with forgiveness. But still she had hoped, until at last she knew it wouldn't happen, and then she fell asleep. When she woke it was quite late; she hadn't remembered to draw the curtains and the sun was shining on her face. Arundsen had gone. It was all over; the memory of the day before was like an open wound in the mind. It throbbed and seared with pain, and she dragged herself upright and then sank back against the bed, as if the effort to get up was more than she could make. The room was empty, like her life. Tormented by conscience, Mary had tried to steel herself against the inevitable by imagining how she would feel when

Arundsen had done the right thing and gone back to his wife.

Nothing had prepared her for the reality. She had been lonely for most of her adult life until he came into it. Her marriage had been a vacuum, punctuated by interludes of nightmare. Since her divorce she had leant to live in isolation, seeing people but never being intimate with any of them. Arundsen had changed all that. He had changed her attitude to life. She had shared with him, and learned the great happiness of giving freely. Her body and her mind had discovered what love meant in practical terms, and it was not a lesson which either would forget. She got out of bed and wandered to the dressing table, instinctively brushing her hair. He used to sit up in bed drinking coffee and watching her. He had loved her hair; when they made love he used to twist it through his fingers, drawing it over her face like a curtain. He wouldn't let her have it cut, and in the three months they had been together it had grown a little too long. She turned and looked behind her at the empty bed. That side of it was still to come. And that would be a very special hell. She moved very slowly, the listlessness of despair dragging at her limbs. She went into the bathroom and opened the medicine chest. It was an automatic search among the pill boxes and little bottles. There were no sleeping pills; nothing but his Alka Seltzer and three aspirin tablets. There was no quick escape. She turned on the bath taps and watched the water spilling down into the bath cavity, filling it slowly.

The bathroom door was open, and she heard the telephone in her bedroom start to ring. It wasn't Arundsen. She said that aloud before she picked up the receiver, but still her hands were shaking.

'Mary?' Phillip's voice said. 'Are you alone?'

'Yes.' She had to repeat it because he said he couldn't hear. 'Yes, quite alone.'

'I thought he'd be in the office by now. It's all fixed for next weekend. I'll meet you at Claridges' Buttery at twelve-thirty on Friday and give you all instructions then. And bring your luggage with you.'

'All right,' she said. 'I'll be there.'

'Thank you, my dear,' he said. 'How are you – you sound as if you've got a cold . . .'

She couldn't tell him Arundsen had gone because she'd have to tell him why. He had forbidden her to tell anyone about Washington, and she understood that he was protecting himself as much as her. At least she hadn't let him down.

'I haven't a cold,' she said. 'I'm just tired. I had a late night.'

'Very foolish.' His tone was slightly disapproving. 'You'll spoil your looks if you cut down on sleep. Eight hours is the minimum. I'm very grateful to you, Mary. And don't worry about anything. It'll be perfectly easy for you.'

'I'm not worrying,' she answered. 'I'm sure it will. After all, it's not like the first time. I'm rather looking forward to going. I've always wanted to see Berlin.'

It wouldn't be the first time; she had played the mean little espionage game for six long months, listening to conversations, issuing invitations to people as instructed, knowing that some trap was being laid for them. What she was doing was worse, at least it seemed worse, in spite of Phillip's reassurance. She would have to actually give them something having smuggled it out of her own country. Arundsen had been wrong. He should have turned her in. People like her, cowards on the run from life, were never to be trusted. She didn't know how she was going out, but it must be by air. She got dressed, forgetting the bath. She would fly out and discharge her debt to Phillip. Phillip had been her only friend. He hadn't turned her out, and walked away in disgust like the man she loved. He had understood and helped. She owed it to him, and this was one responsibility she meant to carry out. When it was finished she could get on a train, and somewhere on the journey across Germany she would find the courage to open the carriage door and just let go.

Arundsen had spent the night in a hotel. He went back to his office after leaving Mary's flat, and finished off the day's business. He had himself in control, and he concentrated on working as if nothing had happened. He didn't let himself think of her, because when he had to give in and face the situation he knew he'd need to be alone. It never occurred to him to go back to his own home, or to make any move towards his wife. That was finished. Both relationships were finished. His wife and his mistress. He had walked out on them both, and he never bloody well wanted to see either of them again. That was the first thing he said to himself when he got to the fourth-floor single room at a hotel near Victoria Station. It was a massive Edwardian building, with an impressive entrance and thick carpets underlaid with rubber, like a cinema foyer. He wasn't surprised to see a stately potted palm in a corner of the lounge. It was the first place to go he could think of; he needed somewhere to stay, but it wasn't exactly the place to get drunk, and he was going to get very drunk indeed that night. He left his cases in his room, and went out. In the second railway bar a woman tried to pick him up; he glared at her and made a foul reply. Then he was sorry. He should have bought her a drink, bought himself someone to talk to and blotted out that other image which he couldn't keep out of his mind any longer. Mary sitting on one of her pretty gilt chairs with the tears pouring down her face. He'd said to himself he was damned if he would take any notice. He'd seen women cry before, women who'd betrayed their countries and their own men. They always cried when they were caught, thinking it might help them. It never had with him. It wasn't going to change his attitude because the woman was someone he had loved and he was the man who'd been fooled.

And yet she hadn't fooled him. He was lying in his room with a bottle of whisky by the bedside table, and in spite of everything he wasn't drunk enough to go to sleep. He slopped some more whisky into the hotel toothglass, and looked at it. She hadn't fooled him. She'd told him the truth of her own accord. He hadn't discovered her or tricked her into it. She had told him the truth.

A different type of woman would have married him, and kept her secret. What a bloody fool she was, he thought angrily. What a silly inefficient fool to make such a song and dance about it. A wise one would have kept her mouth shut, taken what was going in the way of a stupid bastard like himself, who was good at making love and wanted to keep her for life. But not Mary. Oh, no, not Mary. She had to get herself married to a kink and be blackmailed. And then ruin her happiness and his by telling him that she had been what he most hated in the living world. A Red stooge. When he thought about Dunne it was bad enough. Half drunk, he lay back on the bed and wished he'd taken hold of Mary and beaten her unconscious. Perhaps then he might have been able to stay with her . . . But that was an alcoholic fantasy. He didn't take it seriously. Everything was distorted in his mind; what she had really done, and how much she was to blame – it was all a muddle, and it was growing more confused

134

as he slipped into sleep. When he woke the next morning his head was splitting and his stomach heaved as soon as he tried to stand up. He remembered the afternoon he was going down to Buntingford, and the nagging hangover which was his birthday souvenir. It was only a few months ago, but it seemed like another life. It began with a headache and a sour stomach and that was how it ended. He felt flat and emptied out; there was a blank space inside him where she had been.

Somehow last night he had come through the worst of blaming her, and that morning he could even say there might be some excuse. It was over; that was final and he didn't try to argue it, but some of his bitterness had gone. He discovered during the course of that day how quickly regret could insinuate itself into the vacancy where his reproach had been. He would have to keep hating her. It was the only way to cut the canker out. And loving her was a canker which had eaten very deeply into him. He could stay in his hotel for a week or so, and decide what he wanted to do next. He had to sort out the mess with Joan, and see that she was settled first. He owed her that. The senior partner came through into his office in the later part of the morning; he had some share indexes to discuss, and Arundsen listened to him wearily, hardly saying anything.

'You're looking a bit rough,' the partner said. 'Are you feeling all right, Peter? Want to go home or anything?'

'No, thanks,' Arundsen said. 'I just need the hair of a very large dog. I'll hang on till lunch.'

Why had she done it? He had given up concentrating on his work; he had been able to do that yesterday when the shock and anger acted as a buffer, but now both were wearing off. Why had Mary worked for them? 'I was being blackmailed.' Of course she was; he could imagine how easy it was for them to get something on a man like Richard Wetherby and then apply the pressure to his wife. They had agents among all the better-class prostitutes in cities like Washington; sexual deviations were a favourite lever. The women tipped them off when they had a client of importance with peculiar tastes. And a wife and a family to lose. It was an old and dirty trick, employed by all sides in the game. They had got something on the husband and used it on Mary. He put his head in his hands for a moment. He hadn't even asked her what it was. He hadn't asked her anything; he had just condemned her. But why didn't she go for help? He had put that to her, and the answer was pathetic in its honesty. 'I couldn't. I was too ashamed.'

It was the answer most people would have given. He left his office and went to the nearest city pub; he couldn't eat anything and the smell of food made him sick. He went to the public bar, where he wasn't likely to see anyone he knew, and slowly drank a double brandy.

He wasn't angry with her any more. He was angry with himself for behaving badly to her, walking out without seeing if she needed anything; after all, they had been together for a time, and she had loved him. He was sure of that. He had been a bastard. There was a telephone in the corner. He put his glass down and looked over at it; he even counted the change in his pocket. But he didn't ring. He couldn't go back to her. He felt as some men do when they find their wives have slept with someone else. She was defiled. She had worked for the opposition, and Arundsen had spent half his adult life fighting them. He knew what they were and what they did. He had friends who had been taken and disappeared; he had proof of men in public life whose probity had been an obstacle to their political intrigues, and these men had been assassinated, as callously as swatting flies. Human life meant nothing to them, and by *them* Arundsen specified the K.G.B. There was no mercy and no scruple. If Arundsen had loved his work he had also hated the enemy, and this was what had made him such a successful operator. But more than the enemy, he hated his own kind who traded with them.

For them, as for Dunne, he could find no excuse. He could excuse Mary but he couldn't let himself forgive her. He could never go back. He finished his drink, and walked slowly back to his office. He had his hotel bedroom to go home to, and beyond that he couldn't think ahead.

CHAPTER SEVEN

'I am looking for Countess Graetzen,' the man said. He smiled at the manageress of the pension in the Rue de la Liberté. She was a dour woman, and she did not smile back. He was an ordinary-looking man in his forties, with a self-effacing manner that encouraged her to be surly.

'She's not here,' she said.

'Oh, what a pity. I've come from Marseilles specially to see her,' the man said. 'When did she leave, madame?

'This morning,' she said. The Countess had come back the previous night, so drunk she had fallen up the stairs and lain sprawling on the half-landing, until Madame and her husband had hauled her on her feet and guided her into her room. There had been no need to tell her to leave the pension. She had come down very early, to their surprise, paid the bill and left in a taxi.

'You don't know where she's gone? It's very important.'

'I've no idea. Probably back to England. She said she lived there.'

'Thank you.' He gave her a little bow, and put his soft hat on, pulling it down to a correct angle on the centre of his head.

In the street outside there was a green Citroën waiting. He pulled open the left-hand door and said to the driver, 'Too late. She's gone. You go to Orly. I'll go to Le Bourget. We might just catch up with her.' The car began to move away as he slammed the door shut. He stood on the pavement, his arm raised to hail a cruising taxi. 'Le Bourget, and hurry,' he told the driver. 'Fast as you can. I've got a plane to catch!'

When the Countess had woken up that morning she couldn't remember at first where she was or where she had been the night before. Slowly the confusion cleared, leaving her brain defenceless before the onslaught of her hangover and a crushing sense of despair.

She had uncovered Phillip Wetherby as the contact between Dunne and the Russians. A chance in a million had betrayed him; beginning with her making friends with Arthur and the first hint that he knew something about Dunne which he had never disclosed. And from the scruffy bar of the Fox public house she had gone on to Paris, with the postcard opening yet another door, until the last of all had closed behind her – the manager of the little Malakoff Hotel.

'That is the Englishman. The gentleman who brought M. Dunne back here.' He hadn't hesitated over the photograph. He had recognised Phillip immediately. As he had said, it wasn't an ordinary face.

She had got very drunk that night, but nothing could stop her trained mind from marshalling the facts in one damning sequence after the other, before the brandy blacked her out. Phillip had been seeing Dunne in secret; he had never mentioned seeing him to anyone or pretended that they had more than the briefest acquaintance. A chance meeting once during a conference held at S.I.S. headquarters in London. That was all. He had been in such close contact with Dunne that he had followed him to Paris. To keep an eye on him, of course. Once you had got your hooks into someone you had to make sure they didn't just go off somewhere and get away from you. You followed them up. You went to dirty pubs with them and sat while they got drunk. You talked and encouraged them to talk back. You made them feel you were their friend. You conned them into trusting you, and above all you kept the contact going. How Phillip must have hated it all. She had smiled in bitterness as the thought of how his fastidious nature must have been outraged by the excesses of Jimmy Dunne. Even those in the Firm who didn't know him personally knew all about him. He was dirty, he was drunk, he befouled the English language with obscenities every time he opened his mouth.

Phillip must have loathed every moment of it. But what a prize – what a coup to get Dunne to turn bad and go over to the opposition! How long had Phillip been a traitor – how many years had he been working for them? And why? As she threw her clothes into the suitcase, the Countess paused, one hand supporting her pounding head, and asked the question out loud. Why had he done it? None of the usual reasons fitted in with him. He didn't need money; he, above all men, with his upper-class background and hatred of disturbance, wouldn't have been converted, like a modern Saul on the Damascus Road. Phillip wasn't a Communist. He was just a traitor. And suddenly she understood it all, because the key was in the clue that he had laid against himself. He had gone bad because he was bored and vain. He had been retired, and so he went to the other side because it pleased his professional vanity to pull the rug from under his own people's feet. And because he despised them he had given that description of himself, and then sat back to watch the fun. It must have amused him to resurrect her, and give her the job of tracing the mysterious Englishman. She could imagine him laughing. He must be very secure to take even such a tiny risk, and that kind of security only came with long practice. Phillip hadn't suddenly gone over; he must have been working for them for years. She had found some loose aspirins and swallowed them with tepid water from the washbasin tap.

She remembered the temptation to drop the whole thing; it had come on her yesterday on her way to the Place Malakoff. For a friend who was in trouble she might just have done it, if she owed them what she believed she owed Phillip Wetherby. But then, of course, she had realised that she didn't owe him anything. He had been using her, not helping her. Even that wouldn't have made her damn him, in spite of the sickening hurt to what was left of her self-respect.

But that was not why she was leaving Paris and going back to England to denounce him. There wasn't just one reason, there were many. They came crowding on her in the stuffy bedroom, parading themselves before her eyes. The flames licking up into the black night sky as Warsaw burned, and her patriots perished in the blast and glare of German artillery, while from across the Vistula the Soviet armies watched and waited till the slaughter was complete. Men she had known after the war – their faces came and mocked her. They were all dead faces, and only one was living, and this passed in a wordless scream, echoing in a mindless vacuum of induced madness.

One or two women, friends, Poles who had done too well in the war against the Nazis and must be extinguished quickly because they pointed to another leadership. Murder and blackmail and terror in the name of universal brotherhood. The Countess put on her coat, checked that she hadn't left anything behind her, and faced her own ravaged reflection in the dingy glass above the washbasin.

It wasn't personal any more. Her pride didn't matter and her future had never been more than a shadow in the bottom of a brandy glass. That was all over. She felt no malice and no pain on her own account. But for those others and for all the crimes committed daily against the peoples of the earth the Countess knew that Phillip Wetherby had to be stopped. She had paid her bill and taken a taxi to Le Bourget Airport and bought herself a ticket on the mid-morning flight. There was an hour to wait, and she sat down in the large open lounge, an unread copy of *Figaro* rolled up across her lap. Her head ached and the thirst was coming back. There was a couple sitting near to her, on the seats opposite, a red-headed woman and a dark man; the woman was holding a very dark child in her arms, and it was screaming, one fist shoved into its mouth. The noise was like a buzz saw, cutting into the top of her head. She closed her eyes and wondered why the mother couldn't hush the child. Other passengers were looking at the couple. They were flustered and the man bent over his wife and whispered something. She answered him irritably, and went on rocking the baby backwards and forward, patting its back. It went on screaming at what seemed to the Countess a more frenzied pitch.

A man in a dark suit, with a buff mackintosh on one arm, got up from the seat two down from where the Countess was sitting, and said to the couple, 'Excuse me, madame. There is a crèche downstairs where you could leave your baby. We have nearly an hour to wait for this flight.'

The woman muttered something and got up, looking round helplessly for the sign that showed where the crèche was, and her husband got up too and said loudly, 'I'm going to have a drink. I'll order something for you too.'

That was what brought the Countess to her feet. She followed him across the slippery floor to the bar, and ordered herself a large cognac. It went down her throat like milk, and she was still dry, as if the place were a desert and the pain in her head was increased by a malevolent sun. She had to work out what to do when she got back. It wasn't so clear-cut, this duty to show Phillip Wetherby as a double agent for the Soviets. It might have sounded simple enough to an amateur, but to a real professional like Katharina it was not. If she made the obvious move of going to the Major-General's department, and telling them that their former chief of the Eastern European Section was a traitor, they'd say she was drunk and kick her out. And tell Phillip, of course. She was discredited, labelled unreliable, unemployable, a pensioner of Wetherby's because he was sorry for her. She could imagine how much sympathy she'd get with her story. They wouldn't even listen. And when Phillip knew she wouldn't get another chance. She hadn't been afraid for some years; it was an emotion which had been left out, and sitting at the bar at Le Bourget Airport she was suddenly afraid, just as she used to be during the war when she was operating in France. She ordered another brandy, forgetting that it was her third. The man with the mackintosh was having a drink too. Thank God that child had been taken away. If Phillip got a whisper that she had been to see anyone or tried to make an accusation he would alert the K.G.B. people in England. They wasted no time. She was safe for the moment, so long as she said nothing to anyone.

There was a call for the London flight, but she didn't hear it. She took a full glass back to the central lounge with her and sat down to try to think what she could do. Her head was aching gently, and the brandy was sending messages of comfort and relaxation to her brain.

She took a long swallow and leant back. She couldn't go to the Major-General; he didn't know her, and he wasn't a man she could approach. None of her old friends were in the department now; they were gone, or retired, like George and Françoise Geeson. Would they believe her? Would they give her the chance to explain to them what she had found out and how, without putting it all down to an alcoholic fantasy. She didn't know. She couldn't be sure. She finished her drink and looked at her watch. She had missed her plane. It didn't matter; there were plenty of others. She needed time to think; but first she needed time to rest, to let her head clear a little. A drunken sleep is not sleep at all; she was dull with tiredness from the night before, and a little drunk, too, from the cognacs. Perhaps if she settled back and slept a little while it would be better. She could catch a later plane to London, and make up her mind what to do during the flight. And not drink any more.

She said that to herself for emphasis. She had to stay sober now or she wouldn't have a chance; nobody would want to give her a hearing anyway, and one whiff of liquor would send the doors slamming in her face. She leant back and closed her eyes. The man with the buff mackintosh let his paper down an inch and watched the back of her head. In a moment or two it rolled slightly to one side, showing she was asleep. The lounge was full of people. There was nothing he could do. He would have to get on the plane with her.

Phillip had arrived at the hotel first. He went into the Causerie, and took his table for two; he ordered a glass of dry sherry and settled down to wait for Mary. The restaurant was full; he looked round him, noticing one or two people he knew, and smiled, waving his hand to one couple. It was one of the best restaurants in London, managed with the elegance and comfort which made Claridges itself a haven for the rich from all over the world.

It was famous for its enormous buffet table, rich with the best varieties of smörgåsbord, at which the customers helped themselves. Some of the more impecunious smart young men brought their girls to lunch there because there wasn't any limit on the amount of food you could eat from the cold table. The price remained fixed.

Phillip liked the Causerie; it was pleasant to have a light lunch and its position was central to the best part of London. He looked at his watch. It was 12.50; Mary was not usually late.

He had her first-class air ticket in his wallet, and the address of the hotel in West Berlin where he had booked a room for Friday night. Ivliev had been told to expect her on Saturday; she could come across with a coach load of sight-seers and get off at the Adlon Hotel. They would pick her up there. In the inside pocket of his coat he carried a medium-sized buff envelope. It was sealed and unaddressed, but there was nothing inside it but folded sheets of the *Sunday Times* Colour Supplement. He saw her come through the door and pause, looking round for him. She was wearing a dark green woollen suit, and a little round mink cap on the back of her head. He saw several people stop eating, and watch her, as she asked the head waiter where his table was. She was a beautiful woman, and unlike so many women of her class, she knew how to walk. He half rose from his chair as she move with gentle grace across the floor towards him.

'I'm so sorry I'm late,' she said. 'I got a taxi in plenty of time but the traffic was awful.'

'It always is at this hour,' he said. 'Sit down, my dear, and join me in a glass of sherry. Or do you want something else?'

Now that she was close, he saw how white she was, and the dark hollows under her eyes. 'I'll have sherry,' she said.

He frowned. 'You look exhausted,' he said. 'What have you been doing? Aren't you feeling well?'

'I've been sleeping badly,' Mary said.

'You're not worrying about this trip?' he said. 'There's nothing to worry about, I promise you. It'll be the easiest thing you've ever done. Of course, Mary, if you've changed your mind, and you'd rather not go . . .' He left the sentence half finished, and sipped his sherry.

'Of course I want to go,' she said. She put her hand on his arm, which was unusual because she knew he disliked being touched. 'I told you, Phillip, I'm not worried about it in the least. I just haven't been sleeping, that's all. It's nothing to do with the weekend.' She took her hand off his sleeve and brought some cigarettes and a lighter out of her bag. Phillip showed no sign of the sudden panic she had caused him. 'Is there something wrong with you and Arundsen?'

They couldn't have broken up, not now, at the last stage in the plan. That was just impossible. Mary looked at him and lied.

'No, nothing like that. We're fine. I told him I was going to see my cousin in Dorset; I said she'd had a baby.'

'Good.' Phillip relaxed inwardly. Now that the moment of tension was over he realised how much he had enjoyed it. How insufferably dull life would have been without the constant move and counter-move, like a lethal game of chess. He leant towards her. 'I'll explain all the details for you first, and then we'll have a nice lunch in peace. Here is your plane ticket; it's the Lufthansa flight from Heathrow, and it leaves at four-fifteen. You should arrive at Tempelhof by six-thirty or so. I have booked you a room at the Hotel Am Zoo, just off the Kurfuerstendamm. I know it, and I'm sure you'll be comfortable. The food is simply excellent, but if you want to go out somewhere there's a very nice restaurant on the Kurfuerstendamm itself, called the Emilion. I can really recommend the German cooking there. I used to dine there twice a week when I was in Berlin in the fifties, and I went back there last June, when I made a trip there, you remember. Just mention that you're my niece, and they'll look after you. Hadn't you better write down the address?'

She nodded and wrote down the name of her hotel. 'I won't go to the restaurant,' she said. 'I'll probably feel like an early night.'

The waiter had brought her sherry and she drank some of it. It was pale and tasted bitter; she hadn't been able to eat anything since Arundsen left. The drink would go to her head unless she sipped it slowly.

'When do I go across to the East?' She didn't feel nervous now. She didn't feel anything except heavy and dead, like someone who knows they have a certain time to live and are resigned to dying. This would be the last treason, the last shame. It was an odd sensation till one got used to it, this determination to get out of life. Arundsen had left her, despising her, unable to forgive. And he was right, because there was the envelope on the table in front of her, with Phillip's fingers just touching the edge of it, and Phillip explaining how she got a tourist ticket at the hotel to go through the Wall on an excursion, and wait at the Adlon Hotel until someone contacted her. Then she had to give them the envelope, and that was all. 'You can take a taxi to the checkpoint, and walk through; you can get on a flight on Monday morning,' he was saying.

'I'm very grateful to you, Mary. This will set us both free from now on. I promise you that. We'll never have to speak of it again.'

'I thought that last time,' she said. 'I hope you're right, Phillip. You're quite sure it wouldn't be easier for me to own up about Washington? I can still do it – I'm not afraid any more. Then you wouldn't have to give them this.' She looked at the envelope, and wondered what was in it. When he had first told her, Phillip had said it wasn't really important, and she knew he was in a position to judge. He was only being blackmailed because of her initial act, and he had never once reproached her.

She looked at him and her eyes filled with tears. 'I'll go and explain everything,' she said. 'I'll keep you out of it, Phillip, I promise you. I'll say they've approached me a second time. Please let me do it. Don't deal with them. Don't give them this!'

He waited a moment before answering. He saw her brush the tears away, and blink back others.

'You're a sweet person,' he said gently. 'And I know you're trying to help. But it's no good. You don't know what you're dealing with. I told you that day at Buntingford that nothing in the world would be worth the disgrace of my name and our family's reputation. And believe me that's what would happen. Your poor little lies would be torn to shreds in a few minutes. And pictures of Richard with that prostitute would be posted to every department head in S.I.A. I couldn't survive it, my dear. If you want to help me, and I know that's what you're trying to do, hand over this envelope at the Adlon. That's all I ask of you. Surely you trust me to know what's best? Do you think I'd really give them anything important?'

'No,' she said. 'No of course you wouldn't. I know that. I'm sorry, Phillip. I was probably being stupid.'

'I appreciate the offer,' he said. 'But just do as I've told you and don't worry. Now,' he changed his tone, speaking almost briskly, 'let's go over and choose something from the smörgås-bord. It looks delicious.'

They spent the next hour and a half talking about trivialities. Phillip ate well because the contrasting dishes pleased his palate, and didn't press Mary, who managed a little of the complicated hors-d'oeuvres and then left it. They talked about the alterations he was making in the picture gallery at Bunting-ford. Three of the lesser Italian Masters were being auctioned in London. It was a pity, he confessed, but there were signs of dry rot in the timbers of the roof above the Great Hall, and this would be expensive to put right. Also some of the brickwork of the east front needed re-facing. Anyway, he hadn't liked the paintings very much, and it allowed him the pleasure of replacing them one day with something better. They had coffee, and she smoked continuously.

The restaurant began to empty out; there were gaps in the bright patchwork of the smörgåsbord table, and two waiters began removing the empty dishes. Phillip looked at his watch. It was 2.30.

'Have you got everything with you? Suitcase, passport?'

'Yes,' Mary said. 'Only one case. I shan't need much. I left it at the desk outside.'

'Then I think we'd better be going. You don't want to rush getting to the airport. I'm sorry I can't drive you down, my dear, but the Geesons are coming for the weekend, and I've got to go straight down.'

It was late afternoon when the Countess woke. The lounge was still crowded with people, but they were all changed from those she had seen before she closed her eyes. She went to the counter and explained that she had missed her original flight. The clerk was slow and irritable; passengers who missed the plane were a nuisance, especially women passengers. They were always more troublesome than men. She watched the Countess with the blank, hostile look which begged for an excuse to be unpleasant, and when this didn't succeed either, she retaliated by being as slow about making out a new ticket as she could. She even disappeared behind the counter into the little office, and powdered her face, just to keep the customer waiting. When she came out and started on the ticket the next plane was at six o'clock. When the Countess moved away, the clerk found a man standing in her place. He pushed a rolled-up mackintosh on the ledge and asked about the next flight. She made him out a ticket for the same plane, and when he said thank you she didn't answer. She had taken the job because she spoke perfect French, and she liked living in Paris. The trouble was simply that she hated passengers. From her side of the counter they just weren't members of the human race. It was surprising how many members of the staff felt the same way.

The Trident was three-quarters full, but because she boarded at the first call, the Countess got an outside seat. She settled back, buckling the seat-belt round her waist, and adjusted the seat-back for take-off.

She had always liked flying; even the three perilous trips by Lancaster from Kent to France during the war had excited her. She remembered the last one, six months before the Allied invasion. There had been four agents in all, a radio operator, two couriers and herself, who was to act as liaison. That was where she had met Duclos; he was in the Maquis group which she was sent to contact. It was a pity she hadn't been to his home and met his family. She made up her mind to write to him and apologise. He would understand that something important had come up. She looked round the smoothly decorated pressurised cabin, its walls painted a soothing baby blue, piped music drifting over the passengers to create a calming atmosphere before take-off, and smiled, thinking of the stark inside of the Lancaster, the freezing cold which became a bitter chasm of wind and blackness as the door was slid back before they jumped.

'Will you adjust your seat, please, madame. Upright, before take-off!' The air hostess was bending over her, her pretty face smiling and impersonal as an advertisement for a deodorant.

'I'm sorry,' the Countess said. She had made the same mistake on the flight from London.

'It's a new rule,' the hostess said. She was polite but very firm. 'It's safer. Let me do it for you.'

The Countess sat with her back straightened against the impact of a crash, and began to read the copy of *Figaro* which was dog-eared and very curly at the edges from being rolled up all day. The man in the dark suit, with the mackintosh, passed down the aisle and took the seat behind her. She didn't see him, and it wouldn't have interested her if she had. Forty-five minutes later they touched down, and in the same time it had taken for the plane to cross from France to England the passengers passed through the Customs into the main building. The Countess went to a bookstall and bought an *Evening Standard*. She stood for a moment counting her change, and then, picking up her one case, followed the sign marked 'Telephone'. There were four empty booths in the line. The man who had followed her from Le Bourget couldn't get into a vacant one beside hers for a few moments. He waited, unable to see if she were speaking because she had turned her back. When a man came out of the booth on the left of her he pulled his hat down over his face and sprang inside. He lifted the receiver and stood, slightly angled so that he could look through the glass wall between them.

The Countess knew the Geeson's telephone number; she had put her money on top of the machine and was waiting for an answer. She had decided to get in touch with them during the flight. George worried her; he had been such a brilliant operator himself and so successful now. He might go out of his way to be kind to her because she was down, but it didn't mean he'd take her allegation seriously. She wanted to see Françoise first and to talk to her. It might be doing it in a hurry, but she felt instinctively that she shouldn't wait. This wasn't something she could sleep on now; her nerve had deteriorated long ago. She wanted help and she wanted it quickly. The phone went on ringing. Buzz buzz. Buzz buzz. She waited for a full five minutes and then put down the receiver. Next door the man saw her do it, and saw the money; whoever she had been ringing, there had been no answer.

She hesitated, trying to think what to do next. Her hands were shaking and she knew with desperation that unless she saw somebody that night she would go home and get drunk again. Wetherby had nearly cured her; she had been able to control it, perhaps in time she could have beaten it completely, but now that prop was knocked away. She had no obligation to pull herself together. She didn't owe him or anyone anything now. But she had a job to do, and if she gave way and climbed inside a brandy bottle she would never do it. She knew this, and she knew herself. She wouldn't be able to hold out for too long; she couldn't take the strain any more, and what she knew about Phillip Wetherby was a crushing responsibility. She lit a cigarette, staying on in the booth, trying to decide what to do next. The Geesons were out. It was Friday. They were probably away. Damn them. They might even be down at Buntingford. And then she thought of Arundsen. They had been lovers once; he would listen to her. He wouldn't want to believe her, but he would listen because he was a professional, like herself. He would know what to do next; the Major-General's people would listen to someone like Arundsen. Thank God she had thought of him. She knew his address and began looking through the directory. The man in the next booth watched her dialling, saw the money waiting on top of the little square box, and wished he'd taken a chance and given it to her at Le Bourget, while she was asleep. It would have been dangerous, but not as dangerous as letting her get the information through before the job was done. He felt sweat coming out of the pores in his neck and under his hatband. He looked at her half-hidden profile with hate.

Arundsen's flat number rang half a dozen times before Joan answered it. She had been watching a news programme on television, and wondering why she didn't switch it off and read. It was boring and she never watched anything 'heavy' as she described it. That used to be Arundsen's choice. He had found world events interesting. She had always thought them dull and rather a waste of time. It wasn't as if ordinary people could change anything anyway. Now that she was alone, she kept the television on most of the evening, looking at everything. It was so quiet in the flat if she just sat and read, or knitted. When the telephone rang she was glad. Her friends had been very kind when they knew she was alone. The excuse that Arundsen was away on business hadn't held up for very long; she had told first one friend the truth and then found it easier to tell them all. He had another woman and they were separated. Everyone sympathised and told her to come round to them and not sit on her own. For the first month she hadn't been so lonely. But now the invitations were slowing down; people were getting used to her being deserted, and very gradually they began to desert her too. She relied on the telephone to fight her bouts of depression and isolation. She rang people up and had a chat and then it was possible to turn off the lights and go to bed.

She didn't recognise the voice at first. 'Is that Joan? This is Katharina Graetzen. How are you?'

Joan felt herself redden. It was that bloody Polish woman Peter used to work with. One of the Buntingford/Wetherby clique. She had always disliked her, and deliberately froze her off when Peter tried to have her round. Her voice was unfriendly. 'I'm very well thank you.'

'I wonder if I could speak to Peter?'

Joan was suddenly so angry that she almost banged the receiver down. How dare she ring up! How dare anyone connected with that damned dirty organisation of his ring her telephone and ask to speak to him! 'No,' she said. 'I'm afraid you can't. He doesn't live here any more!' Then she did ring off. She went back to her chair, turned up the volume on the television set, and suddenly began to cry.

Katharina put the telephone back. The man saw her do it and calculated by the few seconds she had spoken that nothing of importance had been said. There hadn't been time. Probably whoever she wanted wasn't there. He saw her pick up her bag, and he slipped out of the booth behind her as she began to walk away.

Arundsen had gone. The Geesons were away. The Countess walked out of the building and shivered in the cool air. It was past seven o'clock and already dark. The porters hadn't bothered with her because she had only one light case. She stood hesitating on the edge of the pavement, thinking who she could try next. Bill Thomson – Alex MacCreadie . . .

'Taxi?' The cab was in front of her, and she looked up. She was a fool; the charge of going into central London was over three pounds and she was short of cash. She could have taken the airport bus. It was too late now. 'How much?' she asked.

'Four quid.'

She shook her head. 'I haven't got that much. It's too expensive.'

'Suit yourself,' the driver said.

'Excuse me, wait a moment.' The man had come up to her, and he took off his hat. He was in his early forties, dark and slightly built. He looked a typical French bourgeois businessman.

'I also want to go to London. Perhaps we could share?'

'Why not?' the Countess said. 'They are such robbers, these drivers. I refuse to be robbed like that.'

They got into the next taxi, and she was surprised to find that he jumped inside in front of her. He apologised quickly. 'Pardon, madame.' He sat in the rear seat on the right, and she on his left.

He gave the name of an hotel in Piccadilly, and she called through to the driver to take her to Fulham first.

They moved down through the narrow roadway from Number 1 Building, the scream of an incoming jet overhead, and the man gave a little shiver. 'It's cold tonight,' he said. He pointed to the partition at the driver's back. The narrow glass slide was open.

'Do you mind if I close that? There is a draught.'

'Not at all,' the Countess said. She looked at him for a moment, frowning. There was something familiar about him. Not the face, but the appearance in general. It was the mackintosh.

'Did you come from Paris?' she said.

'Yes. I think we were on the same plane.'

They were travelling down the underground tunnel, and the lights were so bright they filled the cab. He had the mackintosh over his knee, and she noticed that he was wearing gloves. Her head was aching and she thought suddenly that she would have to face Arthur if she went to the Fox for a drink. And she hadn't made contact with anybody yet. It was all still in front of her. As they came out of the tunnel the contrasting darkness hit them; the inside of the cab was light one moment and then almost black. When he moved she knew in the same second what was going to happen, but it was too late and he was much too quick. His left hand closed over her mouth and the six-inch knife blade rammed through her clothes between the fourth and fifth rib into her heart. He was right-handed and couldn't have done it from the left side. That was why he had got into the taxi first. He held her till she died, which was only a few seconds, and she made no sound. He let her lean back against the side of the cab, and left the knife in her. It helped to check the bleeding. Then he opened her coat, very carefully, and ripped her underclothes, watching the driving mirror. The driver didn't look up once; they were moving out on to the motorway and gathering speed. He looked at the dead woman and was satisfied. The coat was drawn over her, hiding the evidence of an apparently vicious assault. It was one of his trademarks, and he often used the technique to disguise the nature of a K.G.B. job on a woman. He had been a professional killer for eighteen years. In his teens he had worked in the black market in occupied France and graduated to dirty, vicious little jobs with the Vichy Militia. From there the Russians had picked him up, and now he was one of their best men. He ran a drapery business in the Rue Coligny, across the left bank of the Seine, and he had been married for ten years, with one child. He had a bank account in Lausanne where the K.G.B. sent his special fees. He settled back in a corner of the taxi, and glanced at his watch. The trip had taken nearly half an hour, and they were just coming over the steep rise that ended the motorway. He had to wait until they were caught in the traffic before he could move. He didn't look at the Countess again. When they turned into the Cromwell Road he put on a pair of spectacles with heavy rims, and as the cab slowed to a crawl in the rush-hour traffic, he edged forward on his seat, blocking the driver's view of the Countess. She leant back limply in the corner, her eyes open, her face dim and peaceful in death. At the second traffic lights he opened the slide communicating with the driver, pushed two pound notes through and said, 'This is impossible! I'd be quicker by Underground. Take the lady to Fulham, I'm getting out here.' He was gone so quickly that the driver hardly saw him; he had nothing but a glimpse of a face over his shoulder; all he would remember afterwards were the glasses. The other passenger was still there. He slipped into gear as the lights changed and drove off.

On the opposite side of the road the man hailed a taxi. He had taken off the glasses and he wore the mackintosh. It was reversible and looked like an overcoat.

'London Airport,' he said. 'As quickly as you can!'

'Would you like a drink?' The B.E.A. stewardess stopped by Mary Wetherby's seat and smiled. It was an odd smile which appeared to have no relation with the rest of her face. It clinked on and off like a neon sign; in repose her face was distant, even sad.

'No thank you.' Mary shook her head.

'Tea or coffee?' The ghastly smile increased. The passenger must want something.

'Nothing, thank you,' Mary said again. She turned away and looked out of the window. The sun was setting, turning the small oval window into a palette of brilliant fiery colours. Dark clouds crept ominously up the edge of the red sky; in a few minutes they would enclose the plane in prehistoric darkness. It was a moment that had always frightened and fascinated her. The immensity of the sunset was impossible to visualise from ground level; only in the suspension of the sky itself did the puniness of man travelling through it like a dust speck, impinge upon the consciousness. She watched the colours slowly fading, the black horizon creeping further and further until there was only a thin crimson line, and then it was completely dark.

The captain's voice came over the intercom. They would be landing at Tempelhof in twenty minutes. She had tried to read the paper, and the new edition of *Queen* magazine, but it was impossible to concentrate. She found herself reading the same item twice over without having absorbed a word. She sat through the flight and let her thoughts go freely through the agony of losing Arundsen in a way they hadn't been able to do before. She was thirty, and her life was over. She wondered how people felt when they had success and happiness to look back upon before they died. Perhaps this made them brave, this ability to measure achievement in their past. Perhaps it made them cling to living and fight off the inevitable illness, the steady move down to the terminus of death. If that was so then she was lucky. She had nothing to regret but regret itself, and there was nothing left behind her any more than there was anything in front.

She had been loved, and she had loved. That was surely something. How many people went through the full life-span without being able to say that, or even knowing what they'd missed. Arundsen had loved her, even though it wasn't a love strong enough to face the truth, and still survive. It wasn't his fault: she hadn't been worthy of this dream, and perhaps it was truer to say that human beings loved the dream in each other, not the reality. Only a child calls forth the absolute love that doesn't need illusion, and she had never had a child. She thought how gay Phillip had been at lunch. Perhaps it was because he saw how nervous she was; he wanted to make her feel at ease. But he was still very carefree, as if the enormity of treason didn't weigh on him at all. He was an odd man. An odd, cold, puzzling man, with generous impulses and unexpected kindness. She owed him a great deal. She owed him her safety for the last two years; the haven of Buntingford, the silence which had never probed beyond the evidence of those dreadul photogaphs. He had given her shelter, and a curious, remote affection, until Arundsen came into her life.

Some incidents in the three months they'd been together stood out in sharper definition than the rest. The walk round the lake at Buntingford, watching the lone swan sail down to meet his mate. Arundsen laughing at the legend that the beautiful mute birds sang before death. The gunshot from the wood after she had told him about Richard Wetherby. She remembered his tenderness then, the threat to kiss her if she cried. He hadn't cared about Richard, or what her life with him had been. His love was already strong enough for that, even before they became lovers. It was the dirty act of treason that he couldn't take – how lucky for him that he had left her. Now he would never have to know about the dirtier and bigger treachery – the envelope in her travelling case. Then there was the walk through Malmaison, holding hands in Josephine's fantastic red and gold bedroom, draped from the ceiling like a tent, laughing because the bed was so small. And the morning a few weeks ago when they had woken within minutes of each other; he had turned her round to him and made love to her without saying a word. It was the most tender thing that they had ever done. Afterwards he had grinned at her, looking much younger with his hair on end, and said, 'Good morning, darling.'

She hadn't been up to his standard. It was the true answer to her exile from happiness. He was a strong man, and he couldn't understand how anyone could be less strong; nothing in the world would have made him do what she had done. He couldn't sympathise with her shame, or appreciate what the exposure of her husband would have meant to her. And she couldn't blame him for not understanding. She had failed him because she was made of weaker stuff; he had been right to reject her. Her presence on the plane proved that.

She had once seen a short film of an experiment with mice; it was a fifteen-minute documentary filling in before the feature movie. There was a mouse in an elaborate trap of little passages, all but one ending in a cul de sac. She remembered how the mouse fled up and down, blindly fleeing without direction or hope, until it lay exhausted and quivering in defeat. Ever since that telephone call in Washington she had been like the mouse in the movie; running blind, without a chance of escape. Phillip had said it that afternoon, sitting in the cloistered elegance of Claridges. 'You don't know what you're dealing with.' And it was true. She had never known, never really understood. When they came with the photographs she had imagined she could buy them off. But there was no end to the payments and no limit to the price. She didn't believe Phillip when he said they would be free after she made this delivery. She didn't believe he thought so himself; it was just another subterfuge to comfort her and give her courage. He would never be free, so long as what she had done could be used against him. If she were dead it would be easier for Phillip too.

The lights above the seat flashed on. Cigarettes out. Fasten seat-belts. The captain's voice crackled through the intercom again. The city of Berlin was just below them; the glittering glow-worm pattern of lights spread out to the right of them as the plane banked before the run in. Mary fastened her seat-belt. Ten minutes later the Trident landed.

She went by airport bus into the centre of the city. Modern skyscraper buildings reared up like Christmas trees; the broad streets were lined with shops, open and filled with every kind of goods. The pavements were thronged with people and the cafés were doing capacity business. They turned up along the Kurfuerstendamm, the two-mile-long avenue which was the city's shopping and entertainment centre, and again it reminded Mary of Christmas: Regent Street and Times Square at their most extravagant. Everything blazed with lights, everyone seemed to be hurrying towards something. The traffic streamed along with intermittent hooting, as if they were part of a gigantic carnival, in a never-ending Mardi Gras. There was an enormous circular glass-walled complex, and beside it the first reminder of the city's death under bombardment in the last phase of the war. The shattered steeple of a great church pointed to the night sky above the modern octahedron.

A middle-aged German was sitting on the seat beside her; he saw her look back as the bus went on its way. He had been in the plane and passed some of the journey looking at her because he thought she was very beautiful.

'That round building is the Europa Centre,' he said.

'Is it? It's enormous.' He had a pleasant face, without the

154

glasses so many German men seemed to need. As a nation they must have the worst eyesight per head of the population in Europe. It was a silly observation and it almost made her smile.

'And that's the Kaiser-Wilhelm Gedaechtris Kirche behind it,' the man said. 'It was partially destroyed during the bombardment of Berlin. We have decided not to rebuild it. We want to leave it as a monument. Is this your first visit to Berlin?'

'Yes,' Mary said.

'You must visit the Europa Centre. It has some excellent fashion stores and the restaurants are marvellous. Each one is different. There is a French one, and Italian one, even an English pub. There is a skating rink, and a night-club. The Centre has everything.'

'It sounds wonderful,' she said politely.

'It is,' he said. 'Are you staying long?' She *was* very beautiful, he said to himself, confirming his earlier judgement, and she wore a nice scent. He had been on a business trip to London and had further business in Berlin before going to his home in Munich. He wondered if she would accept an invitation to dinner. He had noticed her legs in the plane.

'Just the weekend,' Mary answered.

'I'm also staying a few days here. Perhaps I could show you something of the city. I'm not a Berliner myself, but I know it very well.'

'That's very kind of you, but I'm joining some friends.' Men had tried to pick Mary up all over the States; whenever she travelled alone there was always one prospector prepared to pan for a night's gold. She knew what to say to them by heart. The German didn't persist. He had tried, but without much hope. He had never had an Englishwoman. They were supposed to be very cold and rather ugly. He felt he should have tried to sit next to her on the plane and start from there.

The bus drew in at the other end of the Kurfuerstendamm, and he got up. He gave her a little bow.

'*Auf wiedersehen*. I wish you a pleasant stay.'

'Thank you,' Mary said. She got off the bus and collected her case. There was a lot of guttural noise, and laughter. She had never thought of the Germans as people who laughed. But then the Berliners were supposed to be different. She had heard them described as very gay. She found a taxi and gave the address of her hotel. Even the taxi driver spoke good English.

'If you want to go out later tonight,' he said, 'I can take you on a tour. One hundred marks, and that can include some night-clubs. I can show you everything in our city. If you want an escort I can arrange it.'

'No thank you,' Mary said.

'I can give you a good time,' he said. He looked over his shoulder at her and grinned. He had strong teeth, very white and regular, with sharp blue eyes and a lick of blond hair straight across his forehead. He was good-looking and young, like an animal; he did a good trade with women tourists, especially the Americans. He took a commission from an escort service, and he did some very professional escorting himself, which included a personal service at a special price, if the customers were interested. He ran a couple of girls on the side and raked in a steady thousand marks a week from each of them. They worked hard for him because he was good to them and kept them happy. He glanced into the driving mirror at his passenger. Very nice; he wouldn't charge for a 'fick' there.

'No,' Mary said again. 'I'm not going out, thank you.' He smiled and shrugged agreeably. There hadn't been much hope, but nothing tried for, nothing got.

'Here's your hotel, Fräulein. That will be eight marks.' She got out and gave him the money. He grinned again at her and winked. 'Enjoy your stay in Berlin. My name is Rudi. If you change your mind this evening, if your gentleman friend wants to take you somewhere, just ask the head porter. He knows where to find me. Everyone knows Rudi.'

The bright blue eyes raked over her, frankly friendly and admiring. The doorman was taking her suitcase out of the taxi; behind her the hotel's plate-glass doors were being held open for her. At that moment she had never felt more lonely in her life. She looked into the man's face and understood why women did such things. There was no gentleman waiting for her. There was nobody in the world waiting for her anywhere. Except across the wall in East Berlin. The thought of the tour and the ride with a busful of sightseers was suddenly too much for her. That was how Phillip had arranged it but she couldn't face the prospect. Go in the morning, he had said.

Get there and wait by the Adlon just before twelve.

'I want to go out tomorrow morning,' she said. 'I want to go into the Eastern Sector. Can you take me?'

The young German raised one yellow eyebrow and pushed out his full lower lip. 'Why don't you take a tour? It's very simple. The hotel arranges everything. Taxis don't like going there.'

'I don't want to go on a tour,' Mary said. 'Can't you take me?'

'Yes,' he said. 'I can. There's very few of us who'll go over there. Most will take you to the checkpoint and after that you have to pick up a cab on the other side. But I'll take you in if you like. What time do you want to go?'

'About eleven-thirty – My name is Mrs. Wetherby. Ask for me at the reception.'

'Okay.' He gave her the benefit of his wide smile, and tipped his cap. 'Tomorrow at eleven-thirty. Then maybe I can show you *West* Berlin in the afternoon? *Auf wiedersehen.*'

He drove off whistling, moving the cab slowly away into the traffic so that he could watch her. Very nice; very good class. And very nervous about something. Sontag would be interested to hear about her.

CHAPTER EIGHT

The Countess was buried in the Catholic section of Ealing Cemetery on one of the finest autumn days in the month. September had been overcast and chilly, but the morning of her funeral was bright with sunshine and the sky above was dappled with scudding, fleece white clouds. In films and books it always rained on these occasions, and the mourners stood grouped around the open grave with black umbrellas mushrooming over their heads. Arundsen stood a little back from the ugly oblong pit and the coffin wrapped in the Polish flag which waited at the edge. There must be about fifty people there, he thought, not counting the Press, who were hanging round in the background because the officiating priest, also a Pole, had refused to conduct the service if they took photographs at the grave.

All the people she had worked with were there that morning. Bill Thomson and the MacCreadies, the Geesons, Françoise pale and with red eyes, and of course Phillip Wetherby. There were a group of Poles, and a representative from the Major-General's department, and even an anonymous man from the Foreign Office, representing God knew what. Everything had come out in the newspapers. There had been photographs of Katharina as a young war heroine wearing her George Cross, stories of her exploits during the war in France, and inevitably the details of her decline. The inquest had uncovered a lot of it: reading the papers Arundsen had felt like vomiting. It made a sensational murder case, the story of the brave and beautiful Polish aristocrat who had come down to the gutter, and died as the victim of a sex maniac in a London taxi. The verdict was murder by a person unknown, and a large-scale hunt was going on for a man with spectacles and a foreign accent. A mound of wreaths was arranged on one side of the grave, many of them made up in the red, green and white Polish colours. The Polish community had turned out for her in strength; he recognised a famous war-time general who must have come from France to pay his tribute. There was one wreath on her coffin in the shape of a cross, made of white roses and lilies. It carried the General's card and would be buried with her. He knew from the newspaper reports that her medals were inside the coffin.

When they had been lovers he sometimes sent her roses; he had ordered them for her now, tall and red and very expensive. He had written '*To Katharina, in memory*,' on the back of a visiting card. The priest's voice was raised, intoning the sonorous Latin burial service. Arundsen bent his head and tried to think of something that might do as a prayer; it was so long since he had even thought of such a thing that all he could remember was the Our Father, so he said that for her under his breath, feeling a hypocrite as he did so. He had never known the Countess to go to Church or indicate that she had any religion. And this religion was the same as Mary's, with its foreign, ritualistic formula for burying the dead. He had hated it and been jealous, thinking it was a barrier between them. But it had dignity, he had to admit that. It had solemnity and style, and he was suddenly glad that this was how Katharina's body should be treated. It would have made him sick to think of a nice, clinical cremation.

There was a man standing a little behind him on the left, and Arundsen could hear him blowing his nose and snuffling. The coffin was lowered, and he saw George Geeson put an arm round his wife. When it was over, the crowd hesitated, waiting for the priest in his black and gold vestments to leave the grave. The man behind Arundsen moved closer. It was Arthur, and he was crying. He held a round posy of pink and white carnations in his hand, tied with white ribbon.

He glared at Arundsen. 'God rest her,' he said. 'All those things they said were bloody lies. She was a real lady!' He wiped his eyes with a large handkerchief and stepping forward, dropped his flowers into the grave.

Then everybody began to break up into little groups, and the photographers moved in, taking pictures of the wreaths, asking the Polish general to pose. Arundsen found himself with the Geesons and Thomson. They stood around, waiting for Phillip Wetherby to join them. He was saying a few words to the General.

'Awful business,' George Geeson said. 'Poor girl. We won't hang around; I think Françoise has had enough this morning. Say goodbye to the Chief for us.' He took his wife away, his arm still round her.

'Hello, old chap,' Bill Thomson said. He held out his hand and Arundsen shook it.

'I can hardly believe it.' He kept shaking his head. 'She must have been mad to pick someone up like that.'

'She gave him a lift from the airport,' Arundsen said. 'It was a chance in a million; anyone could have done the same. It wasn't a pick-up.'

'Doesn't matter much now,' Thomson said. 'What a way to finish. Poor girl.'

He echoed Geeson, and at that moment Phillip Wetherby joined them.

'It was good of Kormeski to come over,' he said. 'I'm glad so many people turned out for her. Look at those scum over there, trampling on the wreaths!'

Sightseers had begun to drift in from the cemetery gates; they were crowding round the flowers and watching the earth being shovelled into the grave.

'George said she was working for you,' Thomson said. Phillip shrugged. 'I made up something for her to do. Just to help out. But it was hopeless. She was beyond it. I asked the department to keep it quiet about Paris, and tell the police not to stir it up. There wasn't any point. It could have happened to her any time, in her own lodgings. That kind of thing is an occupational risk. Thank God she didn't suffer, anyway.'

They began to walk towards the cars parked outside the gates. Thomson turned to Arundsen. 'I've got to get back. Come and have lunch next week. I'll ring you. Okay?'

'Yes,' Arundsen said. 'Or I'll ring you.'

'I could do with a brandy,' Phillip said suddenly, when Bill had gone. 'Come back to my club and have something, Arundsen. I'd like to talk to you.'

Arundsen had never been to Phillip's club before. It was quiet but impressive, with the atmosphere of calm that comes from tradition and exclusiveness. Phillip ordered a small Martell for himself and a large one for Arundsen.

'Do you mind if we don't talk about Katharina,' Phillip said abruptly. 'I find it so upsetting. I was really very fond of her, you know.'

'I know,' Arundsen said, 'I think we all were.'

'I was surprised to see you there,' Phillip said. 'I thought you must be away.'

'No,' Arundsen answered. 'Why should I be?'

'Well, I've been trying to get hold of Mary and there's been no answer at the flat for the last week. You needn't be embarrassed, my dear Arundsen, I know all about your little "arrangement". When there was no answer I thought perhaps you'd gone to fetch her and the two of you were having a holiday. So I stopped worrying.'

Arundsen put down his drink. 'Worrying about what? Fetch her from where – I don't understand you.'

'Oh.' Phillip waited. 'Oh, you mean she didn't tell you? I thought she must have done. She rang me last week and said she was going away for a few days. She sounded very odd on the telephone, as if she was upset.'

There was a look on Arundsen's face which hadn't been there even when they buried the Countess. 'Where did she say she was going?'

'Berlin,' Phillip said. He sipped his drink and let the pause develop. Arundsen had changed colour; he looked grey.

'Do you know why she should go to Germany at all?' Mary had said she'd told a lie about going to a cousin. Arundsen seemed to know nothing about any absence.

'No,' Arundsen said. 'No, I can't think of any reason.'

He reached out for his drink and kept his hand steady. It had begun to shake while Phillip was talking.

'I've no idea.' He paused for a moment and then said it very quickly, rushing over the words, 'We've broken up. I'm not living with her any more.'

He saw a strange expression on Phillip's face; it was as if he had been slapped, and the upper part of his body gave a little jerk. But it passed and left nothing behind it to show that Arundsen had said anything unusual. He could have kicked himself for putting it so crudely. He knew how Wetherby valued finesse.

'I didn't know that,' Philip said. 'I wouldn't have bothered you.'

'You're not bothering me,' Arundsen said. 'When did she go?'

'On Friday last. Funnily enough, it was the day Katharina was murdered. She rang in the morning and said she was going that afternoon. She sounded very peculiar, as if she was in a nervous state. I said I thought it was an extraordinary place to go – she hates the Germans – but she wouldn't tell me anything or say why she was going. But she did say she'd be back on Monday and would ring me. Since then there hasn't been a word. I got so worried I contacted the West German police and they traced her to the Hotel Am Zoo. That was yesterday. The manager there told me she'd spent Friday night there and gone out the next morning in a taxi to the Eastern Section. And she hadn't come back. Her luggage was collected the day after that.'

He waited, watching Arundsen. For a moment he had thought the whole plan was going to disintegrate when Arundsen said they had split up. But not any more. He had seen men look like that before.

'I think she's in some kind of trouble,' Phillip said. 'I think I'd better go out there and find out what *has* happened. It's just possible some damned fool at S.I.S. has picked on her and sent her out to do a job. She met lots of them through me, you know; there was one Foreign Office chap who used to take her out to dinner. They just might have gone behind my back and involved her in something.'

Arundsen hadn't been looking at him. It wasn't the British who'd got Mary involved. Wetherby might think that because he didn't know the truth. She was in trouble; he was right about that but wrong about why. After four years they had come back to her again. They never let go; she was alone and someone had come to the flat, as someone had come to her in Washington, and put the pressure on her. And she had no one to turn to for help because he had walked out. She had gone to Berlin for them, and they had kept her there. He felt as if he were going to be sick. He wasn't listening to Phillip now, or even aware of his surroundings. He could only see Mary in the drawing-room, submitting to his judgement, with the tears streaming down her face, and hear her saying 'I knew you'd never be able to forgive me,' and hear his own voice, bitter and condemnatory. 'I ought to turn you in.'

'What did you say?' Phillip asked.

'I said "Christ",' Arundsen answered him. 'I was just thinking out loud.'

'You look rather done up.' Wetherby spoke sympathetically. 'It's that wretched funeral. Finish your brandy. Don't worry about Mary. I've told you, I'll go out and see what's happened to her. There may be a simple explanation for the whole thing.'

'Maybe,' Arundsen said. 'Maybe not. When someone goes over there and doesn't come back it only means one thing. Those bastards have got her. Will you do something for me?'

'If I can,' Wetherby said.

'Let me go after Mary. Don't go to our people about it, let me handle it from now.'

'You said you had broken up,' Wetherby said. 'I presume that means Mary left you?'

'No,' Arundsen shook his head. 'I left her. If I hadn't this couldn't have happened.'

It was like being on the rack, and turning the pulleys up another notch. He had left her, abandoned her. He had spent the last week brainwashing himself that he didn't really care, that the ache in his body was just sex and the ache in his heart could be willed away and flushed out with whisky.

She was in Berlin and she hadn't come back. Her luggage had been collected from the Hotel Am Zoo. She had crossed through from West to East and vanished. Something had happened; she must have tried to cross them, or defy them. So they had kept her there. He couldn't think beyond that. The sweat was coming out over his forehead, and two cold trickles ran down into his collar. He wiped his face with a handkerchief.

'I don't think you should get involved,' Wetherby said. 'After all, you said yourself that Berlin could be dangerous for you.'

'Not as dangerous as for Mary,' Arundsen said. 'I'm going to get her out. As for getting involved . . .' He lit a cigarette, his face hidden between his cupped hands over the flaming match. 'I love her.'

'I can't argue you out of it? You're determined to go in yourself?' Arundsen threw the match away and stood up.

'I'll be on the plane tonight,' he said. 'Thanks for the brandy. And don't worry. I'll bring her back.'

'I'm sorry you have to stay with us, Mrs. Wetherby. Our headquarters aren't exactly luxurious.'

Colonel Ivliev leaned back in his armchair and smiled at Mary sitting opposite to him. He invited her for tea, or on occasions to have lunch with him, and the meal was served in his office in the Karlshorst. He was very polite, explaining courteously why it was necessary to accommodate her in the K.G.B. headquarters, making her restriction on leaving the Eastern Sector sound like a request. It was all done with the minimum display of force and the maximum security. When she left her cab down the road from the Adlon, telling it to wait, she had expected to deliver Phillip's brown envelope and then go back across the checkpoint. They had picked her up in a car and driven her away, polite but firm, as if they were adults dealing with a child, and brought her to Ivliev at the Karlshorst.

He had insisted on giving her lunch, and spent most of the meal asking her impressions of West Berlin. It had been unreal, like a dream from which it was impossible to awaken. She had interrupted him over the coffee. 'Here is what you wanted,' she said, and put the envelope on the table. He had taken it, and thanked her. He hadn't opened it or said anything.

When she said she had to go, that she would have lost her taxi, he made her a crisp little bow, and said he would arrange transport back to the West for her, but it was necessary for her to stay as his guest for a few days. Her uncle, Mr. Wetherby, had sent a letter asking her to do so. It was his turn to give her an envelope, and then the two men were beside her and she was being taken out of the office and up in a lift. They left her in a bleakly furnished modern room with a bed, and indicated that the bathroom was two doors down the corridor. The letter was from Phillip and it was very short.

Do whatever they tell you, and don't worry. You can trust Ivliev. That was all. She had opened the door and seen the passage outside was empty. No one was watching her, the door hadn't been locked. But she was a prisoner, and she knew it. The only way down was by the lift. If she tried to go out she'd be stopped at the entrance and brought back. She had gone slowly into the dismal room, and sat down on the bed to read Phillip's letter once again. *Do whatever they tell you.* It sounded so simple, as simple as the truth of her situation which was that she had no alternative. The Russian Colonel had been very pleasant but she had never known real fear until she sat opposite him, eating a lunch which had been ordered against her will. He was going to keep her there, and Phillip had known this and sent his three lines of writing to warn her not to disobey. She stayed where she was and trembled for a long time. She had given them the envelope. Why couldn't she go back? Why – why – why . . . she sprang up suddenly, panic flooding into her mind, and tried to push the window up, to lean out, to scream for help. But it was sealed, and immediately she stepped away, knowing the stupidity of such a gesture. No one would help her even if they heard. She was in the heart of organised terror. There was a knock on her door, and she swung round, mastering her nerves. It was one of the men who had collected her. He was a German, with a thin, sallow face, and a military bearing which showed through his pose as a civilian.

'My name is Brückner. You would like to take a drive through the city? This way please.' It wasn't a request, it was an order, and he stood back from the door, waiting for her to pass. She had gone with him, silent and bewildered, hoping for a moment that the plan had changed, that she would be sent back. But the truth was as literal as the man's few words.

They took her for a drive round the city, and the German sat beside her, pointing out objects of interest in his nasal English. It lasted an hour, and then she was brought back to the Karlshorst and up in the lift again. A nightdress and some necessities like a toothbrush and a comb were in the room. The German explained that her own luggage was being collected, and apologised, bowing like the Colonel. A tray was brought to her, with a half-bottle of champagne, and a message from Colonel Ivliev, hoping she was comfortable. The German had been assigned to her, and he was very polite. He opened the champagne for her, and turned away diplomatically when she began to cry. The Colonel was taking proper care of her. Her room was one of a section used only by V.I.P.s or senior K.G.B. officers. She was an honoured guest, and she had no reason to sit on the bed and cry. He decided it was safer not to comment, and went out. That was her first night but it was not the worst. The worst came after three days, when she was invited down to Ivliev's office to take tea.

Mary had often despised herself for being a coward, but by the time she had sat down opposite the Colonel and accepted the glass of tea with its crescent moon of lemon floating on the top, she had mustered her courage, and he was aware of a quivering defiance in her face.

'Colonel Ivliev, I want to ask you something. Why are you keeping me here? I gave you what you wanted, exactly as I was told to do. Why can't I go home?'

Ivliev drank his tea and waited. He was in no hurry to answer; besides, the pause would take her initiative away. She was a very beautiful woman, but there was a decadence about her which almost repulsed him. She was too slim, too over-bred, too feminine and nervous. It wasn't a type he knew well, but he had enough experience to admit that such people often displayed extraordinary courage at the precise moment when they should have cracked. He didn't like Mr. Wetherby and he had precisely the same objections to his niece. He knew all about her, and her unwilling cooperation in Washington. She was a traitor, like her uncle. Throughout the whole complicated negotiation with Phillip, and the setting up of the plan to capture Arundsen, it hadn't occurred to Ivliev that Mary Wetherby didn't know her uncle was working with the K.G.B. He thought Phillip Wetherby had shown great ingenuity and considerable luck in establishing her as Arundsen's mistress. She would make a tempting bait for most men. He also approved Wetherby's caution in not telling her why she had come to Berlin. But he saw no point in concealing it any longer. She was being very well entertained, and it irked him that she should badger his men with demands to go home. Now she was badgering him. She kept on referring to the brown envelope. In his view there came a time when an agent had to be properly briefed. It was now safe to brief Mrs. Wetherby.

'Will you please answer me?' She spoke again, breaking the silence he had deliberately let lengthen into minutes.

He got up from his chair and went to his desk. He took the brown paper envelope out of a drawer and handed it to her. It was still sealed.

'Open it,' he invited. 'Please.'

She tore at it, and the contents spilled out over her knee. The snipped-off newspaper pages and the coloured advertisements floated round her feet. She picked a sheaf of them up and stared into the Russian's face. He watched her with interest and without smiling.

'What is this? This is just rubbish, bits of newspaper!'

'Exactly. You're not very experienced, Mrs. Wetherby, or you would know we don't expect agents to carry secret information in a large sealed envelope! No, I'm afraid your uncle was not quite honest with you. He didn't tell you the real purpose of your visit here.'

She said nothing; she was watching him with eyes that were dilated as her instincts began to rise in horror, like the invisible hairs on the surface of the skin.

'Your purpose was to bring *somebody* to Berlin, not *something*. Somebody we are very anxious to talk to; somebody your uncle assured us would never be induced to come here except to rescue you. Do you understand me now?'

'No,' it was a whisper. 'No, I don't. I don't know what you're talking about. Who is this somebody?'

'The man you have been living with. Peter Arundsen,' the Colonel said. 'We want him very badly. Mr. Wetherby promised to get him for us.'

The shock was so extreme that she betrayed no visible reaction. She went on sitting still, her eyes fixed on the Russian, white and expressionless, the last emotion, hostility, still showing on her face.

'He didn't tell me,' she said. 'He said it was the envelope.'

'Your uncle is a very cautious man. In the past when he was working against us we had reason to respect his caution. Even more so now that he's on our side. He never makes a mistake, Mrs. Wetherby. It's nice that you should be working with him. It keeps it in the family.' He smiled at her, and two gold teeth winked at the side of his mouth. 'Would you like some more tea?'

'No thank you.' She opened her hands and moved them from the arms of the chair into her lap. 'Now that he's on our side.' Phillip was working for *them*.

For a second, perhaps two seconds, she had an overwhelming impulse to leap to her feet and scream and scream, and then heave the samovar of boiling tea at the Russian with all her strength.

It was hysteria, and it passed as quickly as it had come. She conquered it, and no sign of that desperate moment's panic showed on her face. She kept still and held on to herself very hard.

The Colonel poured himself another glass and spooned sugar into it. He dropped a fresh slice of lemon into the tea and sipped it.

'We are keeping you here for security,' he said. 'The West has a number of agents operating here, and we don't want them reporting your presence. Not till I hear from your uncle that Arundsen is on his way. Then we will display you, so to speak. Are you sure you don't want another glass of tea – a cigarette?'

He was watching her through his pale eyes, probing without pity.

'Is there anything the matter? You seem upset.'

She shook her head. They were going to kidnap Arundsen, using her as bait. Was this the price Phillip had agreed to pay them – was that why he had lied and given her an envelope full of old scraps of newspaper . . . Because he knew she wouldn't go if he told her the truth? That was too simple. It didn't fit with the way the Colonel talked about him. 'On our side.' There wasn't any mention of negatives or blackmail. There never had been any blackmail. It was all lies. And the Russian spoke as he did because he thought she knew about Phillip. He thought she was working with him. Keeping it in the family.

'You're not worried about Arundsen?' Ivliev asked. Mary matched his look with a cool stare of her own.

'I've been much more worried about myself. Why didn't my uncle tell me? I've been imagining all sorts of things the last few days.'

'I'm so sorry,' the Colonel smiled. 'But this is a very important mission. We had to be as secure as possible. After all, you might have been a sentimentalist about bringing Arundsen over to us. Women do get involved with the men they sleep with; it can put them at a serious disadvantage.'

'Well, it doesn't worry me,' she said. 'Not all women get emotional about a casual lover here or there, Colonel. Anyway, I don't. But I'm curious about one thing. What do you want him for?'

Ivliev lit a long cigarette and drew on it, inhaling a mouthful of the dark smoke. The brand was too strong for Mary; they made her cough.

'His friend Jimmy Dunne would like to see him. It would raise his morale to see his old friend Arundsen again. For this reason alone he is very important to us. And, of course, we will want to ask him a few questions.'

For a moment his attention switched away from her, back to the latest reports on Dunne from Kalitz. They were not encouraging. He had deteriorated in the last weeks; he spent his time sunk in silence, so deeply depressed that they had been forced to give him some E.C.T. therapy, which had badly affected his memory. The effect was temporary but it had upset Ivliev's general, who sent a biting memo to Berlin, asking how long they must wait before Dunne could be put to work. At the present rate of progress they would be left with a useless psychological wreck. When was Arundsen coming?

Ivliev had been worried, both by the reports and by the General's attitude. It didn't help to be disliked by a superior; the job itself depended on results and a high quota of successes. All his achievements in the past could be nullified by a failure which would cancel out Dunne's value. He didn't allow himself to think of failure. Wetherby said he never failed, and now it was on Wetherby that everything depended. He looked at the woman in the armchair. She was very beautiful.

Wetherby was certain that Arundsen would come after her, no matter what the risk to himself might be. And Ivliev believed in his judgement. Whereas he didn't quite believe the woman when she said she didn't care what happened to her lover. Women were usually incapable of real neutrality in sexual relationships, unlike men, to whom the act could mean as little as going to the lavatory. It might be true; she looked cold enough, she and her uncle were of a kind. Her face showed nothing. Every time he saw her she was pale; it was her normal colour. But anyway she would be watched. Ivliev had two maxims in his job. Never trust anyone completely and never trust anything to luck.

'My uncle should have told me,' Mary said. She shrugged and tried to smile at him. 'I've been rather frightened,' she admitted. 'How long will I have to stay here?'

'Mr. Wetherby said he would wait a week before he begins to move Arundsen. That gives you three more days, perhaps. As soon as we hear he is on his way we will install you at the Budapest Hotel in a very comfortable suite, where he will be sure to find you. It's not quite up to the standard of the Adlon before the war, I'm told, but nicer than your present quarters. We're not used to entertaining ladies.'

'I'm afraid I've been a nuisance,' Mary said. She was relying on blind instinct now, and a lifelong training in social grace. As a girl she had been taught never to show boredom or gaucheness with people, and, above all, never to expose nervousness or fear. It was a spartan tradition, fast dying out in the generation which was growing up after her, but it was all she had at that moment, and it was all she needed. It was a code of conduct that baffled Ivliev in Phillip Wetherby, this calm acceptance of a situation, the opaque shield of rigid good manners. It deluded him in regard to Mary. He had never met anyone like her before.

He stood up and made his brisk little bow and handed her over to the K.G.B. escort, Brückner, who took her upstairs in the lift to her room.

She behaved very carefully when she was alone. Everything she had ever read about hidden microphones and cameras came into her mind as the door closed behind her, inhibiting every action, making her afraid to look in the mirror or turn on the light. She sat down on the bed, and lay back with her eyes closed. She began to shake, and this lasted for so long that she forced herself to get up and move round the room. There was a pile of magazines, travel and general interest papers, most of which were in French or German. She opened one and pretended to read it. Phillip was a traitor. Phillip had lied to her from the start, pretending that he was being blackmailed on her account, tricking her into going to Germany so that the Russians could hold her, and Arundsen would follow.

The lines of print were blurred and dancing in front of her; she felt a wave of sickness coming over her, and fought it down, not daring to give way because they might be watching, and they would know that she was nervous, that her callous attitude with Ivliev was just an act. And they mustn't know. They mustn't see any sign of weakness, or they would know she was an enemy and not an ally, like her uncle, Phillip Wetherby. An ally. She felt hatred surge in her and then repulsion as if she had put her hand on a snake. He didn't matter; already what he had done and what he was were unimportant beside her overwhelming terror for Arundsen. Arundsen, who was being manœuvred into following her, eased into a trap from which he would never escape. She lay down again, her body taut with the sensation of being watched by eyes hidden in the room. She had so much to remember of her time with Arundsen, from that first day walking in the gardens at Buntingford, when it all began, to the night they had talked about Jimmy Dunne, with her own confession still unspoken, and he had said Phillip had tried to get him to go back to East Berlin. He had joked about the special kind of Red Carpet which would be waiting for him if he did . . . He knew his danger, and what must have been Phillip's first attempt to trap him hadn't worked. So she had provided the means; she with her unlucky love affair, breaking up his marriage, unsettling his whole life. She heard the door open and sat up; it was her dinner, with the inevitable half-bottle of champagne on ice. She shook her head, and the German said sharply, 'You are not hungry?'

'I have a headache,' Mary said. He was watching her, and he had the same icy look as the Russian. 'Could you get me something for it? Some aspirin or something? Leave the champagne please, I'll have a glass of that and then go to bed early.'

'You are not well? You want a doctor?' He couldn't speak without barking at her, even when he was trying to be polite. He wasn't human enough to dislike, or even to fear, as she feared the Colonel.

She made a gesture, as if he were being rather foolish. 'Good heavens, I've just got a headache. All I need is an aspirin. And some good news.'

'What news do you expect?' he asked her. Everything she said would be reported to Ivliev.

'That a certain person comes to Berlin and I can go home,' she said angrily.

'I will get you some tablets for a headache,' Brückner said.

She drank some champagne, and swallowed the pills, thinking that never in her life would she be able to bear the taste of the effervescing wine she used to love. Then she turned off the light and lay in the darkness, her head throbbing. She had ruined Arundsen's private life, trying to hide from herself and her own weakness in his strength. God in his mercy couldn't allow her to be the means of his complete destruction. God, whom she had forgotten and ignored, was still the source of all compassion, the final appeal against the wickedness of humanity. She put her hands together and tried to pray, but nothing came except a confused repetition of the same anguished cry. Please God don't let him come, please God don't let him come . . .

And then suddenly, as if the frantic plea was answered, Mary stopped. The whole plan was based on a single premise. Arundsen loved her, so Arundsen would risk himself to rescue her.

But Arundsen didn't love her. He had left her, disillusioned and contemptuous. Even if Phillip went to him with a story that she was being held in East Berlin, as he must surely mean to do, Arundsen wouldn't imagine there was any danger. He would think she was doing another job for them, just as she had in Washington, and poor old Phillip didn't know. For all his cleverness, Phillip had overlooked the vital point. People change. Lovers cease to love. A month ago, three weeks ago, the plan would have succeeded; Arundsen would have rushed into any danger for her sake. Phillip knew his man when he counted on that. But a man can stop loving a woman in a day, and leave her without a word for the rest of his life. It had been very, very clever, but it was going to fail. Arundsen would never come.

The hypersensitive microphone in the reading lamp picked up a deep, peaceful sigh, and the sound of her turning over to go to sleep. She lay very quietly saying the rosary on her fingers with a thankfulness she hadn't known since she was a child.

The headquarters of the West German Intelligence were in Berlin in a twelve-storey industrial building, the first eight floors of which were occupied by legitimate businesses. The upper floors housed the Eastern European Section and the head man used an office with a panoramic view of the city to the south. Arundsen was shown into his office, and noticed that one whole wall was a window with the maximum glass and the minimum framework. It was a little bizarre, as if the room had only three solid sides and a step forward would mean falling into the street below. The German who came and shook hands with him was a man of his own age, as near as Arundsen could judge. He knew all about him from Bill Thomson. He had been in the Feldwebel at the end of the war; even before the surrender he was working with the Allies. He had a thin face with sharp features, and crisp, greying hair cut close to his head. He was known by the name Sontag; it was said that even Kiesinger himself called him by it.

'I spoke to Bill on the telephone,' he said. 'I promised I would give you all the help I could. You know we worked very closely together after the war, Herr Arundsen, and we became good friends. I'm happy to welcome any friend of his to Berlin. Would you like some coffee?'

'No, thanks.' Arundsen hadn't slept; he had spent the remains of the night at his hotel, reading and smoking until it was light. Then he had a bath and shaved, and waited by the telephone until it was time to call Sontag's number. He was grateful to Bill for helping him with the introduction. He had been in a hurry and there wasn't time to go through the ordinary channels via the Major-General's office; anyway, he didn't want to go to them for help. Mary was in trouble, and it wasn't the kind of trouble which would call forth much sympathy in official quarters. It was lucky he and Bill had patched up their row. Bill hadn't argued with him; he'd come up with Sontag and said to go ahead, he'd get in touch and warn him Arundsen was coming. The West German previous chief had retired not long after Arundsen resigned from the Firm himself. He had never come in contact with Sontag during his active days. And for the purpose of crossing the Wall, George Geeson provided him with a false passport, which he sometimes used himself. Arundsen's photograph was in it now.

'I've been reading about you,' the German said. 'We have a long report on the Rodzinski business. Our friends across the Wall were very angry about that. I assume you're not planning to go back?'

He watched the Englishman, Bill Thomson's warning in his mind.

'Help him all you can, but try not to let him run his head into anything. He's like a bloody madman at the moment.'

'I don't know,' Arundsen said carefully. 'It depends. Did Bill explain why I'm here?'

'He said you were looking for Mrs. Wetherby, who arrived here on the 19th and hadn't returned.'

'She checked in at the Hotel Am Zoo on the Friday night, went out on Saturday morning to go into the Eastern Sector and never came back. Somebody collected her luggage. Her uncle found this out because he was worried when she didn't come back to England. She was supposed to stay for a weekend only. That's all I know at the moment, but I've got to find her.'

'This is a personal matter, not an official one?' Sontag asked.

'Yes,' Arundsen said. 'Just personal. I'm on my own.'

'I think I can give you some news then.' The German pressed a button on his desk. 'But it doesn't sound encouraging for your friend.'

'The taxi driver who took her across Checkpoint Charlie works for us. He made a report on it. I'll send for him and you can question him yourself. I do suggest you join me in some coffee while we wait.'

Twenty minutes later the taxi driver Rudi came into the office. He was respectful, and kept calling Sontag Mein Herr, but the gutter cheerfulness kept breaking through, and he grinned at the Englishman.

'Tell this gentleman exactly what you told me,' Sontag said. He sat back in his chair behind a small desk littered with files and a green telephone side by side with a black one. He was very unmilitary; he slouched in his seat, and his papers were untidy. Arundsen rather liked him.

'I picked up the English lady and drove her to the Am Zoo,' Rudi said. 'She didn't want to go out again that night but she engaged me to take her across to the East the next morning. Very few of us will do that, you understand. There are regular tours for foreigners, and most of the drivers in Berlin refuse to go over there. I'm one of the two or three who do.' He glanced over at Sontag.

'Where did you take her?' Arundsen asked him.

'Through the checkpoint; that was okay, foreigners don't need a permit, and then I left her at the Adlon – it's in ruins, you know. She told me to wait at the corner.'

'Did she have anything like luggage with her – a small travelling case – anything a woman would take who might expect to stay overnight?'

'Nothing.' Rudi shook his head. 'Just a little purse, that's all. And a big envelope. She told me to wait for her; she said she wanted to go back to the West.'

Arundsen lit a cigarette; the atmosphere in the room was still. The windows sealed off all noise from below.

'Tell me exactly what happened,' he said.

'I let her out about a hundred yards away from the Adlon. She walked up the street and waited. She looked at her watch, and I remember I looked at mine. It was just after twelve. She had told me to wait round the corner, and she'd come and find me. I went round the corner but I came back, so I could see her. It looked funny to me. After maybe ten minutes or so, I saw a Zim drive up and stop. She was waiting by the kerbside, looking round, walking a few steps up and down. I saw two men get out of the Zim and go up to her. They took her away in the car.'

'Was there a struggle?' Arundsen lit a second cigarette off the lighted butt of the first.

'She didn't make any trouble,' Rudi answered. 'One of them was holding her arm. She didn't look as if she wanted to go with them. But it wasn't a kidnapping. There were two of them and they just persuaded her.'

'I can imagine,' Arundsen said. 'Did you recognise the men?'

'I didn't need to.' The driver shrugged. 'I knew what they were. But I thought Herr Sontag might be interested so I followed them. They took the lady into the K.G.B. Headquarters at the Karlshorst and that's when I got to hell out and came back.'

'Thanks.' Arundsen looked up at him briefly and then away. He saw the German behind his desk make a movement, and the driver went out, pulling on his cap as he went.

'I warned you it wasn't very good,' Sontag said. He

wondered whether he should offer the Englishman a drink; he looked as if he needed one.

'They've arrested her,' Arundsen said. 'They had her stuff picked up from the hotel. They're holding her over there.'

'Do you have any idea what for?' Sontag asked him.

'No.' Arundsen shook his head. 'Her uncle's Phillip Wetherby; he used to be head of our Eastern Europe section in S.I.S. after the war. It could be something to do with that. Maybe they think she knows something – Christ, it could be anything!'

'It appears she went to meet someone,' Sontag said. 'And they were waiting for her. People undertake the most stupid things; we've had American students with C.I.A. stamped all over them crossing into the East and the Russians swallow them up like a spider catching flies. A friend might have asked Mrs. Wetherby to meet someone over there, a relative, take them a letter, just speak to them – it could be the simplest explanation like trying to do someone a good turn. Unfortunately, the opposition don't have much faith in human nature. I doubt if they'll believe her story. Whatever it is.'

He was watching Arundsen very carefully as he spoke, at the same time preserving a detached attitude with just a little sympathy showing through. The whole thing stank. The woman had gone over on some kind of mission, probably for British Intelligence, and been immediately arrested. Sontag's opinion of the way in which the British conducted their affairs these days had progressed from alarm to outright contempt. He kept his own people clear of them wherever possible. They were quite capable of sending an amateur on a damned stupid assignment which had probably been known to the K.G.B. before she ever left England. He didn't want to distress the Englishman, but after a week in the Karlshorst there probably wasn't much left of the lady worth rescuing. Phillip Wetherby's niece; of course, that was the explanation. She had been picked on that account. The British had always relied on family connections. And Rudi said she was carrying an envelope. Sontag sighed, and decided that Arundsen had better have something to go with his coffee.

'You said this was a personal matter, Herr Arundsen.' He came round from his desk with a glass of cognac in his hand and gave it to Arundsen. 'I know how you must feel, but please take my advice. Take the next plane back to London. There's nothing you can do for your friend now.'

'I expected that,' Arundsen said. 'There wasn't much anyone could do for Rodzinski, was there? I'm not asking you to help me, you've done all you can, just letting me know where she is. I said I was on my own.'

'I don't usually involve my department in outside affairs,' the German said. 'And this is nothing to do with us. But Bill Thomson is a very good friend of mine and I promised to help you. I will see what we can do for your Mrs. Wetherby. We will make contact over the Wall and see if she can be released. Why don't you go home and leave it to us?'

'Is that what Bill told you to do? I know the old bastard – anything to keep me out of it. No thank you.' He swallowed the cognac and got up. 'I'll do this myself.'

'In that case,' Sontag said, 'you had better sit down and we will discuss what help you'll need. And you'll need help, Herr Arundsen. I know you're retired now, and one forgets a little, here and there. But Colonel Nickolas Ivliev is better than he ever was. They're all better. Faster, more efficient and backed by some of our best men – I mean that in the espionage sense. Some of the cream of our S.D. went over to them in '45 to save their necks. They know you, Herr Arundsen. And they have very long memories. After all, they found poor Katharina Graetzen after all these years.'

'What do you mean?' Arundsen stood still; Sontag had dark eyes, and they were focused so intently on him that he was suddenly irritated.

What was he saying about the Countess – what did he mean – they'd found her?

'What do you mean,' he said. 'Who found her?'

'The K.G.B.,' Sontag answered him. 'I read about the murder, and I remembered all about her. She was high on the Gestapo list during the war. It's the first time they've used that particular man in England. The sex crime is his trade mark. Do you mean to say you didn't know they were responsible?'

'I don't believe it,' Arundsen said. 'She hadn't been working for years . . .' He stopped, remembering the conversation in the cemetery. Phillip had given her something to do.

'Are you saying the K.G.B. killed her?'

'I have a dossier of similar murders in France and Western

Germany that are identical in every detail, every victim was a Western agent. The man is simply an assassin. The assault is faked afterwards. But it frightens women. That's its purpose.'

'Jesus,' Arundsen said slowly. 'If it's true, that's another one I owe them.'

'Will you let us help you?' Sontag asked.

'No.' Arundsen was moving away from him towards the door. 'I may be retired but I know the fewer people involved in this sort of thing the better. One is just the right number. And do me a favour. Don't try and put a man on me. Just forget all about it. Thanks very much. Goodbye.'

Sontag watched him open and close the door without saying anything. The Englishman moved very quickly, and lightly, for a strongly-built man. Sontag knew the type. They were tough and dangerous, and they worked best in very small groups under critical conditions. One man like Arundsen could be worth a dozen men in the right situation. But taking a suspect from the Karlshorst was not quite the same as smuggling out Janos Rodzinski. You couldn't get a woman over the Wall with grappling hooks and knotted rope. There were no gaps, no blind spots. German escapers had fallen like rotten apples under Vopo gunfire, and made the world's Press in dramatic pictures the next day. But they made it dead. It was crazy, and could only end one way. But he had promised Bill Thomson, and he kept his word. He went back to his desk and picked up the telephone.

'Good morning. I hope you slept well.'

Mary was already awake when the tray with her breakfast was brought in. It was served by a woman, who repeated the same formula every day without expecting a reply. But for the last three nights Mary had slept very well indeed. She looked rested and her eyes were calm, without the shadows of strain beneath them. The little microphone recorded her movements during the day when she was alone, and it picked up tunes that she hummed to herself while she was reading.

Ivliev had all the reports on his desk, including the meticulous impressions of her German escort, Brückner. Mrs. Wetherby was no longer anxious on her own behalf, and she was certainly not showing signs of anxiety on behalf of Arundsen. Her whole attitude was relaxed and relieved.

She had told the truth. What happened to Arundsen was not important to her. Ivliev accepted this, because he knew that the exceptions only proved the rightness of the general rule. This was one woman to whom a lover meant nothing compared with her own safety. She wouldn't try to warn him. A little before noon the German knocked at her door. She expected the inevitable daily drive, and met him with a smile.

'Would you please pack everything, Mrs. Wetherby. You are leaving us this afternoon.'

'Leaving you? You mean I'm going home?'

'Not quite yet,' he smiled at her, expecting her to be pleased.

'You're moving to the Budapest Hotel this afternoon. Your friend arrived in West Berlin last night.'

She turned away from him, pretending to look round the room, her voice carefully pitched, forcing herself to remain calm, and knowing that if he saw her face he would see the truth behind the lying little laugh she gave.

'I shall miss it here. You've been very kind.' Now she was able to face him, and she betrayed nothing. Arundsen had come. Arundsen. Arundsen. It was like a cry, which surely a perceptive ear must catch in the quiet room; surely the bounding heart-beat must be audible, echoing the name again and again. He had come to find her. She smiled into the sallow face with all the strength of her love, and it was strong enough to make the smile seem real. If they mistrusted her, Arundsen's last hope was gone. They'd make sure she didn't get a chance to warn him.

'I've done my best,' Brückner said. 'Colonel Ivliev sends his regrets; he won't be able to say goodbye to you himself. He's very occupied.'

'It doesn't matter,' Mary said, and thanked God that Ivliev wouldn't have to be deceived. 'You can say goodbye for me. I'd better get my things packed up. What time are we going?'

'In half an hour. I will come back for you.'

Arundsen had booked in at a small private hotel off the Bismarck Platz; he used to stay there when he made a trip to Berlin. He and Rodzinski had got very drunk there after their escape, and he knew the proprietor very well. He was paid by the Allies and the West German Intelligence, and he had a particular reason for keeping straight which was nothing to do with money. The Russians had raped and shot his two daughters during the occupation, and his only son had been killed on the Eastern Front during the war. After coming back from Sontag, Arundsen went round to his office behind the reception, and put down two thousand marks.

'I need a Lüger plus silencer, and a suit of clothes made in East Germany. Will this be enough?'

'The Sicher D. Boys can get them for you for nothing,' Otto said. 'If you're going where I think you are you'll need papers too. It would take some time to get those for you. Maybe a week or more.'

'I'm not working with anyone this time,' Arundsen said. 'And I don't want your people putting their noses in; I've already told them so. I haven't got time to frig about with false papers. I just want the gun and the clothes. Can you do it?'

'How long have I got?'

'Tomorrow.'

'*Jesu Gott* – that's no time at all.'

'Look,' Arundsen leant towards him, 'you can do it, Otto. I'm going to give those bastards a real smack in the balls. The gun and the clothes. By tomorrow.'

'All right.' The German shrugged, and then nodded. 'Leave it to me. I'll get them. The gun is easy; it's the suit that will be difficult.'

'Try a few East German refugees,' Arundsen said. 'I'm going out now, Otto. I'll be back in a couple of hours.'

He went for a walk towards the Kurfuerstendamm. It was a cold morning but the day was bright and the city sparkled in the sunshine. There were always crowds in Berlin. Even a few years after the war, when it was still fifty per cent rubble, there was a bustle about it which belied the ruins and the fact of defeat. The place had been full of American and British troops, and beyond the huge Russian war memorial, the sullen troops of Soviet Russia stood on guard. Berlin had been an exciting city; Arundsen had come to it fresh after Hong Kong and the atmosphere was the most exhilarating thing he could remember. It was at the peak of the Cold War; the place was crawling with spies working for anyone who would pay them. Murders were frequent; the blackmailer flourished and the profiteer engorged himself on the needs of the civilians and the occupying troops. Arundsen had come in as part of a trade delegation, following on from his post in the Far East and spent six months investigating a lead which ended in the Atomic Research Station at Harwell. He spoke perfect German, Italian and French. Like Dunne he had been a language scholar at Cambridge, and he had entered the Firm through the auspices of a middle-aged don who had been a distinguished member of S.O.E. It all came back to him as he walked down the immensely wide central thoroughfare, humming with traffic; it was as if the years since his marriage had never existed. His job with the brokers was as dim a memory as his marriage; even his son was a figment of imagination. The only reality was the present, and the pain inside him was growing harsher as the mental pictures flashed through his mind. Mary being arrested. He could see that black Zim and the two men, one on each side, urging her into the back of it. He could see her face as clearly as if he were standing on the pavement, watching it. What he wouldn't let himself imagine was the sequel at the Karlshorst. He was not a squeamish man; he had seen unpleasant things done to people in the course of his career and been able to forget about them. But the thought of Mary with bright lights and heavy shadows standing over her was something he couldn't admit to his mind. He walked on, his head a little down, not really seeing anything, the busy crowds brushing past him. She had been decoyed into coming over; probably the same blackmail threat as before, and when she got there they grabbed her. He stopped in front of a smart shoe shop and paused by the window. It was the first time he had tried to reason it out; when Phillip told him she was missing he hadn't even bothered about why she went to Berlin. He had taken it for granted that it was Washington over again, and that was enough. He hadn't cared what was behind it then and he didn't care now. He didn't care what Mary had done. If someone had proved she was a willing agent from the start he still wouldn't have given a damn. It was a shock, this revelation of how much she really meant to him. He waited by the window, staring at the expensive shoes imported from Italy without seeing any of them.

His patriotism, his training, his hatred of the enemy – they were of no consequence to him now. She was the only thing in the world that mattered to him. If they came to him now, and offered her in exchange for everything he knew, for every friend he'd ever had, he would have made the bargain. The idea of offering himself to Ivliev on condition that they let Mary go free came to him in the same moment, and he began to walk slowly. Ivliev wanted him very badly. He would be tempted. And being tempted he would agree. But he wouldn't keep the bargain. They only kept bargains where their own top agents were concerned. Mary and he were small fry. They would promise anything, and then keep her to use against him. There wasn't any honour at their kind of level. He hadn't got a plan beyond crossing the Wall and slipping away from the party of sightseers. It was the only way to get into the East because it was the most obvious, and wouldn't arouse anyone's notice. Hundreds of people from all over Europe went over Checkpoint Charlie just to be able to say they'd done it, did a quick trip of the Communist sector and then came back. He could go in that way, and with Otto's clothes he could stay there. If he got Mary out of the Karlshorst there was a place where they could hide out for a few hours. If it was still there. But why should it be? He was thinking in terms of eight, ten years ago. He stopped and swore at himself. A woman with a large shopping basket bumped into him and glared. What a fool. He should have taken Sontag's offer. He should have let them help him. How the hell could he go back to a place he hadn't seen for years and expect the same set-up to be operating still. The K.G.B. could have cleaned it out after Rodzinski. He had rushed in like a bloody idiot, so crazy to get to her that he would have wrecked the slightest chance.

Sontag was right. He had retired and he wasn't what he used to be. He hailed a cruising cab and went back to his hotel.

The receptionist called out to him as he went upstairs.

'There's a telephone message for you, Herr Arundsen!'

He came back again and looked down at the paper with a few lines scrawled on it in Schrift, and a Berlin number.

When he dialled he came straight through to Sontag's office.

'You said you didn't want us to interfere,' the German said. 'But I thought you should know your friend moved into the Budapest Hotel this afternoon. We have a man there. She's not under restraint, but she's being watched.'

'Thanks,' Arundsen said. 'That should be easier than their headquarters.'

'It looks like a trap,' Sontag said. 'And they've put her in

181

as bait. They could be waiting for you. Have you thought of that? I can only advise you again. Don't go near it.'

'Thanks,' Arundsen said. 'I'll let you know when we get back.'

CHAPTER NINE

Mary booked into the Budapest as an ordinary traveller. The K.G.B. officer Brückner stood beside her, helpful and polite, while she registered under her correct name, and then he escorted her with the manager up to her room on the fourth floor. It was indicative of her importance that the manager himself came with them; he asked her several times if everything was satisfactory, but his eyes kept blinking towards the German for approval. He knew that this was a K.G.B. booking, and in spite of his professional suavity he showed that he was frightened.

'This is a better room than your last one,' the escort said to her. She looked round it; it was pleasant, but well below Western standards for a first-class hotel. There was a private bathroom leading off, decorated in a screaming peacock blue.

"It's very nice,' Mary said. 'But will you explain exactly what I'm supposed to do here? Can I go out? Will I be alone?' She took a cigarette out of her bag and held it still while he lit it for her. Her hands were steady, her voice cool. She had to find Arundsen before he found her. The decoy duck was suddenly going to sprout wings. If only they trusted her. Please God keep her hands from shaking and don't let that creature see a flicker of anxiety in her eyes. . . .

'You are free to do what you like,' Brückner answered. 'Provided you stay in the Eastern Zone, of course.'

'I'm not likely to get out of it without Colonel Ivliev's permission,' she retorted. 'You mean I can go sightseeing – shopping?'

'Certainly. I'm afraid we can't provide you with a car. But the public transport system is excellent, and there are taxis.'

'What about the man you're waiting for?' She said it without warning, and she saw the pale eyes flick at her and then away.

'If I'm supposed to catch him for you hadn't I better stay in the hotel? I'd like to get this business over and go home. Wouldn't it be better if I stayed put for him to find me?'

'It's not necessary for him to find you, Mrs. Wetherby.

We will find him. I will leave you now. The restaurant is downstairs. I hope you enjoy your lunch.'

He bowed, and his heels snapped together. He was a man in his fifties; Mary guessed accurately that he had served another organisation equally sinister before he enrolled with the Russians.

She waited for a few minutes after he had gone, and then opened the door. The passage was empty. She came back to her room, and went to the window. It looked out over the main street. The windows opened on to a sheer drop. She went into the bathroom; there was another window, above eye level. She stood on the stool and looked out. It too opened on to a smooth-walled inner well. There was no fire escape visible. Mary climbed down, put the stool back in its place, and stood in the middle of the room. It was easy enough to say she would warn Arundsen. But how? How could she find him before he found her? If she left the hotel she would be followed; that was obvious. They might trust her enough not to restrict her movements, but every movement she made would be watched. They weren't relying on Arundsen getting to her; he had given that much away. They had their own plans for picking him up. All they had to do was watch the hotel. It didn't matter whether she was in it or took a walk down their depressing shopping centre. Arundsen would come to the hotel, and try to contact her. And that was where they would be waiting. They must have men posted near her room, men in the lobbies, more men at back entrances. They must have the whole place ringed, waiting for Arundsen to show himself.

She opened her suitcase and began unpacking. How would he approach the hotel? Would he bluff it out and walk in, and hope to get to her and out again; or would he try to slip in through the back doors and wait till he could find her – none of it seemed possible. It was all too easy, too naive. And Arundsen was a professional. She was thinking like an amateur, her mind a confusion of every spy movie she had ever seen. Surely he would try to come at night. That wasn't being melodramatic; night gave cover. And night was when she might be able to slip out. She wasn't clear how that would help; she had a vague idea, and she was painfully aware of its vagueness, that she might watch for him in the street and stop him. She would know him by his walk, she knew every movement of him, the way he held his head, the trick of sticking his left hand in his pocket and hunching his shoulders when he was going into a building. That was one thing where the K.G.B. were at a disadvantage. No matter how he was dressed, she would recognise Arundsen before they did.

It was a foolish plan, poorly formulated and with great risks inherent in it, but it was all that Mary had, and without it she felt her nerve might crack. If she couldn't pretend there was a chance for him she couldn't face the restaurant, pass the scrutiny of people she knew were watching her. She put the last of her clothes in the chest of drawers, and brushed her hair. She felt nauseated by the idea of eating anything, but the appearance of normality had to be kept up. She went out into the passage, and deliberately mistook the turning to the lift. She went left instead of right, and came to a dead end, with a door on the end of the line of bedrooms with AUSGANG on it. She looked round quickly; there was no one visible. But that didn't mean she hadn't been seen going the wrong way; it didn't mean that there wasn't an observer somewhere who would report her investigation of the emergency exit. She shrugged, as if she had lost her way, and then turned back. She knew it was there; if it was an emergency exit it shouldn't be locked. She made a mental note of where an outside stairs might be, and decided to take a walk that afternoon and see if she could identify it from the street.

At the restaurant door the head waiter met her. He bowed, one arm half extended to show her to her table. Not long after she was studying the menu the manager appeared beside her. He was a small man, somewhere in the middle forties, with glasses rimmed in the palest tortoiseshell, and thinning brown hair combed back from his forehead.

'Is everything satisfactory? Is there anything you would like which is not on the menu?'

'Everything is perfect, thank you,' Mary said. 'I shall choose something light, I think.'

'Some champagne, with my compliments,' the manager said. He snapped his fingers and a waiter came hurrying.

'You're very kind,' Mary said, 'but I don't like champagne.'

'Oh?' The nervous hands flew apart like birds. 'One assumes it is the ladies' favourite. Something else then?' He besought her with his eyes to choose something, to let him be of service. Fear had many faces; it was the first time

Mary had seen it in such an obsequious guise. She suddenly felt sorry for the man, sorry for all of them, living with fear like that.

'Some hock would be nice,' she said, and she smiled. 'Thank you so much.'

'At your service,' he said, and repeated it, giving a little bow. She glanced round the restaurant; there were about thirty people in it; several couples, groups of business men, three officers in Russian uniform and two German girls with them. They were laughing and making a lot of noise in their corner. The others ate in silence or talked in monotones. It struck Mary that she had never seen anyone laugh in East Berlin except Colonel Ivliev. He had laughed, showing that he had gold teeth; she remembered that suddenly. The Russians had a sense of humour. Terrifying as he was, she preferred Ivliev to the German with his death's-head face and snapping little courtesies. She ate some of the first course and picked through the main dish. German food was vinegary and harsh; she had never enjoyed it. The hock was superb. She could walk round afterwards and see if she could find a fire escape that corresponded with that door at the end of the passage. She went out into the main lobby, passing her key across the desk.

'I want to do a little shopping,' she said to the clerk. 'Where would you recommend? I don't know Berlin at all.'

'There are some excellent shops two blocks away; "Exquisite" for ladies' dresses, and the H.O. Geschaefte store. You should find everything you need in those two.' The clerk spoke with brisk hostility.

"Thank you,' Mary said.

She followed his directions, walking slowly past shops which were displaying old-fashioned clothes and shoddy furniture, and the inevitable delicatessen, hung with dark sausages like an uneven pelmet above the shelves. The passers-by were drab and sullen; some of the women turned to look after her with expressions of resentment for her elegant clothes. 'Exquisite' was a large fashion store, stocked with dresses a year out of date, long-skirted and dismal, astronomically priced. She didn't bother to go in. H.O. Geschaefte yielded two ashtrays with views of the Brandenburg Gate and a headscarf with transfers of the East German flag. May paid, and went out into the street again. It was cold and a sharp wind drove round the block; she shivered, turning her coat collar up, and began to walk back to the hotel. She went slowly, pausing to look in windows on the way, hoping she appeared to be taking a casual walk. She passed the hotel entrance and crossed over. There was a tobacconist's shop about fifty yards down on that side of the road. On the opposite side the street divided into a subsection. She could see the side of the Budapest quite clearly. She went into the tobacconist's, bought a packet of 'Caro' cigarettes which she had no intention of smoking, and a copy of *Sybille*, a leading East German women's magazine. As she came out of the shop she glanced up at the view of the side of the hotel. There was a fire escape winding its way up the building; it was located almost on the corner, though invisible from the front. It seemed that it must coincide with the door in the passage.

She came into the lobby and went straight to the desk.

'My key please. Room 439.' The same clerk was on duty.

'You found what you wanted?' The tone was arrogant, and the face matched it.

'Not quite,' Mary said. She felt a sudden anger overcome her, and generations of the privileged answered the aggressive product of the egalitarian revolution in those two words. Hostility and aggression. They had enveloped her from the moment she left the Karlshorst. These people hated foreigners, and they took pleasure in showing it. They also took pleasure in being rude, as if the services they performed demeaned them, and they had to re-establish their self-respect. It wasn't just the national character, dour and unfriendly as it was. The alliance with their political system had produced one of the most unattractive species on earth.

'My key,' Mary said. 'Thank you.' She made it sound like an insult, and then walked to the lift. They were all sullen and unpleasant; all except the wretched anxious manager, trembling in his polished shoes because she was with the K.G.B. He was probably just as unwelcoming to ordinary guests as the rest of his staff. She closed the door and looked round. Her room was as she had left it. There were many weary hours ahead of her before it was late enough to go and try that door. She lay down on the bed, and fell asleep. She woke trembling, her face streaked with tears after a dream in which she had seen Arundsen, but though she tried to scream a warning, no sound came.

Within the hour of his phone call Bill Thomson rang the

bell at the Arundsens' flat. Joan opened the door to him. She looked tired and sallow, as if she spent too much time indoors.

'Come in, Bill,' she said. 'Would you like a drink?'

'No thanks, dear. Come and sit down.'

'What's happened to Peter?' She brought the question out with difficulty, her throat constricted by anxiety. All Thomson had said on the phone was that he was in trouble. It wasn't an easy decision, telling his wife that he was in danger; only the strong possibility that she might be his widow convinced Thomson that he couldn't in fairness leave her unprepared. Separated or not, she had a right to know.

'He's gone off and done something bloody silly,' Bill said. It came out angrily, because he too was so anxious. 'He's gone to Berlin.'

'Oh.'

He saw by her face that the significance of this escaped Joan Arundsen, and was amazed at the gulf which must have existed between the husband and wife. 'I mean I know he said he did something over there and nearly got caught, but that was years ago. It isn't anything to do with that, surely?'

'Not directly,' Thomson said. He was going to have to spell it out, word by word, and the prospect didn't appeal to him.

'But the point is that he should never have gone back. He's on their priority list, Joan. If they get their hands on him – well, we needn't go into that. It's terribly dangerous for him. He must be round the bend to do it.' He paused, finding this the most difficult of all. She brought him straight to the point.

'Why did he go back? Is that what you've come to explain to me, Bill? He's joined again, hasn't he – just as soon as I was out of the way.' It wasn't said with bitterness or complaint. She was stating the facts; the old life was what he really wanted; she had been a stop-gap for the last eight years.

'No,' Bill Thomson said, 'I wish to God he was with our chaps. I'd feel a lot happier. It isn't anything to do with the old business. He's gone after Mary Wetherby. It seems she went over to East Berlin and hasn't come back. He thinks she's been arrested. He told me so.'

'I see,' Joan Arundsen said. She got up and spoke over

her shoulder. 'I'm going to have a gin. Sure you won't have one with me?'

Thomson shook his head. 'I'm sorry to have to tell you all this. I know you've been treated damned badly. But there's a risk he won't get back, Joan. That's why I had to warn you.'

She came and stood in front of him, the glass fizzing with tonic in her hand.

'He wouldn't even go to Switzerland for a holiday with me,' she said. 'I asked and asked him to go and he wouldn't. Isn't life funny?'

'Why don't you sit down,' Bill said. He thought she might be going to cry and he hated women in tears. It always distressed him.

'Don't worry about me,' Joan said. 'I'm not all that upset. I've been alone for quite a time now, and I suppose I've seen things in proportion. He's crazy about her, and that's all there is to it. I've only got to be honest with myself to see he never loved me at all.' She sipped her drink. 'Couldn't you stop him going?'

'I did my best. Luckily he needed my help or I don't think he'd have let me know about it. We happened to meet at the poor Countess's funeral, and we patched things up. Then he got on to me for one thing and another and said what had happened. I've got the West Berlin boys looking out for him, and George and I are flying over. That's another reason I came round. I wondered if you wanted to come with us. He may need someone around to hold his hand.'

She finished the drink and put the glass down. 'You mean I ought to be there to comfort him if anything's happened to her? Or just to watch them walk away together if it's all sorted itself out? No thanks, Bill. I don't think he'd want me either way.'

'I think he might,' Bill Thomson said. 'I felt I should suggest it anyhow.'

'I know,' she managed to smile at him. 'You've been very kind all through this. But I told you, I've had time to think. I don't think there's anything left between us, not now. I don't think there was anything even before she came along. And when I think back it hasn't been much fun for me, either.' She stood up, and he did the same. 'I'm not going after him, Bill. I've got used to living alone. David and I went off to my mother's for three weeks this summer. We were quite happy. I hope Peter gets back. I even hope he brings her with him. But I feel I've had enough. I don't really want to start all over again. It's not much good when the man doesn't want you. As I said, he wouldn't take me to Switzerland for a holiday, but he'll risk his life for her. No thanks.'

'I don't blame you,' Bill Thomson said. 'I don't blame you one bit. Goodbye, Joan. And don't worry. I'll let you know what happens. I'm taking the plane tomorrow and George is arriving late that night. Look after yourself.' He kissed her, and patted her shoulder. She shut the front door and went back to pour herself another drink.

It was 1.30 a.m. by Mary's watch. She had sent down for dinner, unable to face the dining-room that night, and spent the next four hours alternately walking up and down, up and down the bedroom, or looking at her watch to see if it had stopped because the hands hardly seemed to move. The time didn't crawl, or drag or do anything described in the honoured clichés of suspense. It simply didn't pass at all. It was nine when the floor waiter took down her tray – she had flushed most of the food down the lavatory because she couldn't eat anything – and it was still nine o'clock when she looked at least an hour later. It seemed like an hour, but it was only a few minutes and the hands on the watch had actually moved a fraction. She tried to read the magazine *Sybille*, bought that afternoon when she took her walk to find the fire escape, and couldn't understand more than a few words. She had learnt German at school, but it wasn't a language for which she had any sympathy and only the minimum had stayed with her. She went to the window, drawing the edge of the curtain back an inch or so, in case her room was being watched from below, and saw nothing but the street lights and the traffic moving. At midnight she switched off the light and sat in the dark, smoking. By one-thirty she was in her coat, waiting at the door. When she opened it the corridor was empty; a low-voltage lighting system operated in the hotel between midnight and dawn. It gave a dull, yellow light in the passage. She held the door open for a few seconds, listening. There was no sound. She stepped outside, closing it behind her with the key. Still she waited. Nothing. Not a sound which could indicate that anyone was awake or watching her.

She walked down to the left, towards the emergency door. AUSGANG. Exit. It was printed clearly on the door panel. It must lead to the fire escape. If she opened it and found someone on the other side – but there wouldn't be. They were watching for Arundsen to come in, not for her to get out. If she saw anyone near the end of the ladder she could go back. And she would be sure to see them before they saw her. The street below was brightly lit. That would make her clearly visible too. For a moment Mary hesitated, fear nudging her on all sides. Then she reached out and turned the handle.

'It's locked, Mrs. Wetherby.'

She thought she was going to faint. She swung round; Brückner was standing behind her. He caught her by the elbow; he thought she was going to try to run.

'Come in here,' he said. She looked into the pale eyes, deep set in the prominent frontal bone of the skull, the closely cut hair bristling in the yellow light immediately above, and on a wild impulse of terror and repulsion began to struggle with him. He slapped her hard across the face, and pulled her into the room he had come out of. She almost lost her balance, he was so rough. Inside, he gave her a push that sent her reeling backwards; she fell, and he turned and locked the door. She watched him come over to her; he held out his hand.

'Don't try to be difficult or you will be hurt. Get up.' All through the days at the Karlshorst building she had believed that she was fooling him. The sallow North German face was like a mask now; it had been a mask then, pretending to be deceived.

She got up without letting him touch her. One side of her face was stinging from the blow.

'Now,' the K.G.B. man said. 'Explain what you were doing by the exit?'

'I wanted some fresh air,' Mary said. He hit her again, and she cried out.

'Don't lie,' he said. 'You were trying to escape. Weren't you, Mrs. Wetherby? Weren't you trying to escape?'

The room had a bed in it; Mary moved backwards as he moved towards her. She sank down on it, covering her face with her hands. Her mouth was bleeding; she could taste the saline blood. There was no point in lying. He would go on beating her until she stopped. She wiped her lips and looked up at him, ashamed of the tears which were streaming down her face.

'Yes, I was,' she said. 'I was trying to escape. And I'll try again!'

He knocked her back across the bed. The room turned into a mist with darkness growing out of it. She heard his voice from a distance.

'You'll answer my questions correctly, please. Sit up!'

She felt his hands dragging at her, and the effects of the last blow on the side of her head wore off enough to let her struggle upright of her own accord. She was blinded by tears, trembling uncontrollably, and being the expert that he was, he waited. He was taking the right line with her. Women of that class had never been struck in their lives. Shock and degradation were as potent a factor in a beating as the pain itself. A working-class woman wouldn't have collapsed under a few hard slaps. She would have been given them before.

'Why were you trying to escape? Answer me, please, or I shall hit you again.'

He looked down at the woman, half sitting, half lying on the bed, blood staining her mouth, weeping hysterically, and deliberately raised his hand. The reaction was not what he expected. The emotion that blazed up in her was not fear but hatred, and defiance.

'I wanted to warn Peter Arundsen,' Mary said. 'I wanted to save him because I love him. Now you can hit me for that, and be damned to you!'

'I do my job,' the German said. 'There's no need for me to be unpleasant. You've told me the truth at last. I suspected it might be so, Mrs. Wetherby, and so I watched you. Did you really think we'd be foolish enough to take a chance on you?'

'I hoped so,' she said bitterly. 'But I was wrong. I didn't have a chance.'

'No more will he,' Brückner said. 'Unless you stop trying to interfere.' He took a cigarette case out and opened it; he lit two cigarettes and bending forward he put one between her lips.

'I'm sorry I had to hit you,' he said. 'But I had to be sure. Smoke that; you'll feel better. I'll get you a towel.' She tried to take the cigarette out of her mouth, and found it difficult because her hand was shaking, and the room kept moving round as if the bed were on rollers. He came back with a small white towel wrung out in warm water. 'Wipe your face with this. I'll take the cigarette.'

The warm towel was soothing; she held it against her mouth and then over her eyes. Her head throbbed with pain, and her heart was racing till it was an effort to breathe. 'I had to be sure.' She knew he had said that, and apologised for hitting her, but none of it made any sense. What he had said about Arundsen made the least sense of all.

He was sitting down quite close to her, smoking, one leg crossed stiffly over the other.

'If you really want to save Arundsen from being captured, then you must do as I tell you,' he said.

'Who are you?' Mary whispered. 'What is this?'

'I am a friend,' the German said. 'That's all you need to know. You must trust me. You've no other choice. I shall have to report you to Colonel Ivliev for what you did tonight, and you'll be kept in your room. Under my supervision, of course. Now I'm going to take you back and lock you in. Again, my apologies for the unpleasantness. Continue to bathe your mouth with a warm towel and it will help the swelling. Come, please.'

He escorted Mary back down the corridor, one hand holding her arm; and locked her inside. Then he went back to his room and telephoned a report to the Karlshorst that Mrs. Wetherby had tried to get away. She was unreliable, and he had ordered her to be confined to her room.

When it was done, he smoked a last cigarette, undressed and went to bed. Ivliev would get the report in the morning. He had caught Mrs. Wetherby trying to sneak down the fire escape. He had questioned her – the floor waiter bringing breakfast would corroborate the style of that interrogation when he saw her bruised and swollen face – and she had admitted to being in love with their man and trying to help him. He had decided to keep her locked up till Arundsen was caught. After that the Colonel could decide how to deal with her. Lying in the darkness, Brückner wished he knew why she was given so much preferential treatment. It couldn't be on her own account. She was no agent; her incredible clumsiness that night proved that. Someone had sent her out to them, but who that was, the German didn't know. Which was a pity, because it must be someone very important. He had gleaned enough to know that Arundsen was connected with the defector James Dunne, and for that reason alone it was essential to prevent Ivliev getting his hands on him. He had sent the message to Sontag the day he brought Mary Wetherby to the hotel. If he managed to get Peter Arundsen back into the West that would mean another sixty thousand marks paid into his account in Luxembourg. There was half a million marks already deposited there under a different name. He enjoyed calculating the exact amount in English pounds: 50,000 U.S. dollars 125,000. Swiss francs 500,000. It sent him off into a peaceful sleep, like counting sheep. He had been on the West German payroll for the past nine years, and they paid on a princely scale where the information came at his level. The K.G.B. was much like his old work under Kaltenbrunner in Czechoslovakia in '43. It protected him from the consequences of that earlier career, and he had a natural talent which brought him promotion. He had been working with Ivliev in East Berlin for the last three years, and he was doing very well. But the dream which had sustained him since the war was very near becoming a reality. One more year and he would make his escape, and spend the rest of his life in Luxembourg, as a very rich man. Greed had kept him from taking the route out of East Berlin and simply disappearing. The money increased year by year from a nest-egg until it assumed the proportions of a fortune. Big spies were paid big money. The K.G.B. had paid an American agent in a key position as much as thirty thousand dollars a year. But now he was beginning to count the months as well as the money. He wasn't a young man and there were a lot of things he wanted to enjoy. More than anything he wanted the opportunity to enjoy them, and the closer he got to Ivliev and the top, the more dangerous his work for Sontag became. In one year he would be out. Perhaps less. Perhaps six months. He slipped into a deep sleep and began to snore.

The coach tour started at 10.30. Arundsen queued up with about twenty other passengers and took an inside seat on the bus. There were English people and a good sprinkling of Americans, a French couple and himself, all equipped with cameras and the tour itinerary. There was a cheerful atmosphere, rather as if the bus were making a trip to an open zoo. The guide was a pretty girl in a smart blue uniform with a neat little forage cap perched on one side of her head. She smiled round the bus and wished them all good morning. They were starting their tour of East Berlin, and the first point of interest would be Checkpoint Charlie. Arundsen looked out of the window; a middle-aged American man had taken the seat beside him, and he felt the other moving about in an attempt to attract his attention. He should have talked to him and acted normally, but he couldn't. If the American was alone he might well latch on to Arundsen for the tour, and that was the last thing he wanted. The itinerary provided for one stop. Lunch at the Moscowa Restaurant, which was described as the best eating place in the Eastern Sector, frequented by members of the Soviet forces, as if the Russians were the star attraction in the Red Zoo. Lunch, Arundsen thought coolly, was a meal he intended to miss. He wore his Burberry mackintosh and a soft English hat; under the mac he was dressed in the East German suit which Otto had supplied the previous night. It fitted fairly well; it was badly cut, with wide trouser legs, and the shirt and shabby tie came from the same source. There was a cloth cap in the coat pocket.

'I must say this should be interesting.' The American voice broke in on him, and he turned round reluctantly. They were such a friendly people. He had always liked them; it was one of the few things which caused friction between him and Jimmy Dunne. Dunne had come back after a short trip to Washington filled with prejudice, and Arundsen couldn't discuss America without quarrelling with him.

'Yes,' he said, and turned back to looking through the window.

'I was here in '45,' the American said. He was alone and he wanted to share the trip with somebody. 'We had a helluva time. My old man came from Hamburg, so I used to interpret for the other guys. It was a helluva city in those days!'

'I expect so,' Arundsen said.

'I just wanted to see what they've done to the Eastern Sector since then.' The American wouldn't be discouraged. 'Is this your first visit over here?'

'Yes.' Arundsen didn't turn round as he answered. The man beside him cleared his throat as if he were going to persist, and then changed his mind. They came to the checkpoint and stopped. The barriers on the Western side were raised and the bus moved slowly through the neutral space between the Eastern checking post. People were craning round to look out at the first 'Vopos' in their dark brown uniforms, their automatic rifles slung over their shoulders. Two of them came to the driver's cab and examined his papers. The passengers' passports were examined. Arundsen handed over the clever forgery Geeson had given him. The name inside was Salt. One detached himself and sauntered past the bus, looking through the windows, one hand on his rifle strap. He stopped at the window before Arundsen's and stared. There was an English couple sitting in the seat; the wife turned away from the window. The hostile face outside made her uncomfortable. Her husband leant forward and glared back. 'Bloody cheek,' he said out loud. 'What's he think he's looking at.'

Or looking for, Arundsen thought. He moved round and turned his face to the American. He didn't want to start a conversation but he didn't want to face the window. 'Why don't we get on?' he said unpleasantly. 'I'm going to complain in a minute.' The American looked disappointed in him. He was out for a good time, reliving the high days of twenty years ago. He didn't want to pick up this sour-faced bastard, after all.

'Maybe they're pointing a gun at the driver,' he said. He opened his itinerary and pretended to read it. Arundsen had seen the Vopo's shadowy figure pass by his window. They weren't looking for him; the guard had been acting up, putting a scare into the foreigners. No West German was allowed to go across the checkpoint without a special pass, and damned few wanted to go anyway. On the opposite side of the road a line of cars and a returning coach were waiting to come back into the Western Sector. Going into the East was easy; they were held up for only a few minutes; coming out was very different. A Mercedes with French number plates was at the checkpoint. Two guards were standing by the driver, while a third examined the passports of the passengers, and a fourth carried out a meticulous search of the car, beginning with the boot, under the chassis, and ending with a long probe into the petrol tank to make certain it contained petrol and was not in fact a place in which a man might be smuggled out. As the coach moved on through the checkpoint, the red and white painted posts rising up in front of its bonnet, the Mercedes was still being detained; the driver was losing his temper and shouting at the Vopos. The guard with the probe was wiping petrol off it. No refugee was hidden there. The car contained nothing beyond three

French tourists that it amused the German guards to in-convenience.

Arundsen noticed all this; they were hotter than ever on searching every vehicle that left the Eastern Sector. The old trick with the hearse wouldn't get past them now. All coffins leaving for burial in the West had to be left unscrewed. The girl in the forage cap was back in position at the head of the bus. She carried a small amplifier and began her commentary.

'We are now turning up Karl Marx Allee. Most of these buildings were erected in the last three years. During the war the avenue was almost completely destroyed; when we turn right here you will be able to see the Unter den Linden and the ruins of the famous Adlon Hotel. We will be approaching the Brandenburg Gate in a moment.' Her voice went on, the words running over Arundsen. He knew this part of Berlin better than she did. He had spent a week hiding in it before it was safe to take Rodzinski over the Wall. He had the Lüger and two cartons of shells, plus the silencer, in the side pocket of his mackintosh. It would fit in his trouser band under the suit jacket. He had only to think of Mary to realise that the last thing in the world he must resort to was that gun. Rodzinski was a man; a tough, fit professional, an ex-guerrilla fighter who knew all the tricks. Even so, they had gone over that Wall with the Soviets' breath singeing their back hair. He didn't even know what state Mary might be in; a week at the Karlshorst without sleep on a 'restricted diet' could make a wreck out of a woman. He couldn't trust her not to betray herself, not to panic; in fact he could expect her to do exactly what a normal girl would do in totally abnormal circumstances and get them both killed.

They had put her in the Budapest Hotel; unrestricted, Sontag had said, but watched. Arundsen had spent the night thinking out the significance of this, and come to the same conclusion as the German. It was a trap for someone, and they were using Mary as the bait. He swore to himself at the idea of her under their manipulation. She must be terrified; he knew how good they were at frightening women without putting a mark on them. It wasn't funny being Ivliev's prisoner. They had a purpose in seizing Mary; probably the same purpose which had made them send for her again. To get her out to Berlin and then to use her as a hostage for someone or something else. The most obvious answer was to hold her over Phillip Wetherby's head. But they would have kept her under cover to do that. And, anyway, the K.G.B. knew Phillip far too well to imagine that a niece by marriage could be used to blackmail him.

There wasn't anyone important enough to Phillip for that role. He wouldn't like her to be hurt, or tried on some imaginary charge of spying while a tourist, but he'd let them shoot her before he even acknowledged a message from them. Arundsen knew him; he was without heart and without fear where his duty was concerned. The obvious answer wasn't the right one, not while Colonel Nickolas Ivliev was in his old job. He knew Wetherby too.

The less obvious answer, and the one which had occurred to Arundsen as it had certainly done to Sontag, was that the trap was being set for him. They knew about him and Mary, and they hoped he would do precisely what he had done. Rush in after her. Offer to make a deal. He stared out of the window, seeing nothing, not taking in a word of the guide's pat remarks, thinking of Mary with an ache of fear which was so real he could have put his hand where it hurt. His fault. His fault for leaving her, for refusing to see her as she really was in Washington. A frightened woman married to a sexual nut, suddenly confronted by the most experienced operators in the world. And he had blamed her for not acting as he thought she should, for not exposing her husband to some snotty-nosed Embassy official. He could just hear it, and picture it too. He knew the kind of people who went to Embassies like Washington. They wouldn't exactly encourage Mary's kind of confidence from the wife of the Naval Attaché. How many innocent, confused and frightened people fell into her kind of mess because they were innocent, frightened and confused. He used to say he loved her, especially when they were making love, and he was enjoying the benefit of her love, her generous surrender of herself to every mood and demand he made. But when she trusted that love and expected his mercy he walked out, full of self-righteous condemnation and self-pity. He hated himself more and more as the significance sunk in. The thought of Mary tethered like a goat at a tiger shoot threatened to send him mad. If he didn't get her out, then, by God, he'd never come out himself without her.

And if he had been skilful and cunning in the days when his own neck was at risk, his love for her had produced a degree of ingenuity and mental speed which was untapped before. If she was at the hotel, then that's where they would be waiting. Not at the checkpoints, wasting time looking for him among hundreds of tourists and the trickle of West Berliners who used the other checkpoints beside 'Charlie'. They didn't waste time or men unnecessarily. The Budapest Hotel was the hot spot. It was lucky Sontag had a man among them. He must be concerned directly with this operation or he would never have known. In his bed at Otto's the previous night Arundsen had worked out a plan. It was the first idea remotely viable which had come out of the hours spent thinking since that drink with Wetherby after the Countess's funeral. Taking her out of the Karlshorst was an impossibility. Now that he knew she wasn't being kept there, Arundsen could admit that, which he had never dared before. The hotel was different. They were waiting, but he knew it. That helped. He would have to go and get her, and walk out with her. No gun-play, no dramatic midnight rescues, ending in both of them being welcomed by Ivliev in his office, or dying in a scruffy German hotel with the bloody silly name of Budapest . . . Arundsen had thought of his plan and because it was impossible he knew it might succeed.

By midday they had done the first and longer part of the tour. The guide announced that they were arriving for lunch within five minutes.

The English couple in front of Arundsen were the first to move out of their seats as the coach stopped. The man was in an aggressive mood after the incident with the Vopo. 'This had better be good,' he said to his wife. 'If I have any more of their damned sausage dishes I'm going to make a row.'

'Please, dear,' his wife said, 'don't start any trouble. I knew we shouldn't have come here in the first place, but you would do it. Don't let's have any trouble here. I just want to get back to West Berlin, that's all.'

A reservation had been made for them at the Moscowa; a group of tables had been set aside for the coach party, with a good view out of the enormous plate-glass window in the front of the restaurant. It was a bizarre mixture of modern functional and nineteenth-century Russian 'twee', as Arundsen described it. He had a sudden thought of paralysing disloyalty that it was the sort of vulgar tasteless place his wife would have loved. There were plastic balalaikas on the walls, crossed over each other like swords in a baronial hall, and a bust of Tolstoy at either end of the large restaurant room. The carpet on the floor was crimson, thick and rubber-backed like a cinema foyer, there were ugly mock antique chairs and metal containers with plastic flowers on every table. Piped music drifted over the surface noise of people eating. It too had a vaguely nineteenth-century tone, as if Lyons Corner House had opened a branch in Bayreuth.

He didn't go to a table; he went to the bar and ordered a beer. The guide saw him, and he waved to her; she had others to settle down in the restaurant and she forgot about him. He drank his beer, and went into the gentlemen's lavatory. He went into a cubicle, and wasted time until the other single occupant had gone. Then he stripped off the mackintosh, stuffed his soft brown Homburg in the pocket, transferred the gun, shells, and silencer into his waistband and jacket pocket and hung the mackintosh behind the door on the row of hooks provided.

He combed his hair into a centre parting – it was extraordinary what a difference such a simple change could make in a man's appearance – and walked out of the door, through the bar, round the back of the restaurant, where the rest of the party were beginning on the enormous hors-d'œuvres, and out of the entrance into the street. Nobody had even glanced at him as he passed, he looked so typically working-class East German. He pulled the cap on, dragging it down and dead central – there was nothing rakish about the way Germans of his age wore a cap or a hat – and began to walk towards the Karlshorst. It would take twenty minutes, which brought the time to about 12.45. There was no particular hurry, and on the way he stopped at a delicatessen and bought himself a black-bread sandwich with liverwürst.

The Karlshorst was in a busy street, mostly occupied by office blocks, in what had been a smart residential area of the city. It looked no different from the other buildings, except that it was built back behind a wall above head height, with a glass-walled cubicle, bullet-proof and connected by microphone to the main block. Arundsen walked past it, taking his time. Two men were on duty in the cubicle; one wore Soviet army uniform and the other was in the drab khaki brown of the People's Police. He made no examination of the front façade. He turned left and walked round to the side. There was another entrance, also guarded, but he could see that the ground ran down into a slope. And slopes like that were built for garages. It was a curious phenomenon, but a man on guard at a back door was less alert than if he were on duty at the front. Too many cars passed through as a routine; goods vans and messengers were a commonplace. And the heavy brass went through the front. The man on duty in the cubicle at the garage entrance was reading a newspaper. Arundsen made a circuit of the block and came round to the front again. There was a café four buildings down on the same side as the K.G.B. Headquarters. The outside tables had been withdrawn because it was too cold, but there was a big plate-glass window where he could sit and get a clear view of the road. What made it perfect were the traffic lights a few yards down. Arundsen went in, folded his cap away in his pocket, took a seat in a window table and ordered lunch.

His German was faultless; his knowledge and aptitude for adopting the colloquialism and accent of different regions had been one of the reasons for his appointment to the Eastern Europe section when he was with the Firm. He talked to the waitress in the flat, nasal tones of Swabia, and while he dawdled over the menu he kept a watch on the traffic outside the window. It was a chance, and it was quite likely that he would spend two hours spinning out his lunch without seeing anything. But if there was anything to see, then that spot close to the traffic lights was the best observation point in the street.

If nothing came, then he would have to hang around the Karlshorst itself, and that was dangerous. He would be missed from the coach tour that afternoon; they might make enquiries for him, or they might decide, in view of the comfort of the other passengers, to see if he appeared to rejoin them at the checkpoint. He didn't know what they would do, and this was something he had to chance. His guess was that the guide and the driver would wait till they were safely back in West Berlin before they reported his absence. He had the rest of the day, and some part of the evening. After that, if a missing call went out, he would probably be picked up by the Vopos within twenty-four hours. He had decided not to try any of his old contacts. They were probably cleaned up, and all he would find waiting would be Ivliev's men. If they knew where he might go, then he could do nothing but the completely unexpected. They weren't likely to look for him outside their own headquarters. If you want to hide a book put it in a bookshelf. By the time he had finished his food it was nearly three, and the café was empty. Nothing of interest had passed the window. The waitress stood beside him; she cleared her throat and he looked up. 'Your bill,' she said. She was a pleasant-looking girl, with brown hair and bright hazel eyes. Arundsen smiled at her, and got an immediate response. An idea was forming in his mind and he made the smile warmer. He sent his eyes down from her face to her breasts, with a quick flicker towards the part of her which was hidden by the table.

'You do a good lunch here,' he said. 'Not many people today.'

'It varies,' she shrugged. 'Sometimes we're so full I'm run off my feet.'

'What's it like in the evening?'

'About the same. We get some people from down the street, you know, the Karlshorst.' She nodded sideways towards the K.G.B. building. Her eyes were speculative, her mouth still smiling. She put one hand on her hip and stuck her breasts forward. She wasn't a whore, Arundsen knew that. She was just looking for a boy friend; an evening out would be enough. She was an attractive girl, if one liked the dark German type; probably a lot of men tried to pick her up.

'If I came back later on,' Arundsen said, 'would you be here?'

'I'm on duty till nine,' she said.

'After that?'

She shrugged. 'I go home.'

'That's a waste,' Arundsen said. 'What do you do now?'

'I clear up here,' she said. 'The boss goes home till six. He's a real swine; lazy as a pig.'

'I could come round the back and help you,' Arundsen said. He looked at her and she giggled. 'I'll take you out for a few beers tonight, after you've finished. How about that?'

'All right,' she said. 'But you'd better wait till the swine's gone. Then come round the back – it's a green door, and I'll let you in. You can do some of the washing up.' She slid her hand from her hip down the length of her thigh, and Arundsen did what was expected. He pinched her.

'I'll come back when he's gone. In an hour.' He paid the bill and got up; he turned and grinned at her over his shoulder. He couldn't have touched her seriously if his life depended upon it. He hadn't looked at or wanted any woman since he left Mary. But he could stay in the regions of the café and then come back. He needn't be put to the test; even as he thought of it, the incongruity struck him. Love, the emasculator. He went outside and hesitated. A big black car was coming, slowing down before the traffic lights.

Two men were in the back, both civilians, one smoking, the other talking hard. He had a clear view of them. If his luck held, and the impossible plan proved possible, he would be able to identify the one car going or coming out of the Karlshorst, with Nickolas Ivliev inside it. He could hang around and then go back and make false love to the little waitress, with one eye on the street traffic. He didn't wait for an hour; he watched the café until he saw the proprietor come out, and gave the girl's powers of description a high mark. A fat pig; lazy, a real swine. He looked all of them as he moved down the street, a gauleiter of the cafeteria. Arundsen guessed the girl didn't get much in the way of a friendly pinch there.

'You're early!' She seemed pleased, and held the back door open. 'I'm not nearly finished.'

'Never mind,' Arundsen said. 'You just bring me a cup of coffee, there's a nice girl, and I'll wait inside for you.'

'Aren't you going to help me?' She looked arch, and disappointed; she pouted at him, but without malice.

'You don't want me tired out, do you?'

She laughed at him, and shrugged again. 'All right. I'll get some coffee for you. I won't be long.'

He went back to the window, and lit a cigarette. It would be difficult in the dark. Even with the street lights it would be very difficult to see. He was halfway through his cigarette when he saw the stream of traffic slowing down as the lights changed. The grey Zim was on the nearside of the kerb. It was so slow that it almost stopped outside the window; before it moved on a yard or so he had seen Ivliev sitting alone in the back.

He had always been quick to move; he left the table and reached the door before the lights changed. He saw the number plate of the Zim from the rear before it turned into the main entrance of the Karlshorst.

When the waitress came back with a cup of black coffee three minutes later Arundsen had gone. The half-smoked cigarette still glowed in the ashtray.

CHAPTER TEN

'You must understand,' Sontag said, 'we've done all we can.'
He looked from Bill Thomson to the other Englishman; they
were sitting at the bar of the Europa's reproduction English
pub. The place was full of people, few of them English, mostly
German or Americans, and a thick haze of blue cigarette and
pipe smoke drifted in the ceiling under the lights. George
Geeson was a name the German knew very well from past records, but this was their first meeting. They hadn't liked each
other from the first five minutes, and the antipathy was growing. Sontag had found Thomson a congenial man to work with;
there was no residue of malice because they had been on different sides. But Geeson was different. He was cold and busi-
nesslike, and his eyes called Sontag a German bastard without
any effort at concealment. Sontag found this even more irrita-
ting as both men had come to ask a favour.

'I don't know why you let the bloody fool go through,'
Geeson said. 'It's more and more obvious that the whole thing
has been set up for him.'

'I am not Mr. Arundsen's old nanny,' Sontag said. 'He is a
professional with considerable experience. I warned him that
this was a trap, and the woman was just bait, but he wouldn't
listen to me. I don't see what more could be done. After all, he's
not acting officially. He made that quite clear.'

'If they've gone to all this trouble,' Geeson said, 'he must be
pretty important to them. And this isn't vengeance; this is big
stuff. That makes it official enough, in my view.'

'Then why haven't I heard anything from your department?' Bill Thomson could see a line of red creeping up from
the German's collar, and he knew that he was going to lose his
temper.

'Of course you've done everything possible,' he said. 'Without you we wouldn't even know where Arundsen was. But the
real point is this – can your contact help him if he gets into
trouble? If he can't, or he needs a couple of helpers, then
George and I can go in.'

'That wouldn't be wise.' The German made a signal and the
barmaid came over to them. 'You gentlemen will have the same
– good. Two whiskies, one beer. Now, please listen to me. All I

know is that Arundsen crossed over and disappeared from the coach tour. I also know that he had a suit of clothes made in East Germany and a gun. He was reported missing to the police here by the travel agency, and they informed me. It was what I expected. My last report from our contact on the other side was that they had no news of him. So that means he's lying low somewhere.'

'Or your contact's holding out on you,' Geeson said. 'How important is he?'

'Important enough not to be placed in any danger,' Sontag said. 'That's why you gentlemen will do better to stay where you are. My contact is in the middle of this. He had instructions from me to get Arundsen out of East Berlin. If you start interfering you could cause a lot of damage. Serious damage.' He swallowed down half his beer, and looked at his watch.

'I'm not prepared to risk my contact. I have been in touch with London and I have their full agreement. I will stop you and your friend from interfering if it means arresting both of you. With your major-general's blessing. We will give Arundsen back to you.'

'Not without Mary Wetherby,' Bill Thomson said slowly. 'It's both or nothing. I know how Arundsen feels about her. And remember who her uncle is.'

'I guaranteed Arundsen,' the German said. He finished his drink and stood up. 'That's all. Just Arundsen. Forgive me, I have an appointment.' He turned away from Geeson and smiled at Bill. 'I'm taking my wife to the theatre tonight. I'll be in touch with you.'

The noise in the bar closed round them after he had gone. Neither spoke for a few moments. Then George Geeson looked up from his drink and said a one syllable word.

Bill shook his head. 'He isn't, George. He's a top-class man. If he says he'll get Peter out, he will; if it's humanly possible. And if he says he'll stop us going in, he'll do that too.'

'I see,' Geeson said. 'So we sit on our asses here and do nothing? We might as well go home. Fancy our bloody people giving him the carte blanche over us! Wait till they want me to do something for them again!'

'We're retired,' Bill said gently. 'You do the odd job here or there – I haven't touched anything for years. We're not in the picture any more. Sontag's got a man over the other side who really means something. He won't let us stir it up for him because of Arundsen or anyone else. At the same time he'll try and get Peter out in one piece. I know Sontag, and I'm going along with him. Have another?'

'No,' George Geeson said. 'Let's get out of here. English pub my backside – what are you going to do, Bill? Stay on?'

'I think so,' Bill Thomson said. 'As I said to Joan, if anything goes wrong, he'll need someone to hold his hand.'

'You mean if he doesn't get Mary out with him,' George Geeson said. 'That's a nasty thought.'

'I can't say it worries me,' Thomson said. 'She's caused him enough trouble already. If you want to go home ...'

'I'll stick around,' Geeson said. 'Come on, let's go and get some dinner.'

'You're looking better this morning.' The man had made his little bow, and he was looking at her out of his flat eyes. There was a bruise on one side of Mary's jaw, but her mouth was no longer swollen. She looked up at him unwillingly. She had been locked in her room for twenty-four hours; her food brought up by a plain-clothes man who never spoke. This was the first time she had seen Brückner since he beat her up.

'I'm feeling better,' she said. He nodded and smiled encouragingly at her. He pointed to the overhead light, and then to a Gauguin print on the wall, and put a finger to his lips. She understood him; fear teaches at a rapid rate. There were microphones hidden in the ceiling and the wall.

'I hope you realise how disloyal you were, trying to escape,' he said.

'I was frightened,' Mary said, looking upward at the light. 'I wanted to try and get away.'

'You wanted to save your lover,' the German said. 'You lied to us when you said he didn't mean anything to you. That was very foolish. You can't save him. Nothing can save him now.'

'I want to save myself too,' she said, following the lead he had given her, without knowing where it ended.

'Colonel Ivliev sends you a message,' he said. 'He will overlook what you did, provided you give no more trouble. Your friend has crossed the Wall. We should catch him very soon now.'

He nodded, showing that this was the truth, and Mary put both her hands to her mouth; the anguished little cry would go down on the tape recording. 'Then you can go home,' the German said. There was a piece of paper in his hand, and she took it. It was difficult to read because her eyes were flooded with tears.

Trust me, the note said, *and your friend will be safe.*

He took it out of her hand, and their fingers touched. She remembered the vicious blows across her unprotected face, and flinched away from him. He put the note back in his pocket, bowed again and went out. He saw her sink back on the bed and heard the sound of her weeping behind the closed door. They knew Arundsen had come in because the checkpoint guards reported one tourist missing from the returning coach tour. A mackintosh had been found, and a hat, left in the cloakroom of the Moscowa where the passengers had eaten lunch. It was obviously Arundsen who had come through and stayed behind. Ivliev had leaked Mary's presence in the Budapest through channels of his own. Sontag's man had confirmed the leak, and received specific instructions to help Arundsen if he could but without prejudice to his own safety. As a result of Sontag's communication with London, a further instruction had reached Brückner that morning. If Arundsen had a bearing on James Dunne, then he must not be taken alive by the K.G.B. The word 'alive' had been repeated twice for emphasis. In his mind it applied to two people instead of one. He had shown his hand to the woman. Whatever happened to Arundsen, she mustn't be around for Ivliev to question.

He went into the lavatory along the corridor, where he burnt his own note and flushed the ashes down the pan.

At 8.33 in the morning Arundsen watched the grey Zim come out of the entrance courtyard to the Karlshorst. It had gone in with Ivliev sitting in the back; it came out empty and turned the corner to the garages in the rear. The day before Arundsen had bought a car rug. It had given him some warmth during the night, which had been spent behind the refuse bins outside the back door of the café. It was the safest place he could find for the most part of the vigil, because he knew the café was empty after the proprietor left. He had passed most of the early evening at a cinema, where he relaxed and went to sleep. It was after midnight when he slipped round to the green door at the back, and for a moment he thought about the waitress. Lucky for her he had walked out. She mightn't have enjoyed being asked questions by the K.G.B. if he were caught and any connection between them was established.

The place smelt of stale food and refuse, with an acrid stench of cat, but the bins were tall enough to hide him. With the rug wrapped round him Arundsen settled into the cramped space and dozed. Before it was light he rewrapped the rug into a bulky parcel, and by 8.33 he was across the road from the garage entrance to the Karlshorst. The grey Zim went through at some speed; the guard on duty hardly bothered to look up. Half a minute later he was facing Arundsen through the glass.

He saw a shabbily dressed man in a workman's cloth cap, half hidden from the top by a big brown paper package. There was a label from a well-known shop pasted on the front of the package.

'This is for the Colonel's driver,' Arundsen said. 'I just missed him at the front.'

'All right, go on down. Third bay on the right.'

Three steps past the cubicle and Arundsen was inside. He walked down the gradient, cradling the parcel. Behind him the guard might be pushing an alarm button. At any second the entrance doors might close, shutting him in. Men could come running out from the dark mouth of the garages below ground. The slope became steeper, and there were lights burning, showing the bays with the official cars parked in them. Third bay to the right. He turned, noticing that on the left a car was moving out, but on the right the Zim had stopped in its allotted space. There was nobody in sight but the Zim's driver. Arundsen eased the parcel into his left arm, and undid the lower buttons of his jacket. He walked forward quickly, towards the Russian. The car he had seen moving out was going up the gradient, its engine noise accentuated by the underground acoustics.

'A parcel for Colonel Ivliev.' The driver shook his head. 'Give it in at the gate,' he said. His accent made the German hard to understand. Arundsen was blocking his way.

'They sent me down here,' he explained. 'It's a car rug.' He gave it to the driver, almost pushing it at him. The man said something in Russian, took the parcel and turned round to put it in the car boot. As he did so, Arundsen whipped the Lüger out of his trouser band and hit him across the back of his shaven head with the butt end. He died instantly from a broken vertebra. The heavy body sagged against the car, the package slipping to the ground. Arundsen looked once over his shoulder. There was still nobody about. The luck, the crazy million-to-one-against luck, was still holding for him. He dragged the

Russian into the back of the Zim, stripped off his jacket, trousers and boots; he was out of his own clothes in seconds. The uniform was not a bad fit; the man was big-boned, although much shorter, and the boots were tight. He pulled the forage cap over one side of his head, doubled the dead man up on the floor of the back seat, tore the car rug out of its wrapping, and threw it over him. Minutes afterwards the guard in the cubicle saw the Colonel's grey Zim speed up the slope and roar out through the gateway.

Arundsen had a bad moment at the traffic lights. They turned against him, and for a second he pressed his foot on the accelerator, prepared to shoot across them, but he stopped himself in time, and pulled up in the line of traffic. While they were still at stop, he felt a distinct jar against the back of the driving seat. Sweat burst out all over his body. It was many years since he'd hit a man in the way he'd hit the driver. In the desperate hurry to get into his clothes he had taken it for granted that the man was dead. Dead men didn't kick you in the back, and that was what he had just felt. There was something sticking into the base of Arundsen's spine. The Russian had moved. The road ahead was straight for about two hundred yards. He couldn't see a turning, where he could pull in and look under the rug. The lights changed and he moved off. At the end of the street he turned left; his hands were sticking to the wheel, and he began to think the thing behind was shifting. It felt as if the pressure in the back against his seat was changing; the Russian might have been injured and be coming to. At any moment he could lurch up from behind. Arundsen pulled the Zim into the kerb. He got out and climbed into the back seat. People passed in a steady flow, cars overtook him, and a policeman began moving down to tell him to go on. He pulled back the rug. The driver's face was upturned, the eyes wide open, the jaw dropped. His left knee had slipped, and become jammed against the back of the driving seat. There was no fear of him coming out from under cover. Arundsen dropped the rug back over the body, and climbed into the front seat. The East German policeman took in the Soviet uniform and changed his mind about complaining that the Zim was improperly parked. Arundsen started the car, and, gathering speed, made for the Friedrichshain Gardens. It was just nine o'clock in the morning. It was cold and clear, with a pale blue-grey sky which could become quickly overcast. The beautiful gardens were deserted; he drove through the gates and stopped under an avenue of lime trees, their leafless branches stark and angular overhead.

Slowly Arundsen circled the Zim, lighting a cigarette; he leaned against the door, smoking and looking carefully in all directions. The road and the park were deserted. He threw the cigarette away. He put the Russian in the boot, on the pile of his discarded clothes, folding the rug over him, and locked it. Then he searched the uniform pocket for the man's identity card.

Pavlov Vinogradov. His rank, his army number, age, height, distinguishing marks. A small photograph, taken full face. He put it back in the breast pocket, and eased the collar which was tight for him. His right foot was beginning to ache and swell in the dead man's boot. He looked at his watch. He had spent almost fifteen minutes in the Friedrichshain. Ivliev had come to the Karlshorst at 8.30. Arundsen had reckoned on two hours in which to carry the plan through. Having just arrived at his office, it was unlikely that Ivliev would need the car again for some time. Two hours was a generous margin, but he had already wasted three-quarters of an hour.

He checked the petrol tank. It was full. He got inside again and started up the engine. The impossible was becoming the possible. He had got the car, killed the driver; he was on his way. He hadn't believed in it himself, right up till the moment when he cracked the Russian across the neck. He hadn't believed it possible to get this far. For a moment his elation turned into fear; blind, superstitious fear that crawled up and down his body, as it had done when the corpse shifted in the back. The first part had been too easy. Disaster would come with the last stage, when it was Mary's life at stake.

He turned out of the Friedrichshain and up the avenue to the centre of the city, towards the Budapest Hotel.

The manager had moved out of his office to accommodate the K.G.B. officers; a direct line had been established with Ivliev's private phone in the Karlshorst, apart from the outside phone and the internal system operating from the hotel switchboard. It was the internal system that rang. Brückner had been drinking coffee, and reading the morning newspaper. He had made his round of the hotel, beginning with his visit to Mrs. Wetherby, and checking on the men posted at the back entrances and in the foyer, apart from a man who was on duty in a building across the road. Everyone was in place.

Brückner wasn't worried. He had a methodical mind and thirty years' experience of this kind of work. Sontag had given him the solution for Arundsen, and he had worked out his own for Mrs. Wetherby if the need arose. It was impossible to prevent his people from arresting Peter Arundsen if he came near the hotel. He had made the arrangements and he knew how tight they were. Nobody could have got through that human mesh. But even so he could satisfy Sontag, and pocket the thirty thousand marks in Luxembourg. He would arrest Arundsen, and make sure that he was killed during the inevitable struggle. That way he was clear, and though Ivliev might not be pleased, he couldn't suspect Brückner of anything more than a mistake. A dead English agent wasn't any good to Ivliev. Security in West Berlin and London would be satisfied. When the phone rang he answered it. He had been about to make his morning report to Ivliev after finishing his coffee. It was the man he had put on the reception desk, in place of the clerk. 'The Colonel's car is here, sir. They want Mrs. Wetherby.'

He dropped the receiver back on its cradle and stood still. Something had gone wrong. Ivliev had sent for the woman. He must have changed his mind about leaving her at the Budapest after his report on her attempt to escape. His mind whirled from one possibility to the next, blaming himself for telling the Colonel the truth; but if he hadn't reported it someone else would. She was locked in her room, her face bruised and swollen. The manager, the floor waiter – if he hadn't confined her she was fool enough to have tried again and delivered Arundsen into their hands prematurely – there was nothing else he could have done without drawing suspicion on himself.

But he hadn't thought of this. He hadn't thought that Ivliev might decide to withdraw the woman altogether. And if she went back to the Karlshorst and they started asking questions – Brückner carried a small automatic in his pocket. He took it out, checked it and clicked back the safety catch. His face was jaundiced as he took the lift up to Mary Wetherby's room.

'Listen to me.' He spoke in a whisper, bending down to her as they walked along the corridor. He had one hand firmly round her arm, and his breath was on her face. 'Listen very carefully, Mrs. Wetherby. I have just heard that Arundsen is safe. Don't stop,' he pulled her angrily, 'don't say anything, just listen. He's safe, and waiting for you. But Colonel Ivliev has sent for you. He's in a nasty mood. You've got to do what I tell you, you understand?'

Mary didn't answer. She had not been allowed to take anything out of the room. He had told her to put on a coat and come with him, and the expression on his face had warned her not to argue.

'You're being taken back to the Headquarters. You realise what will happen to you? You know what they'll do because you tried to run away?'

They had stopped in front of the lift. She turned to him, she seemed quite calm and unafraid. 'I don't care about myself,' she said. 'Tell me where Arundsen is.'

'Safe,' Brückner snarled at her. 'I told you! Waiting for you! But if they take you back to the Karlshorst you'll never see him again. You've got to escape!'

'I won't do anything that could lead them to him,' Mary said. 'I told you, I don't care what happens to me.' He could have knocked her down at the moment. The lift was coming up; he could see the little red eye winking from floor to floor on the indicator.

'He's in the Western Sector,' he said. 'I had a message. It's all arranged for you to meet him. I'm to get you out. But I wasn't expecting this!' You've got to do as I tell you – you've got to trust me!' The lift doors opened and they stepped inside. He let go of her arm. 'Listen carefully,' Brückner said. 'Don't get in the car. When we get outside the hotel you've got to break away from me and run for it. I'll chase you and make sure you get away. You understand? I'll give you the signal, and then run!' He looked down at her; the hand which had been gripping her arm was in his pocket, the fingers curled round the gun.

'You promise me Arundsen's not here?'

'I swear it,' Brückner said. 'If you get into that car you're as good as dead.'

'All right,' Mary said. They stepped out into the foyer. A middle-aged man and woman were registering at the reception desk; she saw the manager and the hostile clerk who had given her directions the day before yesterday. Nobody was looking at her and the German; there was an air of normality which made her inward panic seem unreal. Brückner was holding her arm again, his fingers so tight that they hurt her. As they walked out into the street it occurred to Mary that they must have looked an ordinary couple leaving the hotel. There was nothing to distinguish them from the people passing by. Brückner saw the familiar grey Zim parked in front of them. The Russian driver was opening the rear door. They were within two or three feet of him. Brückner suddenly loosened his grip on Mary.

'Now!'

She pulled herself free and turned to run, as he had told her, but her high heel twisted. At the same moment the Russian looked up and Mary saw his face.

The gun was half out of Brückner's pocket, but she hadn't moved; he had heard her catch her breath. He was overcome by blinding rage. She hadn't fallen for it. If she'd tried to escape as he told her he would have shot her dead before she'd gone ten yards. She was the only one who knew about him, and now he'd never have the chance to shut her mouth. He spoke to the driver almost automatically.

'You're not Colonel Ivliev's regular driver.' The Russian had come up beside him, and something hard was pressing into Brückner's side. He saw the long blunt muzzle of a silencer. The man was right up against him, shielding the gun between their bodies. 'Get in,' he said. 'Slide over to the front passenger seat and don't try anything.' He spoke very quietly to the woman in English.

'In the back, Mary. And don't worry, everything's under control.'

Brückner got into the front seat, followed so closely by the man in Russian uniform that the gun muzzle was bruising him through his clothes.

'Now,' Arundsen said. 'I'll have what's in your pocket. Very slowly, and butt first.'

Brückner gave him the automatic; he hadn't the slightest intention of resisting. One injudicious move and all that money in Luxembourg would be wasted. Arundsen passed the gun over the back seat.

'Take this, darling. Point it at the back of his head and if he even turns round, pull the trigger.'

'That won't be necessary, Mr. Arundsen,' Brückner spoke in English. 'Mrs. Wetherby will tell you, I am on your side. I work for Sontag.'

'Shut up,' Arundsen said. 'Do as I tell you, Mary. Let him have it if he moves!'

'He said you were safe,' he heard her voice, and saw her in the driving mirror. She was leaning forward, holding the gun in both hands. 'He said you were in West Berlin.'

'Never mind that now,' Arundsen said. 'Be a good girl and don't cry. We've got a bit to go yet before we're out of it.'

'You've got the checkpoint,' Brückner said. He was being careful, the idea of an inexperienced woman with a gun was most uncomfortable. He remembered how hard he had hit her. 'How do you propose to get through that?'

'We'll get through,' Arundsen said, 'because you'll take us. Or I'll make a nasty hole in you.' He looked up quickly in the mirror. She was watching him; her eyes seemed too big in a face that was thin and very white.

'Are you all right?' he said. He saw her nod, and try to smile at him; Brückner saw the look that passed between them.

'I must congratulate you, Mr. Arundsen,' he said. 'How did you get by the reception desk at the hotel? The clerk is one of my best men.'

'He wasn't worrying about me,' Arundsen said. 'He recognised the car.'

'Remarkable,' the German said. 'So simple and so clever. When we get through the checkpoint you must tell me how you did it all. Where is the Colonel's driver, by the way?'

'In the boot,' Arundsen answered. 'It's big enough for two, so just remember that.'

'You don't have to threaten me,' the German said. 'I am ready to defect. It has all worked out conveniently for me. Take the fourth turning on the right and then the second left. We'll get through the Heerstrasse checkpoint. There's less traffic through there. You haven't much time.'

'Why not?'

'Because it's ten-thirty and I haven't phoned in to report to the Colonel. He will check up at the hotel soon.'

Arundsen spoke to Mary. 'Is he telling the truth?'

'I think so,' she said. 'I think we can trust him.'

'How long do we take to get to the Heerstrasse?'

'Twenty minutes, maybe fifteen. It depends on the traffic at this time.'

'We'll go to Charlie,' Arundsen said. 'I know the way and it's nearer. Keep that gun on him, darling. And don't worry; everything's going to be all right.'

He overshot the traffic lights twice, and ignored an angry signal from a policeman on duty. The police knew the Zim, and the city traffic automatically gave place to a speeding car driven by a Soviet soldier.

By ten-forty they were coming up to Checkpoint Charlie.

There was a long queue in front of them, going through the routine search Arundsen had seen on the way through in the coach. The Vopos were opening the boots of cars and pushing rods down the petrol tanks, examining passports. Soviet troops stood by, watching. It could take half an hour or more to get through.

When the German didn't phone through to Ivliev's office a check would be made at the hotel. The result of that check would close every escape route within a few minutes.

He turned to Brückner; the gun was in his hand again.

'Ivliev doesn't queue up,' he snapped. 'Get your pass out, or whatever you carry, and have it ready.'

He punched the horn and held it for a couple of seconds; then he swung the Zim out of the line and put his foot down, alternately hooting as he went up the middle lane between the two opposite traffic streams. In the back Mary closed her eyes for a moment, the little automatic on her lap and prayed. Arundsen's instructions broke in on her.

'Put the gun under your coat. I'll be watching him. Just sit back and look natural. You won't have to say anything. And as for you,' he said savagely to Brückner, 'you blink a bloody eyelash in the wrong direction and I'll blow your insides out!'

Every morning at 10.30 Ivliev paused from his work to drink a glass of tea, and smoke a cigarette. It amused him to copy the capitalist custom of a mid-morning break; it was also the time when he thought most clearly and rapidly about the day's problems.

He had gone through his paperwork in the two hours since his arrival, and it was a rule that during this period he was never interrupted except for an emergency. Then he relaxed with his tea, arranged everything in order mentally, and by 10.45 he was ready for the daily conference with his junior officers. There was a decoded telegram from Moscow, demanding news of Arundsen in even angrier terms than last time. As he had proof of Arundsen's presence in the city, this telegram didn't disturb him. He had prepared a rough draft in reply. The previous day one of his officers, a Major Maximov, had asked why they didn't mount a massive search through the whole sector and bring Arundsen in. Ivliev's answer had been patient and detailed. There was no need to do something which would cause considerable alarm among the population, and which might well drive an experienced agent like Arundsen into deep hiding. He had come to the city in order to contact Mrs. Wetherby. He must believe himself undetected. When he tried to approach the hotel he would be taken. Up to that point Ivliev had thought that the Major was one of his best men. He had shown himself impetuous and rather stupid. That suggestion would delay his promotion by another year at least. Ivliev had a plane standing by to fly Arundsen to Kalitz. He could be superficially interrogated there, but what information he might have was of no importance compared to what his advent would mean to Jimmy Dunne. He had promised Dunne to bring Arundsen to him, and thanks to Wetherby's brilliant manœuvre with his niece, that promise would be kept. Brückner's report on her had come as a surprise. He had really believed that she was as cold and self-interested as she made out. He hadn't liked her for it; it fitted in so well with the upper-class attitude which was especially distasteful in a woman. He liked women to be feminine and domesticated; the aggresively independent woman of modern Soviet ideal was not in accord with his personal preference. He had married a girl who was a medical student, but to his satisfaction she had given up her studies to look after their two children. He had brought his family with him to Berlin. He thought of Mrs. Wetherby, and revised his opinion a little. She had tried to save Arundsen, after all. Women were very difficult to understand sometimes. He would have to keep her in East Berlin until he contacted Wetherby.

He had a feeling that Phillip Wetherby wouldn't be anxious to have her back. And it was then that he remembered something. It was 10.40; Brückner's report hadn't come in. He switched on his secretary's intercom.

'Colonel?'

'Where is Brückner's report?'

'He hasn't phoned in, sir.'

Ivliev frowned. It was unlike Brückner to be late. He had the German obsession with punctuality. 'Get a direct line through to the Budapest.'

A moment later his telephone rang. Three minutes after the start of that call the Colonel's morning conference was cancelled.

The Zim was stopped at the checkpoint. The Vopo sergeant came to the right-hand window and saluted. Brückner held out his pass.

'I'm in a hurry. Tell them to raise the barrier!'

The Vopo called out an order to the man in the guardpost operating the posts, and they began to rise in readiness for the Zim to go through. Arundsen didn't look round. He nosed the car a little forward until it was a bare yard from the demarcation line, its bonnet under the barrier. He had his left foot on the clutch pedal, holding it engaged by a hair, and his right foot pressed on the accelerator. The powerful engine was tugging at the wheels, ready to leap forward the moment the clutch pedal came up.

Mary was sitting back as Arundsen had told her, holding the gun covered by the skirt of her coat. The Vopo sergeant was examining Brückner's identity pass. As her near window was open it was Mary who heard the telephone ring first; it gave one loud, strident shrill. The excited shouts of the man who answered it came just as Brückner's pass was being handed back. There were two Soviet soldiers standing near the car on the left-hand side; they heard the yell of warning first, and the one nearest Arundsen jerked up his automatic weapon and took aim at him, Mary pointed the little gun through the window and fired point blank. The man fell as Arundsen let out the clutch; as the Zim hurtled forward, the second Russian swung his weapon round and sent a burst through the rear passenger window from which the single shot had come.

The barriers were falling, but the Zim had got beyond them; the troops were firing almost in unison at the back of the car. There was an ugly clatter as the spray of bullets smacked against the bullet-proof bodywork. Arundsen drove the short distance at frantic speed, steering the Zim on a wild zigzag. It screeched in a violent skid as they reached the West German checkpoint, and came to a stop that threw Brückner up against the windscreen. Police and frontier guards surrounded the car as Arundsen flung himself out of the driver's seat and wrenched open the rear door.

One of the police had spread his greatcoat on the road and Arundsen had laid her on it. Inside the checkpoint someone was phoning through for an ambulance. Brückner, his nose bleeding into a handkerchief, was explaining who they were. The Zim was halfway across the road, its doors hanging open; two frontier guards were dragging the body of Ivliev's driver out of the boot. The officer in command of the checkpoint had ordered his men to keep back; there was nothing anyone could do for the woman on the ground.

It seemed to Arundsen that they were quite alone. The day was grey and overcast, with a chilling wind that swept over them in angry gusts. He had taken his jacket off and wrapped it round her. He knelt beside her, holding both her hands. His head was bowed and he was crying.

'Oh, don't,' Mary said. 'Please darling, don't do that . . .'

'You mustn't talk,' Arundsen begged. 'You mustn't move. An ambulance is coming – they'll give you something quickly . . .'

'I don't feel any pain. I've got to tell you something . . . it's difficult to breathe. Don't let me go!'

'I'm holding you.' Arundsen raised her very slowly, cradling her against his breast. The greatcoat beneath her was dark with blood.

'Phillip. Phillip's working for the Russians . . .' The words were coming with difficulty, and she stopped for a moment. He didn't seem to take it in. He didn't seem to care.

'You must tell them,' she struggled on, ignoring his pleading to stop, to please not use up her strength. 'You must stop him . . . he tricked me into going. He's a traitor . . .'

'Don't talk,' Arundsen begged her, holding her as if he could contain the ebbing life. 'Don't try and talk. It's hurting you.' Her head turned slightly against his arm and her eyes closed.

'I wish I had a priest.'

'I'll get you one,' he promised. 'I'll get one for you. Just try and hold on.'

Her eyes opened and she looked at him. 'I can't.' It was a whisper. There was an odd expression round her mouth as if she were trying to smile.

'Please . . . please, darling, don't be sad for me. I'm so happy that you loved me. It makes everything – worth while . . .'

'Oh, Christ,' Arundsen was groaning. 'Oh, Jesus Christ.' She raised her hand and touched his face; the fingers were cold and the hand fell back.

'You remember the swans . . .' The words were hardly audible. 'It's not a legend, darling. They do sing . . .'

She died without his knowing it. He went on holding her, kneeling on the road, until he heard the wailing siren of an ambulance. A hand touched him on the shoulder.

'Your English friends are on their way here? Arundsen looked up and saw Sontag leaning over him.

'Come away,' the German said. 'It's all over now.'

The 5.48 pulled into Buntingford Station seven minutes late. The first week in November had been stormy, with sustained downpours of rain that caused some flooding. It had been raining for most of that day and there were large pools of water on the platform where the surface had subsided. When the train stopped the complement of commuters came pouring out, umbrellas and evening newspapers under their arms, filing through the ticket barrier towards the rows of waiting cars with waiting wives inside. One by one the cars were started up and drove away. The train pulled out, heading for the next stop sixteen miles down the line. One man was left on the platform. He wore no hat and carried nothing, not even a paper for the journey. He gave in his ticket to be clipped and dropped the return half into his pocket. The station was empty except for the local taxi which had been booked by telephone. The driver leaned out and called to him. 'Are you Mr. Arundsen?'

'Yes,' Arundsen said. He got into the back of the cab. 'Take me to Buntingford House.'

Coming soon!

ALBATROSS

Evelyn Anthony

Davina Graham has left the service. She has turned her back on her old profession and her old colleagues once and for all. Or so everyone thinks.

In reality, however, Davina Graham has undertaken the most important and most dangerous mission of her career: unearthing a traitor in SIS. She must work entirely on her own against a faceless opponent who might be anyone – even someone she trusts.

Davina Graham's new adventure is her most thrilling yet – a game of cat and mouse that threatens not only national security, but family unity and the relationship that is dearest to her heart.

Publication date: November 1983

EVELYN ANTHONY

Evelyn Anthony is one of Britain's bestselling thriller writers and her books are available from Arrow. You can buy them from your local bookshop or newsagent, or you can order them direct through the post. Just tick the titles you require and complete the form below.

☐	ALBATROSS	£1.75
☐	THE ASSASSIN	£1.75
☐	THE AVENUE OF THE DEAD	£1.75
☐	THE DEFECTOR	£1.75
☐	THE GRAVE OF TRUTH	£1.25
☐	THE LEGEND	£1.75
☐	THE MALASPIGA EXIT	£1.75
☐	THE OCCUPYING POWER	£1.75
☐	THE RENDEZVOUS	£1.60
☐	THE RETURN	£1.60

Postage ‾‾‾‾

Total ‾‾‾‾

ARROW BOOKS, BOOKSERVICE BY POST, PO BOX 29, DOUGLAS, ISLE OF MAN, BRITISH ISLES

Please enclose a cheque or postal order made out to Arrow Books Limited for the amount due including 10p per book for postage and packing for orders within the UK and 12p for overseas orders.

Please print clearly

NAME ....

ADDRESS ....

....

Whilst every effort is made to keep prices down and to keep popular books in print, Arrow Books cannot guarantee that prices will be the same as those advertised here or that the books will be available.